THE PARAMEDIC'S AMAZON

JAMIE DAVIS

The Paramedic's Doom

By Jamie Davis

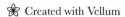 Created with Vellum

Prologue

HANGBE SURVEYED the empty village from the ridge before heading down. She cursed under her breath. She was too late again.

She pulled the Land Rover to the side of the single gravel road passing between the cottages. The police constable's van sat across from her. As she climbed out of the SUV, the Scottish constable got out as well.

"You the inspector I was told to wait for?"

Hangbe nodded, her black braids rattling a little as the beaded ends touched. She pulled back the side of her leather jacket to show her ID badge clipped to the inside pocket. The maneuver exposed the black, contoured body armor she wore underneath.

The constable leaned forward and nodded after a brief look.

She ignored him. The mystery of these disappearances deepened with each site she visited. Hangbe stood in the middle of the small seaside community trying to get a sense of what it would take to clean out a place this size. She counted ten homes that she could see. There could be a few others nestled out of sight down along the water, but probably not many. She guessed less than fifty people had called this community home.

The constable, a heavy-set fellow with a bright red nose and rosy

1

cheeks, took off his cap and scratched at his thinning brown hair. "I have to say you're not what I expected an Interpol special agent to look like."

"Met many of us, have you?"

"Um, no." He scratched his head again and changed the subject away from his surprise at meeting the West African woman in blue jeans, custom-fitted tactical body armor, and a long leather jacket.

He shifted his attention away from her after staring for too long. "Any idea where they all went?"

"I was going to ask you the same thing, Constable. Has there been any trouble among the villagers, perhaps with others living in the towns nearby?"

"No, in fact, I hardly ever come up here at all. The people here have always been clannish and keep to themselves. If they have trouble with one of their own, they keep it within the community and don't call for help."

Hangbe only half listened as she walked down the road. The gravel crunched under her knee-high boots and she cast outward with her otherworldly senses. The Constable had to jog a little to keep up with her long strides.

Common smells and sounds of the seaside met her as she strolled along past the empty homes. A glance to the left and right at the open doors told her whatever had happened had been hurried. Who leaves their homes open to the elements if they're planning to return? Other than that and the missing people, everything seemed the same as the others she'd seen. These small Unusual shifter clans all had similarities, no matter where she encountered them around the world. They'd avoid interacting with nearby humans, keeping up the pretense they were as normal as every other small fishing community.

"When did you first realize something was wrong?"

The constable stopped walking, snaking his forefinger up under his cap to scratch at his head again. Hangbe rolled her eyes, keeping her back to him so he wouldn't see her reaction. It was as if he couldn't walk and think at the same time.

"The first curious thing happened when old Joseph didn't bring in the village's catch yesterday morning. He usually sells it to one of the wholesaler trucks that passes through on their way into the city."

"So you sent out someone to investigate?" Hangbe asked after she realized he wasn't going to continue on his own.

"Oh, no. We figured they hadn't caught anything and left it at that."

She resisted the urge to turn and glare at him. It was almost nightfall the following day. He'd let the trail go cold because he didn't like coming all the way out here to look in on the strange little village and its people.

"So when did you finally realized they were gone?"

The edge of her voice cut like a knife, and the constable bristled a little as he caught the tone of what she said. "Now, look here, missy. I'm a busy man. There were other things to attend to yesterday, and I had no way of knowing there might be trouble."

"When?"

"This morning. When Joseph missed the second day's fish market drop off, I drove out. I thought maybe his truck had mechanical problems. That's when I found it empty. The whole place was just empty. There were thirty-seven people living here."

Hangbe turned and looked back up the street towards her vehicle. "Just like the others."

"What's that?" the constable asked. "There are others?"

Hangbe nodded. "You must have suspected it when you filled out your report and my BOLO popped up in your system."

She'd had her team back in London submit the *Be On the Look Out* notice to all the UK police units for any mysterious disappearances of more than two people at a time.

"I wondered, but we get those kinds of things all the time from headquarters. They rarely apply to the outlying areas in the countryside. We don't pay much attention to them."

Hangbe surveyed the empty village. The open doors glared back at her. Two whole days had gone by. It was unlikely she'd be able to find any evidence of what had happened, even with her special skills. Still, she had to try.

"Alright, Constable. I'll take it from here. I'll loop you in on anything I discover."

"Um, my Superintendent probably wants me to stick around and assist you with your investigation."

Hangbe fixed him with a level stare. "Is that what you want to do?" She reached up and rubbed her middle fingertip across one of the ridged beads on the ornate necklace she wore. The magic worked instantly.

His eyes glazed over and the constable said, "No, I want to go back to the station so I can hit the pub with my mates."

Hangbe nodded, holding his gaze. "Then you should do that. I'll work things out with the Superintendent."

She dropped her hand from the necklace and the policeman's eye's cleared.

He opened his mouth to say something but stopped as if trying to remember a comment that had slipped his mind. He shrugged, nodded once, and walked back to his van.

She waited until the police van was out of sight before she started her search for clues. With her right thumb and forefinger, Hangbe rolled a different bead, this one orange and green with a pebbled exterior, back and forth as she walked back up the street. She took her time, waiting for the images of what had happened here to manifest. Two days was a long time, but if the emotions were strong enough, there should still be at least a shadow of an imprint left.

A few fleeting images of women running from dark figures crossed her path. They never lasted more than a few seconds. She pressed with her will to make them linger. All she got was a stabbing headache behind her eyes. It had been too long. Cursing aloud this time, Hangbe let go of the pebbled bead and stopped beside her car. She shifted her fingers to a different bead, this one black as the moonless night sky. This time the magic worked instantly, and she frowned knowing what she would find.

The tug on her mind pulled her between two nearby cottages and down to the water lapping at the stony shore. Fishing boats sat beached along the strand of shoreline nearby. The pull from the magic took her away from the boats and around a small headland to a small isolated cove. The magic wasn't needed anymore. The gulls and crows battling for scraps from the dead caused enough noise to tell her right where to go to find the bodies.

A dozen men and older boys lay in a heap, huddled together to shield each other from the hail of bullets that had rained down on them from the top of the cove. She knelt down and plucked a shell casing from the stones at her feet. The bastards had stood right here when they did it.

She glanced at the 9mm brass casing in her hand, then slipped it into a small plastic bag from her pocket. She'd submit it for evidence to her superiors. She'd catch the bastards. She always did, eventually. That was why she was given the latitude she had from her bosses, the humans overseeing international crimes against Unusuals. The evidence she gathered now was important. They'd want proof linking the trail of bodies she left behind once she caught up to the ones who'd done this.

Hangbe snapped a few photos with her phone of the bodies and of the surroundings in relation to the boats. That constable wasn't too bright, and she didn't want to have to come back to lead him to what he should have found before she'd arrived. She hoped the sight made him lose whatever he'd had for dinner tonight. She knew her appetite had left for the evening.

Returning to her Land Rover, Hangbe sat behind the wheel giving the village with no name one last look. This trafficking ring was slippery and careful. It was why she'd had little to go on so far. There'd been no concrete leads at all over the months she'd been tracking them down. She just needed one break in the case. One little slip by whoever had done this. Then she'd descend on them like an angel of death. Then she'd show them how an Amazon dealt with those who threatened the innocent.

Chapter 1

THE AMBULANCE VEERED around a car which slowed for no apparent reason. Paramedic Dean Flynn gripped the grab handle beside the passenger door even though his seatbelt was buckled.

"Easy does it, Barry. We need to get there in one piece, or we don't get to help anyone."

Barry, Dean's partner and fellow paramedic grimaced. "Sorry, Dean, I expected them to pull over like everyone else. What's the use of running with my emergency lights and the siren blaring if no one is going to pay attention to it or do the wrong thing when they do hear it?"

"You're preaching to the choir here, bud. If people did what was smart all the time, we'd be out of jobs."

Barry's eyes stayed on the road, though he did smile in response to Dean's comment. He peered through the nighttime street lit by the isolated pools of the streetlights ahead. "Did the printout from HQ have anything else on the patient?"

Dean glanced down at the paper in his other hand and then shook his head. "It just says injured subject from a fall. It could be anything. I'll call in and see if I can get them to give us a clue what we're walking into."

Reaching forward, the senior paramedic grabbed the mic from its clip on the dash and called the dispatch center. "U-191, we are almost on location. Do you have any additional for us?"

"Negative, U-191. Twenty-two-year-old female, injured in a fall is all we've been able to get from the caller. They disconnected and haven't picked up when we called back."

Barry frowned. "That doesn't sound good."

"No, it doesn't," Dean replied. Something about this particular dispatch didn't feel right. Learning long ago to trust his instincts, he keyed the mic again. "U-191 to Dispatch. Requesting a police unit to the scene for a check."

"Received, U-191. Police unit en route."

Dean replaced the mic on the dash and leaned forward to look out into the night as Barry turned off the main road and down a residential street. This was a run-down working-class neighborhood. Four and five-story buildings lined the street. They had broken most up into small apartments with various shops and businesses occupying the first floors.

Barry spotted the correct street number first. "There it is. I don't see anyone out on the sidewalk waiting for us. What's the unit number?"

Dean checked his sheet again. "Apt 3. I'm guessing that's on the third floor. It's usually two per floor in these places and that dry-cleaners takes up the first floor."

Barry pulled to the curb in front of the building and slid the gear lever into park. "Should we go in or wait for the police backup?"

Dean shrugged. "It could be nothing. Maybe I'm still jumpy, even after all these months since the——" Dean trailed off.

Barry finished for him. "Since you stopped the four horsemen of the apocalypse from ending the world as we know it?"

Dean grimaced. He hated it when people said things like that. Not that they were wrong. But to Dean, he'd done what anyone would have in that situation. He wasn't anything special. Besides, there were other people just as valuable there beside him. He couldn't have done it alone. That was for sure.

"Let's stay focused on the job at hand," Dean said. "We'll go in. Just keep your eyes open for trouble. The cops will be here soon enough."

He hopped out and moved back to the compartment doors down the side of the ambulance. He grabbed the med and trauma bags and walked around to the back. Since Barry was driving today, it was Dean's turn to take the lead with the patients. They traded off and took turns every other day, even though Dean was senior to Barry, at least in Station U terms. He'd been working there longer and had more experience handling their supernatural patients.

Barry had already opened up the back and climbed inside to retrieve their heart monitor and oxygen and airway bags. He climbed back out to stand next to Dean on the street. Dean nodded and together they started across the sidewalk with their gear.

The entrance to the apartments above the storefront was up several steps. Dean glanced back at the ambulance. They were going to need the stair chair to save them from hauling the stretcher up to the third floor. He turned to Barry to say something, but his partner had already opened the side compartment housing the folding chair with wheels. It was invaluable to assist them in getting patients up and down stairs safely.

Dean walked up the steps and reached for the buzzer to contact apartment 3. He didn't push the button. One glance at the door told him the door's latch was broken.

Barry stepped up behind Dean carrying the stair chair along with the heart monitor and oxygen and airway bags. With the straps from the monitor and bags across his chest and the stair chair held in front of him, Dean knew his partner was loaded down. He pulled the door open and waited for Barry to enter first before following him inside.

The interior lights did little to illuminate the entry hall. Everything seemed grimy and more than a little run-down.

Dean headed forward to the bottom of the stairs and climbed to the second floor. Apartments one and two were to the right and left. That meant, three was one more floor up, as he'd suspected. He started up the next set of stairs and heard the sobbing right away. It sounded like a woman, but he couldn't be sure.

Heeding his own earlier warning to Barry, Dean proceeded with caution, ready to defend himself or run if need be. As he neared the landing, the door to his left stood ajar. The one to his right was closed. A tarnished brass number four was tacked to the wooden frame above it.

A glance to the left to check the frame above the open doorway revealed no number, though there were holes where the screws had once held a number in place. Still, this was likely the location they sought.

Dean glanced inside, past the partially open door.

A woman sat on a ratty, brown plaid couch in the center of the room. A tall, heavily muscled man in a grimy white tank top paced the floor next to her. She flinched a little every time he walked past her.

"Hi, I'm Dean Flynn," he said as he rapped on the door. "Did someone here call paramedics?"

The man spun around, his motions fluid, almost catlike. Dean, given the type of patients they treated, wondered right away if the guy was a shifter of some sort. There had to be a connection to an Unusual creature of some sort with this call.

"It's about damn time you got here. I've had to listen to her whining for too long as it is."

The woman looked up at Dean, her sunken eyes making the dark circles around them look even worse. Her whole emaciated body looked as if she had had little to eat or drink for days. She clutched her left arm tightly to her stomach and hunched over it.

The guy pacing next to her looked like he hadn't missed a meal in a long while. He wasn't overweight, but you didn't get muscles like that if you missed a lot of meals. Something wasn't right here.

Barry arrived in the doorway.

Dean moved inside to kneel on the floor next to the woman. "Hi, I'm Dean. What's your name?"

"You don't need her name. Just fix up her arm. She had another stupid accident."

"I need to know her name for my report. I'll need yours, too, since you're the one who called us."

"I'm Manton. Her name's Verity. You don't need our last names."

Dean turned back to the woman and smiled. "Hi, Verity. Can you tell me what's wrong? Is it your arm?"

"Of course it's her arm. She was clumsy as usual and fell down. Again."

"I'd like to hear it from her directly, if you don't mind."

Manton stopped, glaring down at Dean. His fists clenched and he loomed over the kneeling paramedic.

Barry must've decided the situation was getting a bit too tense. He came up to stand behind Dean, ready to back up his partner if needed. Dean was glad he was close by. Everything about this call seemed odd. A chill of danger ran down his spine.

"Alright, Verity, why don't you tell me what happened while I get your blood pressure and pulse."

"She don't need none of that. She just needs you to fix her arm."

Manton leaned over Dean again.

Barry slid into place between them, causing Manton to take a step back. "Sir, I'm going to need you to give my partner some room to work. Why don't you show me where she fell?"

Manton muttered something unintelligible in a way that almost resembled a deep, rumbling growl. Dean ignored it and focused his attention on Verity.

While Barry distracted the man, Dean leaned in to take her blood pressure. He pushed up the long sleeve covering her unhurt arm and concealed his gasp with a disguised cough as he spotted the bruises all along her arm.

While he wrapped the blood pressure cuff around her arm, he studied the bruises. They varied in color from deep purple and blue to paler yellow and green, showing various stages of healing. This woman had taken a beating, and more than once judging from her injuries. This didn't happen falling down the stairs, and if she was a shifter, too, she probably healed faster than a human did. That meant these past injuries had been even more severe than he'd normally expect from such bruising. It all had him questioning how today's injury had happened.

Dean glanced at the open doorway to the stairs outside, wondering how far out the police unit was. He couldn't call to check on them over the radio. Manton would overhear him, which might escalate his already edgy temper.

Dean pushed the button on the heart monitor to pump up the automated blood pressure cuff and smiled at Verity. "While that's working, why don't you tell me what happened in your own words."

She glanced past Dean at Manton and then said, in a thick Scottish accent, "It's like he said. I'm clumsy and had a bit of a fall."

"Okay, why don't you show me your other arm. I need to see what I can do about to help you."

She was afraid of Manton. Given everything he'd seen so far, Dean was pretty sure the hulking brute had injured her. There could be any number of reasons she lied about it. It didn't change the paramedic's obligation to help treat her injury at the moment. The circumstances did affect his need to report his suspicions to the proper authorities. He glanced at the door again, wishing the special station U police units arrived soon.

Turning his attention back to Verity, Dean examined her left arm. It was pretty obvious it was broken. The deformity stood out as soon as she shifted her body far enough for him to see it clearly. Her injured arm had as many bruises on it as the other one did.

Dean's anger welled up inside him as his imagination fueled his suspicions. He wished Jaz was here. While he was a healer and not much of a fighter, his wife was a different matter. If Jaz was here, she'd take Manton outside and teach him a thing to two about roughing up women.

Jaz, as the leader of a Hunter Clan, was a formidable martial artist and fighter. Some would say she was also a killer, at least if you were a demon or rogue supernatural of some sort. Dean didn't like to think of her that way, though. She wasn't the same bloodthirsty hunter he'd thought she was when they'd met over a year before.

Dean moved his hands with care as he palpated the injured arm around the deformed area. He could feel the crepitus, the slight vibration from the movement of the broken bones rubbing against each other under her skin. The swelling around the injury was already pretty substantial. It looked like it had happened as much as a few hours ago. Under the bruises, he spotted a unique sort of tattoo on the inside of the forearm. It looked like a panther's head, or maybe a mountain lion of some sort. Did it denote her shifter type?

"Verity, when did you injure your arm?" Dean studied her face, trying to see past her pain and determine what sort of Unusual she was.

"Um," she checked to see where Manton was before continuing. "It happened just before we sat down to eat. Manton likes me to make sure his food is ready as soon as he gets back from work. I was a little late tonight. I guess he startled me when he came home. I just sort of tripped and fell, that's all."

The kitchen table sat a few feet away. Dean scanned the single place setting with a few scraps remaining on the plate. It was clear at least one occupant had finished their meal before calling 911 for the ambulance. He could guess who that was. His anger flared again.

Wrestling his temper under control, Dean smiled at Verity, "I'm guessing from your accent you're not from around here? Where are you from originally?"

Verity shot another look in Manton's direction, then back at Dean.

"Don't worry about him, Verity. My partner will keep him busy talking while we chat. I'll fix it so your arm doesn't hurt as much while you tell me. I hear a bit of a brogue in your voice. Scottish, right?"

Verity nodded. "I came here about a year ago. It's hard to say exactly when. I used to live near the coast on one of the Orkney Islands."

That surprised him. He didn't think there were any big cats native to the U.K. "So you're not a werepanther or some other cat shifter?"

She frowned and flashed a little anger of her own. "No, I'm a Selkie. Why would you think I'm one of them?"

"It's just the tattoo on your arm. I figured..."

Verity immediately swiped at the tattoo with her free hand, as if trying to wipe it away. The anger flared in her eyes again, then faded as quickly as it came.

Dean changed the subject while he worked on stabilizing her arm. "What brought you here to Elk City?"

"Um, I came when I was, uh, brought here. I don't know how long ago it was. I came here to, uh, work. That's why Manton got me; to keep his apartment nice."

Dean doubted she was an ordinary maid. Not in this neighborhood. Plus, no actual maid would put up with the abuse, would they?

He pulled two short, padded splints from the trauma bag and began stabilizing Verity's arm. He started by attempting to align the bones as much as he could, then carefully wrapped gauze around the splints to hold the arm in place on either side of the break.

While he worked, Dean thought back to the previous year. Her words triggered a memory from a refresher class he took at Headquarters. The continuing education program taught the paramedics how to recognize human trafficking victims in the field. This had all the hallmarks of that sort of relationship: The controlling overwatch of the trafficker, the fear and deference of the trafficked, the evidence of abuse.

If he was right, he needed to get her separated from Manton and try to take her to the hospital where he could get her the help she needed. If her trafficker was a werepanther or other were-cat type and she was a Selkie, a seal shifter, it was definitely odd. Shifter varieties like that rarely mixed.

Dean looked back over his shoulder. Barry was doing a good job keeping Manton away, continuing asking questions and jotting the answers in an open note taking app on the tablet. The male shifter kept craning his neck past Dean's partner to see what Dean was doing.

Finishing up splinting the arm, Dean got Verity ready to go to the hospital. She needed an X-ray and a follow-up with an orthopedic surgeon to see if she needed surgery or just a cast.

"Verity, let me pack up my stuff, then I'll help you up and we can head out to the ambulance."

The instant he said she was coming with him to the ambulance, her eyes darted to Manton and then back to Dean. She looked down at the floor. "I may not leave."

"Verity, you need an X-ray for your arm. A doctor needs to look at that break and make sure it'll heal straight. You understand that, right?"

Verity shook her head and behind Dean, Manton pushed past Barry and came over to stand beside the frightened woman.

"She doesn't need to go anywhere. You wrapped her arm. She will heal on her own. You two must go. Now."

The order to leave was as clear as the threatening stance the male shifter had taken. Dean didn't care and opened his mouth to argue. He stopped as a familiar voice sounded from the apartment's doorway.

"Dean, Barry, I was in the neighborhood and spotted your ambulance. You two need any help?"

Officer O'Malley, one of the Elk City police department's special officers dealing with Unusual cases and crimes, stood in the doorway. He placed one hand to rest almost casually on the butt of his holstered pistol as he waited for an answer.

Dean smiled, glad to have O'Malley there at last to give them some support. "Hello officer, I was just telling Verity here that she needed to go to the hospital so we can get her arm checked out. I'm pretty sure it's broken. Her companion is hindering us from caring for our patient."

The officer set his lips in a firm line and nodded.

Dean was pretty sure the policeman understood at least part of the situation. He was as good at his job as the paramedics were at theirs.

O'Malley crossed the apartment to stand next to Manton. He stared into the looming were-cat's eyes for a few seconds, then glanced down at Verity. "You go with these nice paramedics while I chat with your friend here for a few minutes. He can come meet you at the hospital once I'm finished."

Manton started to say something.

O'Malley glared at him and the werepanther backed down.

Dean stood and gathered the gear.

Barry came over and stopped him. "You help her down the stairs. She can walk herself out with you along to steady her. I'll make a couple trips and get the gear loaded up."

"Sounds good. Thanks." Dean turned to the woman and said, "Let me help you up." He offered a hand to her and waited.

This was a critical moment. He knew she needed help, in more ways than one. But, if she didn't want to go to the hospital, he couldn't force her. He forced himself to relax with a deep breath while he waited patiently for her response.

Verity looked at Manton, who stood glaring at Officer O'Malley, then shifted her gaze to Dean. With a small nod, she reached up and took his hand, letting him help her up to her feet. Without looking back, the woman followed Dean out of the apartment and down the stairs to the waiting ambulance.

Chapter 2

IT DIDN'T TAKE Dean long to get Verity settled in the ambulance once he got her downstairs. By the time Barry had everything packed away from their call, Dean had taken another set of vitals and started an IV to deliver an initial dose of four milligrams of morphine for her pain.

"Let's see if that takes the edge off for you. I can give you some more if you need it."

"Thank you, it doesn't hurt so bad."

The way she winced when she shifted in her seat on the stretcher told Dean otherwise. He made a mental note to reassess her pain level in another five minutes. They were about fifteen minutes from the hospital, and he could give her up to ten milligrams without having to call in for a doctor's order.

Given how she was handling the pain so far, he figured it would be enough. They could always give her more once she got to the emergency department at Elk City Medical Center.

The door opened in the cab up front and Barry shouted back through the narrow passageway leading back to the patient compartment. "You all set?"

"We're good to go. ECMC, nice and easy. Mind the potholes, too."

"Already on it, partner. I'll make it a nice smooth ride for you both."

The big ambulance could bounce a bit on its suspension, especially on the local streets with all the potholes after this year's heavy winter. The city was still way behind on filling in all the gaps. Barry would have his work cut out for him trying to avoid them on the way to the hospital. Luckily, they didn't need to rush using their lights and sirens, so they could take their time.

The ambulance started forward. Behind them, Manton ran out into the street, calling for them to stop. Dean turned to the front and called out, "Keep going. He can get his own ride to the hospital."

"I agree," the other paramedic replied from the driver's seat.

Dean nodded at how they'd separated Verity from Manton. It was essential to get her to the hospital alone. Dean would report his suspicions to the nurses at ECMC. The staff had an excellent relationship with local social workers and local shelters. If anyone could get her to safety and in a place where she would open up and tell her story, it was those specialized resources. Dean and Barry had done their jobs by recognizing it in the field. Now they had to follow up and send the report up the chain of care.

It took almost twenty minutes to arrive at the hospital. Barry had taken a round-about route, driving them over some of the better maintained roads rather than going the quickest way. As he backed into an open slot in the ambulance bay outside the ER, Dean gathered his supplies and prepped Verity to go inside.

He'd given her two more doses of morphine, maxing out the ten-milligram dose he could give. It seemed to be enough for now. Verity no longer winced at every movement of the surrounding ambulance.

"Verity, once we get inside, you'll be safe. You can talk to the nurses and doctors in there and they'll help you, with everything you might need. Do you understand? They can help with everything."

"I do. Thank you. Will—" She stopped and looked out through the back windows of the ambulance. "Will Manton be here?"

Dean shook his head. "If you don't want him to come back to your room and see you, they can keep him away. Just tell them what you want. No one can hurt you here."

Verity nodded and fell silent, continuing to search the street outside the back windows.

Dean and Barry unloaded her on the stretcher and rolled her inside the ER. Dean looked to see who the charge nurse on duty was. They posted nursing assignments on the big dry-erase board by the nurses' station. Next to the word "Charge" was the name "Moore."

A smile spread across Dean's face. Ashley was working tonight. He hadn't seen her in a while, but he knew she was taking some shifts at the hospital now that she was back in town.

An Eldara Sister, Ashley was an angelic messenger of the gods or whoever the beings were that lived in the higher planes. In her case, she was one of the Sisters, a healing angel and a more than competent nurse. She had a history throughout time of helping others advance medical and nursing care. She had been one of his companions in the fight against the four horsemen months before.

He smiled as Ashely's tall form walked from behind the counter, a broad smile on her face. "Hey, Dean. I heard Barry on the scanner announcing you were on the way. What do you have for us?"

The first thing Dean noticed was her hair. She'd cut it short, very short, in a sort of pixie cut. It surprised him. He'd never seen her without her long brunette hair, usually pulled back in a ponytail. He had to admit, though; the look didn't detract from her angelic features. He shook himself. He was married now.

He and Ashley had a history, once, long ago. But that was in the past, and Dean had moved on. Now, she and Jaz were close friends, which was more than a little awkward for him at times.

Dean shifted his mind back to his patient. He nodded to the woman on the stretcher beside him. "This is Verity. I'm pretty sure she fractured her arm. She also might benefit from a room with some privacy because of some special concerns."

Ashley's eyes narrowed a little at the request for a room isolated from the others. He hoped she trusted him enough to follow his lead until he could explain the situation.

Ashley smiled at Verity and said, "Take her back to room sixteen. It's near our break room in the rear of the ER, which should be off the beaten track enough to keep her from any prying eyes."

Dean nodded. With Barry's help, he rolled the woman to the room at the back corner of the emergency department.

Another nurse, Barbara, came in as they moved their patient over to the hospital bed. She took Dean's verbal report on Verity's injury. He didn't expound on his suspicions here. He'd fill in Ashley out front and let her handle the relevant referrals. That was her job as the charge nurse.

"Verity, Barb here will take good care of you from here. Don't be afraid to share anything you want with her, or any other people on the staff. You can trust the folks here to take care of you."

Barb was one of the nurses who knew of the existence of Unusuals living among the human inhabitants of Elk City. She'd protect Verity's Selkie identity from the normal human patients in the ER. She'd also work with Ashley to get the girl the help she needed.

Dean and Barry took the stretcher back around front. On the way, Dean heard a familiar voice shouting in the waiting room through a pair of double doors. It was Manton, and he didn't sound too happy and being told to wait there.

"Barry, you got the stretcher and the supply restock? I want to fill Ashley in on the situation with the noise out front. We don't want Manton barging back here without someone to stop him."

"I got it. I'll see you back out at the ambulance."

Dean nodded and crossed over to the nurses' station. Ashley and the others had heard the commotion. As Dean approached, Ashley hung up the phone on the desk in front of her.

"Hey, Ash, that guy shouting out in the waiting room was at the scene earlier. He says he's Verity's boyfriend. Something weird is going on with them and we had a hard time separating him from her."

"I just called security down. Do you think he's got some kind of charm going on or other magic?"

"Not sure. My gut reaction is she's a victim of human trafficking or whatever you call the Unusual version of it."

"They're all humans, Dean," Ashley chided him. "You know that."

"Yeah, I do. Sorry." Dean of all people, having recently found out he was half-Eldara himself, should be more careful with his words. "Anyway, if you can, I'd keep them apart until you can get her to open up about what's going on."

Ashley nodded. "I'll get back to see her myself once we get the guy out front calmed down. I don't want him upsetting anyone else."

"Officer O'Malley came to the scene and dealt with him there. You know him?"

"I do," Ashley turned to one of the clerks seated next where she stood. "Jack, see if you can call in to ECPD's station U team and get O'Malley to stop by if he's in the area. Tell them we have a situation and individual here he just handled at an ambulance call."

Jack nodded and picked up the phone to dial in.

"Uh, I haven't seen you since just after—" Dean said, trailing off.

"What? The end of the world?"

Dean couldn't hide his wide-eyed expression. He looked around at the nurses nearby to see if they overheard.

Ashley laughed, "Don't worry, the whole shift today is clued in. Most of the ER staff is at this point. There was no way to contain everything the four horsemen caused without explaining about the supernatural world all around them."

That surprised Dean. He hadn't heard that before. "Okay, somebody should've passed that down to us."

"I'm sure it's much the same for your colleagues in the Fire Department."

Dean thought about it and nodded. When he'd first started on the job just over two years before, he'd been part of a very small collection of responders and health professionals who knew about the secret world all around them. Since the near apocalypse, it was less of a secret. Having the living dead walk the streets opened more than a few eyes.

Still, the vast majority of the Elk City population had bought the health department line about a viral encephalitis outbreak that caused violent behaviors in those infected.

Deciding to change the subject, Dean pointed to Ashley's head. "I like your hair. When did you cut it?"

"Not that long after things settled down. It has been so long since I've had short hair. It's been at least a thousand years. I'd forgotten how light it makes my head feel. I'm surprised Jaz didn't tell you about it."

"Why would she?" Dean hadn't known Ashley and his wife had been in contact recently.

"Jaz and I have lunch every week or so when she's not traveling. She likes to keep up on what's going on in town from a supernatural perspective."

His wife had not told him about it, and Dean wondered why she hadn't mentioned it.

Ashley must have spotted the perplexed look on his face. "Don't get annoyed with her. No woman likes to remind her husband of an ex-girlfriend, no matter how safe she knows it to be. Don't worry. We didn't talk about you, at least not too much."

She said the last with a little giggle and picked up a tablet computer from behind the nurses' station as two security guards entered through the doors leading to the rest of the hospital. "I have to go help these two deal with the disturbance out front. I'll see you again. I'm on shift all week while a few of the regular charge nurses are at a conference."

"That's nice to know. It's always a relief knowing you're here when we bring in critical patients."

As Ashley left, Dean checked his watch as he headed out to the ambulance. The shift was almost over and that meant he could get home and see Jaz. She'd returned that afternoon from a week-long trip to check on her company's European operations. It would be good to have her home again. She was supposed to be in town for a few weeks this time around. The apartment would be much less lonely with her there.

Chapter 3

BACK AT STATION U, tucked away back in a nondescript industrial park on the edge of town, Dean and Barry got the ambulance parked and restocked just in time for Bill and Lynne to arrive and take over for the next shift.

As Dean entered the crew quarters, a wonderful smell struck him and saliva flowed into his mouth from whatever Freddy had going in the kitchen.

"Freddy, you culinary genius, what glorious thing have you come up with for dinner?"

A shuffling gray form walked out of the small duty kitchen at the far side of the room. "I got some fresh mussels in from Kristof over at Sabatani's. He had some extras in the shipment he just got in, so he called over to see if I wanted them. I said sure. It's a good excuse to make you all a seafood chowder."

Dean gave Freddy a gentle high five. He had to be careful, so he didn't knock anything loose. Freddy was the station's resident cook. He also was a homeless zombie who traded his pre-death skills as a top international chef for a place to live.

"That sounds awesome, my man. Can you put some in a

container for me to take home? Jaz just got back from her trip and I'd like to take some dinner home to enjoy with her."

Bill laughed from where he sat at the computer terminal, checking in with the daily reports. "What's wrong with the rest of us? You too good to eat with us heathens?"

"Leave him alone, Bill," Lynne said. "The two of them are still technically honeymooners."

"It doesn't count if the two of them haven't actually gone on a honeymoon," Bill countered. "Dean can't seem to get his act in gear to plan one."

"Hey, I'm working on it. I've just got to find a time when Jaz is in town for longer than a few days and when I can get off work." Dean wasn't lying, nor was he trying to evade Bill's point. He'd been working through a few ideas on where to take Jaz for a real, honest to God honeymoon. He didn't need his coworkers to remind him they hadn't been able to go away together yet.

Barry came in from the ambulance bay and let out a sigh. "I'm hungry enough to eat an entire hog. I hope you made a lot of whatever it is I smell, Freddy."

"I did, don't worry. I'll have it on the table in a few minutes."

"Don't forget to check for missing bits before you serve it," Barry cautioned. "I found your pinky finger in my salad last week."

Dean laughed. That had been hilarious, even if he'd almost had to Heimlich his partner to clear the choking zombie finger from his throat.

"It's not funny when it's in your food, believe me," Barry chided all of them. "I could have died and then what would you have done?"

Dean waved off Barry's comment. "We'd have saved you just like we do for everyone else. Stop complaining. You can't expect food this good for free and not have some trade-offs." Dean turned to check himself out of the shift on the computer.

Bill finished what he was doing on the other terminal and turned to Dean. "Anything interesting on your shift today?"

"There was our most recent call. It seemed like we'd stumbled on a woman who'd been a victim of human trafficking or something like it." Dean related the events of the last call of the day and what he'd done at the hospital to report it. "I hope she takes the help she's offered."

Lynne shook her head. "I was in that same class as you were, Dean. You heard what the instructor said about the percentages who were rescued and those who opted to remain under the control of their captors. It has conditioned a lot of them to think no one will help them."

Bill said, "Didn't Brynne say something about a few similar calls being reported recently by some of the other shifts? I seem to remember seeing it here in one of her daily updates."

"If she did, I must have glossed over it," Dean said. He'd have to go back and check his email for that notice. "Where is Brynne? Isn't she on as supervisor tonight?"

Lynne nodded. "She'll be here later. She texted me she had a meeting to attend with the Chief before he went home for the night. The paramedic class just graduated, and I think she has her eye on at least one of them for Station U."

Brynne had been Dean's training officer until she'd nearly died from a gunshot wound. Only a last-minute save by her vampire boyfriend had saved her, sort of. Now she was back at work, but she could only work night shifts after sundown, and that limited her contact with the rest of the human fire department leadership who worked during the day.

"What did her email about trafficking say, Bill?" Dean asked.

He couldn't put his finger on it, but the fact that the other station U staff might have had similar ambulance calls told Dean that Verity's plight wasn't an isolated one.

"What are you thinking, partner?" Barry asked. "You think there's some sort of ring operating here?

"I don't know, but if there were, why bring them here where more people know about Unusuals," Dean said. "I could see a regular human trafficking ring setting up shop here. Putting one in place dealing in Unusuals here seems like they're asking for a run in with us or our police counterparts."

"Maybe you should ask Jaz that question," Lynne suggested.

"With her connections both here and abroad, she might be able to find out something."

"I'll mention it to her. I know she'd want to help out. That's not something she has much patience with at all." Dean scanned down through his old emails but didn't see the one to which his colleague was referring. "Bill, I can't find the message."

"I remember it was a Merrow girl they found. She was in pretty bad shape when the crew got to her. I'm not sure if she survived or not. She had numerous health issues when they brought her in." Bill had turned back to the computer. He scrolled down the screen and pointed at one entry. He must have found the email because he clicked on the reference link to open the actual patient report.

"Merrow?" Dean asked. "That's an Irish sea fae, right?"

Lynne nodded. "They're the classic mermaids and mermen you hear about in most sailor's stories. They have tails and gills when in the water, but they can shift to human form to walk around on land if they want, at least for a limited time. There aren't many of them ashore, though. They usually prefer their home waters and communities."

"How did she get all the way over here, then?" Dean asked. "It's strange. I can't help but think there's a connection of some sort between the two calls. Mine was a rare variety of water Unusual, too. This one was a Selkie, a seal-shifter."

Bill shook his head. "They're even rarer than the Merrow are. They come from the islands off the northern coast of Scotland if I remember my legends and lore correctly."

Dean tried to pull the pieces together in his head. It felt like it was all connected, but he didn't have enough pieces yet. "Let's all keep our eyes open and check with the community when we get out and about. Maybe someone has heard something. I'll get with Gibbie and the rest of the disaster CERT response team to follow up for us, too. They've been champing at the bit for a chance to get some action again. Maybe if between us we turn over enough rocks, we'll kick something loose to see the connection."

The others nodded. Dean knew their informal paramedic community in the station would keep an eye out for similar patients and situations. Hopefully, they'd see something else that would lead to a clue.

Freddy came from the kitchen again, carrying a large Dutch oven to the break room table where he set it down next to a bowl of salad and a basket of rolls. He smiled at the assembled paramedics with a snaggle-toothed grin. "Dinner's ready. Get it while it's hot."

"Hand check," Barry called.

Everyone laughed as Freddy held up his hands, displaying all ten fingers, mostly intact. Dean had reattached the detached pinky finger the previous week using some super glue.

Freddy pointed back to the kitchen. "Dean, I have a plastic container back in the kitchen so you can take some home to have with Jaz. I added some dinner rolls and the salad, too. They're in a reusable nylon bag next to the container. Don't forget to bring back the bag and the containers, please."

"Thanks, Freddy. I'll remember. I know Jaz'll appreciate it." Dean stood up and said, "I think I'll get going. I'll follow up later with you all if I find out anything from my wife."

"I'll start an email chain with the different shifts so we can bring Brook and Tammy, along with the backup shift, into the conversation."

Dean nodded and walked over to the kitchen to grab the food Freddie had packed up for him.

Barry, Lynne, and Bill had changed subjects and were grilling Barry about a recent date. Dean chuckled to himself as he headed out to the parking lot. The crews of Station U were a close-knit group. There were very few secrets between them.

As he walked towards his pickup truck, he realized how oddly dark it was. A glance back at the Station told him why. The light on the pole by the building was out. It usually lit up the parking area bright as day. Dean shook his head. He'd have to tell Brynne about it. She'd report it to the industrial park's owners and get it fixed.

Dean turned back towards his truck and set the food containers on the hood so he could reach his keys. He grunted in surprise and pain as something slammed into him. The force knocked him down so hard he skidded on his chest across the asphalt for several feet. It took the wind out of him and he struggled to catch his breath.

Trying to gather his wits while getting up onto his hands and knees, Dean turned his head to see what had hit him. Expecting to see a vehicle, it surprised him to see a dark form stalking his way, red eyes glowing in the blackness of the parking area.

A ripping snarl followed by a guttural voice came from the figure. "You shouldn't have interfered with Verity, human. She was mine to do with as I pleased."

The dark form had gotten close enough now that Dean made out the humanoid form of a werepanther, the cat-like features blending with Manton's human face.

Dean pushed upward, trying to rise to his feet.

Manton took two steps towards the struggling paramedic, kicking Dean in the gut as he rose.

The air whooshed from Dean's lungs as the powerful blow lifted him from the ground and rolled him over and over until he came to rest against the curb beside Barry's SUV.

He put out a hand to use the vehicle to help get to his feet so he could defend himself. Dean didn't have too much hope to hold off an attack by an enraged shifter of any type for long. Still, if he were on his feet, he could make a dash for the station door. Help was there if he could reach it.

Gasping to catch his breath, Dean tried to call out for help. The building was pretty well insulated. He wasn't sure they'd hear him inside or not, but he had to try.

Manton stalked forward; his clawed hands extended towards Dean.

"H-help." He still hadn't caught his breath. The croaking rasp of Dean's voice had little volume, certainly not enough for the other medics inside to hear him. He worked to draw in a deeper breath to call out again.

Dean got to his feet, swaying as he stood. He propped his back against the SUV's rear door to steady himself and let out another pitifully weak call for help.

The shifter came closer and Dean lifted his fists, ready to defend himself as best he could, even if it seemed like a futile gesture.

Manton had almost reached him when a shadow streaked by, coming out of nowhere. It knocked Manton from his feet and sent the shifter rolling across the parking area.

Dean stared into the night, trying to see who or what had rescued him. The shadow moved to his right and he tried to pierce the darkness to see who it was.

"You alright, Dean?" Brynne asked.

He let out a sigh of relief at hearing his former partner's voice. "Yeah, I am now that you're here."

The vampire turned towards the werepanther who had regained his feet. A low snarl came from Manton's throat as he readied himself for a fight.

Brynne rushed forward, moving so fast, she was little more than a blur. She charged the shifter, colliding with Manton at full speed.

This time he was ready for her and took the hit without getting knocked down. For a while, the two of them were an indistinguishable swirling mass of battling darkness in the middle of the parking lot.

Dean considered running for the station door to get more help, but the fight ended before he took a step.

Brynne knocked Manton to the ground. Before he could rise, she kicked him so hard he flew over twenty feet across the parking lot to slam into the wooden telephone pole beside the building.

The werepanther rolled away from the pole and climbed back to his feet. From the way he carried himself, Brynne had injured him, perhaps seriously.

Before she could move in to follow up on her attack, Manton completed his shift to full panther form. The big cat, black as night, ran off into the darkness behind the Station U building.

Brynne stared after the cat, peering into the murky darkness around them. She glanced at Dean. "He's gone. Are you okay?"

"I am now. Thank you for saving me."

"You'll always be my probie, Dean. I'm not going to let anyone hurt you on my watch. Who was that guy? Did you know him?"

"He was the companion of a patient we had earlier. We thought she might be caught up in a human trafficking thing and separated them long enough to get her some help. Ashley was the charge nurse tonight and said she'd take care of it. It looks like she was successful separating them based on what that guy said when he attacked me."

Dean took a step towards his truck and groaned, clutching his ribs. He didn't think they were broken, but he'd be sore for the next few days.

"You're hurt. Come on inside so we can check you over."

Dean shook his head. "No, I'm okay. I'll get Jaz to help me manage the scrapes and bruises when I get home."

Brynne looked like she was about to order him to come inside, but she changed her mind. "Call in when you get home and if it gets worse, get yourself to the ER. Don't be a hero. Got me?"

"Me, a hero? You know me better than that. I'll be fine. I promise."

"I'm serious. Either tell me you'll do as I say, or I'll pick you up and carry you inside right now."

Dean held up his hands in surrender. "I'll call, I promise."

Brynne nodded. Dean picked up his keys from the ground by the pickup truck. He unlocked the doors and put the food inside on the seat, pushing it over to the passenger side as he climbed in.

A glance out the window as he backed out showed Brynn standing there with her arms crossed, lit by the taillights from his truck. He waved before he pulled onto the street and headed home.

Chapter 4

DEAN WINCED as his wife tended to his injuries.

"You should have listened to Brynne. Your ribs could be broken." Jaz wiped at the scrapes on his arms with a damp wash-cloth, cleaning the remaining dirt and grit from the parking lot out of his wounds.

Dean twisted around where he sat on the closed lid of the toilet and probing with his fingertips at his side. "They're not broken. Just bruised, I think."

Jaz snorted in response as she turned to soak the cloth in the sink full of warm water.

Dean knew she didn't approve of his decision to avoid getting checked out any more than Brynne did. He didn't care. He just wanted to eat and get some sleep. There was nothing wrong with him he couldn't deal with in the morning. He'd head in to the ER if it seemed more serious then.

"Tell me who it was who did this to you again? You said it was a werepanther?"

"That's how I'd describe the guy. I knew he was some kind of cat shifter based on what I picked up from him during the ambulance call. Seeing him in the parking lot confirmed it. He was a big black cat. That's a panther, right?"

Jaz nodded; her lips pressed together in a thin line. She dabbed at his scrapes, saying nothing.

Dean knew his wife well enough to know she was plotting revenge of her own against the creature who'd made the mistake of attacking her husband. He didn't want her to go off on some sort of vengeance hunt.

"Hon, look at me. I'm going to be fine. Brynne scared him off and I don't think he'll be back. Besides, he has to know I'm aware of who he was. He's probably a hundred miles away by now, figuring the police are after him. I'm sure Brynne reported it."

"The police are the least of his worries. They won't put a silver bullet in his skull."

"Jaz, seriously, let it go. It's more important that we focus on the good news from the attack."

"Good news? Like what?"

"His attack means we freed Verity of his control," Dean replied. "I call that a win. She can get the help she needs, and the authorities can find out where she came from."

Jaz nodded. "If there's a trafficking ring set up here in Elk City, it's got to be rooted out. There has been no werecat activity from the Cartels around here for quite a while. My father made sure of that. Maybe they think they can come back now that he's dead."

"I didn't know there was a cartel of werepanthers."

"Most of the werecats in North and South America answer to one or two criminal cartels run by old-school families of were-jaguars. They're very rare and supposedly super powerful among their own kind. They have an agreement with Errington regarding this kind of thing. I have to look into this."

"O'Malley was there, Jaz. Let the ECPD handle it. If there's a ring like that operating here, they'll take care of it."

He could tell from her expression Jaz wasn't convinced. She threw the supplies they didn't use back into the first aid kit and dropped it on top of the toilet tank lid. "You know as well as I do how the Unusual community is with getting help from human law enforcement agencies. They're afraid to reach out for help for even the simplest of reasons. Something like this would go unreported by almost everyone."

Dean shrugged. "I had to report it and help Verity deal with it. It's required. Besides, it's just the right thing to do. Brynne's looking into it, too, so that means James and Rudy will get involved. You've got enough on your plate working to get Errington Security's international operations back online. Let someone else handle it."

The Hunter clan leader shook her head, her blond ponytail swaying behind her. "Nope, keeping this city clean of scum like that is as much my job as it is the local authorities. I want this place to be a place of safety and refuge when I come home. It should be somewhere my family and I can relax without worrying about getting jumped in a parking lot."

Jaz turned back to the sink, wringing out the washcloth. She stared in the mirror for a few seconds than sighed. "Look, I'll stand down. Let me have my intel guy check into some things, though. These types move in certain circles. We might be able to get a handle on them where local police investigators can't."

Dean knew better than to argue with her about stuff like this. It was her company, and it was her decision to make if she wanted. He could've had a say, but he'd turned down the executive vice president position she'd offered him. He wasn't ready to give up working on the streets just yet. Of course, that meant he didn't have the right to say no to things like this, other than to express concern as a spouse. The dynamic between them might change someday, but for now it was the way they'd drawn the lines between their two jobs.

He changed the subject. He checked his injured arms. "This is good enough. I feel better already. Let me get a shirt on and we can go reheat the dinner Freddy made for us."

Jaz smiled and nodded. "It smelled good." Anger spread across her face. "I'm glad that shifter waited until you put the food down. If he'd ruined dinner, nothing would keep me from hunting him down."

"Great, at least I know where your priorities lie," Dean said, laughing.

"What can I say? Freddy's food is just that good."

The two of them went into the kitchen and started working side by side on getting the meal together.

Fifteen minutes later, as they sat eating, Dean asked, "Have you thought anymore about getting some time away from work so we can finally take that honeymoon trip we've been talking about?"

Her hesitation to respond was all the answer he needed. "Jaz, you promised. You said after you got back from Europe you'd have some time to do this."

"I know what I said, but I have more on my plate now than when I left. I deal with one issue, and three more crop up. I don't know how my father did it all."

Dean leaned over the table and put his hand atop hers. "He delegated the small stuff to his management team."

"There isn't any small stuff. And there isn't any management team." Jaz shook her head. "There's a rogue pack of werewolves roaming around Eastern Europe. I've had two teams in Budapest go missing while tracking them. I'm going to have to go myself if the head of European ops doesn't get it under control."

"I haven't met him yet, have I?"

"Her, and no, you haven't. I just put Elsa in place two months ago when I found out the last guy, a former German special forces operator, was taking payoffs to look the other way on some of our security accounts."

"How did you find her?"

"Rudy recommended her to me. She's the oldest daughter of the senior pack leader in Belgium."

Dean's eyebrows shot up. "You hired an Unusual for the job? That's pretty progressive of you considering where you were on the subject when we first met."

Jaz smiled. "I've had a change of heart. After all, I'm married to a half-Eldara."

"I might as well be plain old human if I'm going to keep getting my butt kicked by every evil bad guy to come along."

"I've offered to teach you some weapons and self-defense techniques. I could get you a concealed carry permit once you're trained."

Dean shook his head. "No, you know how I feel about this. I'm a healer, not a fighter. Let's just call it a division of labor in our marriage. One total badass is enough."

"Flattery will get you nowhere, dear. I'm serious. You need to be able to protect yourself. You'd think after everything that's happened to you over the last year and a half, you'd understand that."

"Nope, we both have our roles in this family. I'm happy with the way things stand." Uncomfortable with the talk about weapons and fighting, Dean shifted the conversation. "So this Elsa you hired is a Lycan, just like the ones you're trying to hunt down? It seems like she'd be a good fit if she's willing to do the dirty work. Most werewolves I know don't like packs breaking the rules. It only draws unwanted human attention."

"The biggest problem is getting the strike teams to listen to her. That she's both a woman, and a shifter is causing a problem among the older, more established members."

"They listen to you, right?"

"Mostly," Jaz replied and held up her hand. "Before you say anything, I'm dealing with the ones who are the worst. It's not just my gender. It's my age, too. They don't think I have the experience to lead the organization. I've got some ideas on how to show them I'm the boss in more than title only."

"How?"

"That's one reason I've had to keep going back over there. I've fired three of them so far, and two of those poached their friends from the team to go into security operations for themselves. I can't afford to lose experienced hunter team members. This whole last week, I've had to run damage control to keep the bulk of the remaining strike groups from running and hiring out for someone else."

"What does this Elsa say you should do?"

"She suggests hiring more Unusuals to fill the gaps, but I'm worried it will cause more problems than it solves."

Dean shrugged. "It seems to me that the people you're losing are dead weight, not the cream of the crop. If these losers are quitting because of their prejudice, they aren't going to be open-minded when on an operation either. I say good riddance. Let Elsa put together hybrid teams so everyone learns to trust each other."

Jaz paused, considering Dean's suggestion. "You're just voting for Elsa to take over the hiring so you can keep me home here with you."

"Of course I am, but that doesn't mean I'm not right. Let her do her job. Have her send regular reports for you to review but, let her have full control for a while and see how she does. It works for us in the fire and emergency medical services. The Chief has to let the line medics have the option to be unconventional sometimes. A good leader trusts her crews to use their own skills and intuition. They know best when to be creative and when to follow the letter of the rules."

Jaz stirred her spoon through the remains of the stew at the bottom of her bowl. "That might work. I have to go to Ireland next week and handle the opening of a new branch office there," Jaz said. "Elsa will be there, too. I can have a chat with her about what you've said. I'll see what she thinks about giving her more latitude in operational decisions and hiring."

"Perfect! I could go with you."

"Go with me? Why?"

"We can kill two birds with one stone. You can go do your grand opening thing and meet with Elsa. Then we can take a few days and tour the Emerald Isle. I'll bet if we ask Dougie down at the Irish Shop, he'll even let us use that magical doorway in his place to travel to Dublin."

Jas smiled. "It would be nice to take a little time. A few days wouldn't kill us. When's the last time you talked to the leprechaun?"

"It's been a few months, but he's always said I could use the portal again if I needed to. It worked out well the last time with the CERT team. We went to debrief in a pub on the other side after the Barrens fire."

Jaz smiled. "Well, I guess it's a date, then. You set everything up with Dougie and I'll make arrangements for a hotel and transportation while we're in Dublin."

"Perfect," Dean said. He forgot how sore he was from the fight earlier. He stood and leaned over the table to kiss Jaz. "I'll get to show off my hot hunter wife to everyone we see."

"Who's saying I'm not going to show off my new boy toy, too."

They both fell into a round of chuckles and cleaned up their dinner. Dean tried to hide his pain when he moved and hoped he'd heal up before the trip came around. He didn't want to go on his honeymoon all gimpy from this injury.

They finished the dishes and got ready for bed. Dean pulled out his phone and sent off a text message to Dougie to check about taking the secret portal doorway in his shop to Ireland.

It pleased him he'd been able to get his wife to slow down a little and spend some time vacationing. They both could use a break and she was the type to work all the time if someone didn't make her slow down. It would be the perfect opportunity for both of them.

Chapter 5

THE NEXT FEW days flew by as Dean and Barry continued running the routine calls that made up the bulk of their days. Most were a lot like the current call on which the pair found themselves.

"We're almost there, Barry. You grab the med bag and monitor and get inside. I'll bring in the rest of the gear. This chest pain patient sounds like she's in the middle of a major cardiac event."

Barry nodded. "The additional dispatch information was pretty detailed. It's weird, don't you think? Who notifies the 911 operator they have chest pain, radiating pain down the left arm, and diaphoresis?"

Dean shrugged as he turned off the highway and down into a residential neighborhood. "Beats me. Maybe they have some medical training of some sort and knew what to tell our dispatch team. Either way, if it's accurate, we'll need to make sure they don't code on us before the hospital."

Barry pointed out to a house on the left. "There. That one is number 874."

Every one of the Victorian homes sat on large, grassy lots with trees lining the street on either side. Because the homes sat back off the street, it was hard to spot the house numbers from the road.

Dean squinted in the darkness and tried to make out the numbers by the door.

"How can you even see that? Those numbers are tiny."

"I didn't look up at the house. Look down at the curb. The house numbers are stenciled there beside each driveway."

Dean grinned. "Good catch, partner."

He pulled into the driveway and Barry hopped out of the passenger seat to grab his gear and go. Dean worked quickly but didn't rush. He pulled out the stretcher and lowered the wheels until it stood by the rear of the unit, ready to go.

Loading it down with the airway bag and trauma bag just in case, Dean unhooked the stretcher from the rear of the ambulance. He wheeled it towards the house across the grassy yard when he spotted a familiar white van parked on the street in front of the home.

As if on cue, a middle-aged, slightly balding man came down the house's front stairs and jogged towards Dean, waving and offering a broad smile to the paramedic.

"Gibbie, what are you doing here?"

"Oh, I was just here for my weekly reading. When I got inside, she wasn't looking so good."

"And this woman's our patient?" Dean asked.

"Yeah, the Yakshini who lives here."

"The what?" Dean wracked his mind to remember where he'd heard that word before. He did regular research on the Unusual community, but there were a lot of creatures to learn about, especially when you added in all the international variations on the theme out there.

"The Yakshini, the woman inside. The Yaksha are a variety of Asian shape shifter. Tahira works as a Buddhist spirit finder. She helps work on people whose souls are out of alignment with their karma."

"But you're not a Buddhist, Gibbie. You once told me you didn't follow any religion since you became a vampire."

"Oh, it's not a religious thing. I'm just coming here so she can help me find my soul mate."

"You mean like a sort of dating service?"

"Yeah, but much more reliable than any of those online things. I tried the swipe left and right thing for a while, but none of them ever swiped me the right way."

"I wonder why," Dean muttered under his breath.

"Hey, I heard that." Gibbie pointed to his head. "Enhanced vampire ears, remember?"

"Sorry, Gibbie. Here, help me get this gear inside and then you can help us get her ready to go to the hospital."

"I don't think she's going to want to go. She didn't want me to call you in the first place, but I could tell her heart wasn't doing well. I could hear it sort of skipping beats and running real fast."

It sounded to Dean like she might have atrial fibrillation going on, but he'd need Barry to confirm it with the heart monitor. His partner knew what he was doing and probably already had the monitor hooked up and running a check on the woman's heart. No matter how good it was, Gibbie's enhanced hearing wasn't a reliable clinical benchmark.

Once he and Gibbie got the stretcher inside, Dean left it in the entry hall and entered a room filled with velvet upholstered furniture and stained-glass appointments to the windows and lampshades. Barry had already hooked up an old gray-haired woman to the heart monitor, as expected. The tiny, white-haired woman leaned back on an ornate, red divan.

Barry pushed a button on the screen to run a twelve-lead EKG. It looked at multiple areas of the heart at one time rather than just one tracing at a time. It would give them a better picture of what they had here.

Barry glanced at the printout as it came out the front of the machine and looked up at Dean. "A-fib. Draw me up some Cardizem while I get the IV started."

"Got it. Gibbie, help Barry get the IV line and bag ready to go."

"Will do, Dean."

The vampire started assembling the intravenous line tubing and inserted the spiked end into the opening on the plastic one-liter bag of saline fluid.

Dean smiled as he opened the med bag to draw up the syringe of medication Barry would use to treat the woman's rapid and irregular heartbeat. Training Gibbie and the others as Community Emergency Response Team or CERT members had been one of the best ideas he and Brynne had come up with during their time together as partners. The team had come in handy around town on more than a few occasions.

Once the IV was ready and Barry had taken another set of vitals, Dean handed over the medication and Barry began administering it via the IV tubing running into the woman's arm.

Dean reached out and held her other hand to comfort her. A spark flew between them as he touched her fingertips. Instead of jumping and pulling away from the surprise shock, her fingers clutched at his with surprising strength. He stared down at his hand and then up at her face.

The Yakshini's eyes bored into his. "Eldara-spawn, you must save her. It has fallen to you to rescue her amidst the sandy caves. Many things hinge upon your success."

Her eye still wide and wild, she turned to Gibbie. "The one you seek will soon be here, child of the night. Watch for the sign of the golden eagle."

As soon as the final words left her mouth, her eyes rolled back in her head and she slumped to the side. Dean searched her wrist for a pulse, staring at the heart monitor. A more-normal rhythm had replaced the irregular heart rhythm.

He waited to see if there was a pulse to match what the monitor showed. Dean followed the mantra taught him long ago. Treat the patient, not the monitor. He breathed a sigh of relief when his searching fingertips found a sudden, strong pulse in her wrist, matching what he saw on the screen. Nice and regular.

"What was her pulse like when you first came in, Barry?"

"Rapid, thready, and weak as hell. I almost couldn't find it."

"Well, it's nice and steady now. The med converted the rhythm."

"But I didn't give it yet." Barry held up the full syringe Dean had handed to him moments before. "I started to but stopped when she started talking to you. Her voice went all weird and I forgot what I was doing."

"Well, whatever happened, it converted. It doesn't explain why she's unconscious. She might have thrown a clot and had a stroke. Let's get her loaded up and out of here."

"What was that she called you?" Barry asked.

Gibbie beat Dean to an answer. "She called him Eldara spawn. That means Dean's dad is the Archangel Gabriel."

Barry shook his head. "I still don't know if I can get used to having a partner be able to do super stuff like that."

"Trust me, Barry. I didn't get anything fun from my sperm-donor of a father. I'm a normal guy, just like you."

"I don't know, Dean," Gibbie said. "You did use your powers to stop the end of the world."

"That wasn't what happened, believe me. Besides, you weren't even in the room when it all went down."

"No, but I know what Ingrid said about it once you all came back outside."

"She exaggerated everything," Dean snapped. Gibbie's eyes widened at the sharp retort. Dean realized he'd spoken louder than intended and drew in a deep breath. "Look, let's focus on the patient. Help us get all this stuff packed and loaded up. Barry and I will get her on the stretcher and into the ambulance."

Gibbie nodded. Despite his attempt to make it right, Dean saw the hurt reflected in the vampire's eyes. He hadn't meant to lose his temper like that. Something about thinking about Gabe and how he'd tried to end the world stirred up angry emotions inside him.

Gabe had wanted to stick around a little while to help Dean after they defeated the horsemen. He'd nipped that idea in the bud right away. His father had tried to trick him into starting the last battle between good and evil. The archangel wanted to bring on the end of the world to further some heavenly destiny or something. When Dean had figured a way to stop either side from having their way, he had made it clear he wanted nothing to do with powers from heaven or hell.

And now this woman had pronounced a prophecy of some sort

over him. All the supernatural stuff lately sickened him. He wanted nothing to do with any of it, at least where it intersected his personal life. Pushing thoughts of his father from his mind, he focused on helping Barry roll the woman out to the ambulance. He'd ponder what the woman had said later. Right now, he had a patient to care for. It was more important to stay on target and get her to the hospital alive.

By the time Dean pulled the ambulance into the bay at ECMC ten minutes later, the woman had awakened in the back of the unit. She chattered away at Barry about her grandchildren and other random things during the last half of the drive.

In the ambulance bay at the hospital, Dean opened the back doors to unload the stretcher. The Yakshini smiled at him, as if she'd never seen him before. She nodded a greeting, but there was no mention that she'd said anything to Dean. He didn't want to bring it up.

Had he imagined all of it?

They rolled her into the hospital and Barry took charge as the lead paramedic on the case, giving his report to the nurse once they had moved the woman to a bed.

Dean took the stretcher out to make up the sheets.

Ashley spotted him from behind the nurses' station and came out to say hi. He stood by the stretcher in the corner tucking the edge of a white hospital sheet in under the mattress.

"Dean, what happened to you?"

"What do you mean?" Her concerned tone startled him.

"There's Dweomer around you. It looks recent."

Dean checked behind him. Was there something there? "What are you talking about? What's a Dwoomer?"

"A Dweomer. It's the magic residue of a spell. Did someone cast something on you during this call?"

Dean thought back to the spark he'd felt between him and the Yakshini. "I didn't think so, but there was something that happened. Can you tell what it is? It's not a curse, is it?"

"I don't think so. I don't sense any ill intent." Ashley leaned forward with her head tilted up slightly as if she were trying to smell him. Maybe she was. He didn't know all the abilities the Eldara Sister had.

"Well, what is it? I can't be running around with some spell ready to go off at the wrong time."

"Did she say anything when she put the spell on you?"

"She made some sort of prophecy about me being Eldara spawn or something like that. She said I have to rescue someone in a cave filled with sand. It was all nonsense. She was in the middle of a major cardiac event. As soon as she said it, she fainted. By the time she got here, she'd forgotten all about it."

Ashley nodded. "I think the Yakshini cast a Geas on you."

She'd used another word he didn't know. It sounded like "gesh." "Okay, are you going to explain that to me, too?"

Ashley looked around and pointed to the EMS break room by the ambulance door. "Come in here. I'll try to explain it to you where no one is listening. This is serious."

Dean didn't like the sound of that. He didn't have the time to lift some sort of curse. The local witch's coven had become a little gun-shy when it came to casting spells when he was around. Bad things had a way of happening when they did.

He followed Ashley into the break room with its computer terminal and half-size fridge stocked with soda and water for EMS crews between ambulance calls. "Okay, I'm here. Tell me what it is."

"A Geas is a special kind of magic that isn't used much anymore. It imposes an obligation on the recipient that can cause conflicts until they complete some sort of quest that resolves the obligation."

"Wait, so I'm bound to complete some sort of quest whether I want to or not?" Dean started pacing back and forth beside Ashley.

"Hold still while I try to figure it out. It usually won't work if it's something totally against your moral code, so you can stop worrying about that." Ashley reached out with both hands to grip Dean's head while she leaned close with her eyes closed.

At that moment, Barry walked into the EMS break room, took one look at the two of them and pivoted around 180 degrees back out the door. "Uh, sorry, I didn't see anything."

"Dammit," Dean said, pulling away from Ashley's hands. "Now Barry's gonna think I'm cheating on Jaz."

Ashely laughed, "Nonsense, Dean. He knows you better than that. He should know me better than that, too."

"I've got to go. If you figure out what's going on with this Geas thing, let me know. I'll try to see if Jaz can do anything about it. She's got to have a hunter charm or something I can use to block it."

"Don't be so sure. This is an ancient magic spell. It's better to figure out exactly what the old Yakshini meant when she cast it."

Dean nodded. "Maybe I'll come back here after work and visit her in her room upstairs after she's admitted." He broke out in a sweat as anxiety rolled over him.

"Dean, take a breath. This isn't the first time you've stumbled into something like this. You know when the time comes, you'll know what to do. It's part of who you are."

Dean shot Ashley as sideways glance and paused at the door. "You know, Ash. It would've been nice of you to tell me you knew who my father was all along. It's the one thing that sours my memory of our relationship a little when I think about it."

"It wasn't my place, Dean. I didn't know at first. By the time I figured out who you were, I'd gotten close enough to realize you weren't ready to know."

"Maybe, maybe not. That wasn't yours to decide. You still should have told me."

Dean left before Ashley could say anything else. He still had to deal with what Barry thought he saw. Once he put that fire out, he had to figure out what the Geas magic had done to him. Things had been normal for the last few months since they'd defeated the four horsemen. He'd thought maybe he was beyond this sort of thing for a while.

He should have known better.

Chapter 6

OUT ON THE hospital ambulance ramp, Barry stood beside the unit chatting with one of the hospital security guards. He smiled as Dean approached. "You get finished with everything you wanted in there?"

"Ha, ha, Barry. I know what you think you saw in there, but it was nothing. She was trying to figure out what kind of spell Tahira cast on me back at her house."

"Oh, is that all it was." Barry laughed and rolled his eyes.

Anger bubbled beneath the surface as Dean struggled with what to say. Then saw Barry smiling and realized his partner was teasing him. He forced a laugh. "Yeah, that's all it was. You're lucky, Barry. You try to run into one of your exes on a regular basis and see if you don't get caught in a potentially awkward situation sometime."

"Dean, if I had exes as hot as yours, I'd be getting caught in awkward situations all the time. You're a better man than I am."

"You've got that right. Ready to go?"

Barry pointed to the security guard. "In a second. You remember Verity from a few nights back?"

Dean nodded.

Barry continued. "Dirk here told me that her boyfriend came

into the hospital late last night, threw some people out of his way and dragged her out here to the street. A few bystanders saw him force her into a black SUV before it drove away. The staff called the police, but they didn't get here in time to do anything but take a statement."

"Really? Why didn't Ashley tell me?"

Dirk said, "She wasn't working yesterday. She might not know."

Dean shook his head. "I'd hoped getting Verity here would finally get her to a safe place."

The hefty security guard shook his head. "That guy she was with was super strong. He tossed my partner aside like he was a rag doll. He's still upstairs with some pins in his leg because of it."

"Damn, Manton came back even after Brynne ran him off. I thought he'd be long gone by now."

"Too bad Ashley wasn't here."

Dirk shrugged, "Good thing, she wasn't. He'd have hurt her just like everyone else who tried to stop him."

Dean resisted laughing. Dirk wouldn't understand why he thought what he'd said was funny. Dean knew the Eldara would have been more than a match for the werepanther if it had come to a confrontation. It was likely the shifter had waited until she'd left on purpose just to avoid running into her.

As Dean thought about Verity, a vision of a different girl, younger, with red hair popped into his head. A strange, warm tingling sensation ran up the back of his neck. It raised the hairs there and despite the warmth of it; he shivered. Tahira's voice came back to him as if played back on a recording in his head. "Eldara-spawn, you must save her. It has fallen to you to rescue her amidst the sandy caves. Many things will hinge upon your success."

The voice trailed off in his mind and the sensation faded.

Barry stared at Dean. "You alright, partner? You just turned white as a sheet."

"Uh, yeah, just trying to shake of the weird stuff that woman said to me back at her house."

"Oh, about you being the chosen one and all?"

"She didn't say that, and you know it."

48

Barry raised his voice into a loud falsetto. "Help us, Obi-Dean. You're our only hope."

"Hilarious. Get in the unit. We need to get back on the street. You're the medic on call tonight. Maybe it'll be nice and quiet for you."

Barry groaned at the use of the "Q" word. "I'll get you for that, Dean. Now you've doomed us to the shift from hell."

As if to punctuate his words, their radios chirped with alert tones and the dispatcher called out their unit number. "U-191, are you back in service?"

Dean smiled and reached to key the mic clipped to his uniform shirt by his collar. "Affirmative headquarters."

"U-191, respond to the scene of a house fire at 8713 Cree Terrace for burns."

"U-191 responding."

Barry grunted, "I hate burns."

"Me, too," Dean replied. He walked to the driver's side of the ambulance and climbed in. Once Barry was in and settled, Dean started up the unit and pulled away from the hospital on the way to their next call. Even as he drove across town to another set of patients and more injuries, a nagging notion floated in the back of his mind, wondering where Verity was and if she was alright.

Chapter 7

DEAN REGRETTED USING THE "Q" word on Barry by the end of the shift. Every EMS provider knew that word brought on a very real jinx everyone feared. Even though they were supposed to get off work at six the next morning, Dean and his partner didn't get finished with their paperwork until nearly nine.

A glance at the clock as he clicked send on the last report made Dean wince. It was late, and he had a lot to do. He leaned back in the seat with his arms raised over his head and stretched.

Barry glanced his way from his seat behind the computer work-station beside him. "Dean, I hope my eyes aren't as bleary and bloodshot as yours are."

"They're worse, I'm betting. You had most of the patient care tonight. I was just the driver."

"Yeah, well, I'm gonna go home and climb in my bed and not come out again until this time tomorrow."

"It will be good to have the day off. I've got to get Jaz and I squared away for our trip."

Barry smiled. "Yeah, that's right. You two are finally going on that honeymoon thing. You'll have to tell me how it is. I might want to check out using that magic doorway with my girlfriend, too."

"Which one is it this week?" Dean quipped.

"Aw, you're just jealous that I can still play the field while you're tied down to the same old woman for life."

"I'd be careful who you call 'the same old woman,' Barry. If Jaz finds out you called her old, you might have to move out of town for a little while."

"You wouldn't tell her, would you?"

Dean laughed. "What happens at the station, stays at the station. I wouldn't throw you under that bus. My wife can be a stone-cold killer if she wants to be."

Barry laughed, too, but there was a hint of desperation behind it. He knew Dean wasn't kidding. Jaz was, after all, a trained Hunter.

Dean stood up and went over to grab his coat. "I'm out. You're all finished, too, right?"

Barry nodded. "Yeah, I just need to email the training officer about an upcoming slot in a class he's teaching. I'm behind on my continuing education. As soon as I'm done that, I'm out of here."

"Good, get home and get that sleep. You look like hell."

Barry chuckled and waved as Dean headed out to his pickup truck. He needed to pick up a few things on the way home and then he was going to hit the sack, too.

At least that was the plan.

As Dean drove home, he found his mind drifting back to Verity, wondering where she was and if there was some way to help her. He became so lost in his thoughts, he soon discovered he'd driven off track instead of going straight home. He found himself in an old, working class neighborhood on the northern edge of Elk City, down by the river front.

"Damn, I'm more tired than I thought," Dean muttered to himself. He needed to get some sack time.

His phone chirped and he clicked the hands-free button to pick up.

It was Jaz.

"Dean, what are you doing up there on that end of town. Did you get called out on another run?"

He'd forgotten she had an app that could track his phone's GPS. "No, I just got distracted by something and sort of got turned around. I'm getting back on the expressway now. I'll be home in fifteen minutes. I'm sorry."

"I blocked out time this morning to plan that trip to Ireland. I've got a call coming up I can't miss, so we're going to have to reschedule if you don't hustle home."

"I hear and obey, Ms. Errington."

"That's enough of that. Just get home. I'll make you some breakfast. I'll bet you're as hungry as you are tired."

"Take that bet and you'll be correct. Oh, and thank you in advance for breakfast. I'll be home soon."

Jaz hung up and Dean twisted his head around to find the fastest way back onto a main road. He passed several streets before he found what he was looking for. Turning the corner next to a run-down warehouse, Dean saw the intersection for Philadelphia Road three streets away.

He smiled as he thought about eating one of Jaz's omelets soon. It would fill the empty pit in his stomach. The hunger distracted him from the tugging in the back of his mind, telling him to turn around and go back to the building on the corner.

Chapter 8

DEAN DROVE up and entered his code into the keypad by the entrance to the Errington Security parking lot. After the gate opened, he pulled his beat-up pickup truck into a spot amidst a row of immaculate black SUVs.

Jaz had offered him the opportunity to get a new car or to just take one of the company vehicles on multiple occasions. She kept telling him he was in the family now and since it was a family-owned company, that gave him the right to drive anything on the lot. Dean still resisted, and he didn't know why. Deep inside, he'd like to drive something new.

Maybe stupid pride kept him from driving a vehicle he hadn't paid for. It might be a minor distinction to some, but to Dean, it was his last holdout against the massive monetary difference between what he made working for the Elk City Fire Department and Jaz's income as the head of a Hunter clan. Most of that income came from her international security and executive protection enterprises.

Dean grabbed his coat and duffle bag from behind the seat and headed into the building. He needed to swap out the clothes so they could go in the laundry.

Inside the employee entrance, the guard at the desk smiled and greeted him. "Good morning, sir. You're running a little later than usual for this shift. Rough night?"

Dean chuckled. "Yeah, you might say that. And Jed, you don't have to call me 'sir'. I've told you I'm fine with you and the others calling me Dean."

"I appreciate you saying that, but I can't. The boss says you're to be treated the same as her. That's all the reason I need. It's not like I want to get on her bad side. She signs the checks."

Dean sighed and returned the guard's smile. "I get that, Jed. I don't like it when I'm on her bad side either. Have a good day. I hope your shift goes by quickly."

"Thank you, sir. Get some sleep."

"Thanks," Dean replied as he punched the button to head up on the elevator. The doors opened right away, and he stepped inside, hitting the key for the fourth floor.

All the apartments were on the top floor. His and Jaz's place was the largest, but there were smaller ones used to house visiting company personnel from other regions. He stepped out into a hallway and walked all the way down past a series of doors on either side until he reached the door at the end. He reached down to pull his keys out. The door opened before he could get them.

"Hey, babe," Jaz said as she stepped aside to let him come in. "I have breakfast on the table. Come on in and eat something. You'll feel better."

"I hope so. I've been out of sorts all night."

"Why?"

Dean hesitated. He'd talked to her earlier to tell her he was running late, but he didn't tell her about the spell Tahira put on him. She saw through his evasion right away.

"Dean, what aren't you telling me? We talked about this."

"It's no big deal. Ashley said a patient put a Geas on me. I'm sure it'll work itself out."

"A Geas? What for?"

Dean shrugged. "She pronounced some sort of prophecy on me and then fainted. When she woke up, she didn't remember any of it."

"That's obviously bull. Where is this woman? I think I need to have a little talk with her." Jaz's hand rested on the Glock holstered on her hip. She wore it always, even in the apartment. Dean thought it was overkill, especially with all the muscle working downstairs around the clock.

"Jaz, calm down. We've talked about this before. There have to be boundaries between us at home and from our work. I can't have you flying off the handle every time I get roughed up by a patient or something happens to me on the job. I can take care of myself."

"Apparently not. This is why I wanted to get you a protection charm of your own. Its spells would have probably stopped this magic from affecting you."

"I told you why I can't have that. If one of the patients spots it and recognizes it as a Hunter charm, it'll ruin my credibility with them as a healer. It's bad enough I'm married to a Hunter."

Dean winced as soon as he heard the words leave his mouth.

Jaz glared at him, staring down from where she stood across the table from where he sat with his breakfast. "I'm sorry if my family's calling bothers your precious patients. Maybe you should have thought about that before you married me."

"Jaz..."

"I've got some work to do down in my office. Get some sleep. When you wake up, we're doing whatever it takes to get this spell removed. Be ready."

Before Dean could say anything else, Jaz stormed out. She slammed the apartment door hard enough that a picture in the hallway crashed to the floor. The sound of the frame's glass breaking punctuated the sudden silence after her exit.

For a few seconds, Dean considered running after her and apologizing before she got on the elevator, but his stubbornness wouldn't let him. He shoveled another bite of the omelet into his mouth.

He frowned as he chewed. It felt like chewing cold rubber now, and it wasn't any tastier.

He shoved the plate towards the center of the table. Maybe she'd settle down about this and realize he could handle it himself while he slept. They were supposed to pack up that afternoon so they could head over to the Irish Shop first thing in the morning. That was contingent on whether they were still talking to each other, of course. He got up and went to clean up the broken glass before heading to get some sleep.

He stripped off his shirt as he walked down the hallway to their bedroom. He finished getting undressed and climbed into bed. Tapping the small remote on the nightstand, he keyed the button that activated the automated blackout curtains and turned off the lights. Dean pulled the covers up around him and closed his eyes.

His sleepy thoughts drifted back to images of Verity, except it didn't look exactly like her. Her face kept shifting into someone else, someone younger. The girl wasn't alone, but danger seemed to stalk around her. The shifting face steadied into Verity's again as the viewpoint widened. There were others who looked enough like her they could be her sisters. They all sat on a concrete floor with their backs against a cinderblock wall. For an instant, before he drifted off to sleep, she looked up and stared back into his eyes. It was almost as if she was trying to say something to him, but he fell asleep before she started.

The dream stuck with Dean after he got up that afternoon and through most of dinner. It set off a sour mood and his surly, one-word responses to Jaz's attempts to make conversation set her off, too. The thoughts distracted him, and he didn't even notice her mounting anger.

Jaz stood, clearing the dishes. She stopped and stared at him. "Dean, what is going on with you tonight? Are you still annoyed with me from this morning? You're the one who should apologize to me."

"It's not that." Another image of the girl who wasn't Verity popped into his head. He shook it off. "I am sorry about this morning. What I said came out wrong. You know I appreciate all you're doing to change the way Unusuals perceive hunters. I should support that better."

Jaz didn't say anything. She nodded and took the plates she held into the kitchen. Dean grabbed a handful and followed her, setting them down on the counter beside the sink.

"So?" Jaz asked.

"So what?"

"So, what is bothering you, then? You aren't usually like this. What else happened at work?"

Dean struggled with how to explain what he'd dreamt. It was just a dream, after all.

"I didn't sleep well today, that's all. I guess I was anxious about our trip to Ireland tomorrow."

Jaz put down the plates. "Dean, I told you. I have two meetings in Dublin, that's all. After that, I'm all yours for three whole days. Promise." She crossed her heart with a finger.

"Well, as long as you promise. We've had so little time alone together like that. It's okay for a guy to get a little nervous about things like this."

Jaz let out a laugh. "Like what? It's not like it's a real honeymoon. We've been married for months now, and we lived together before the wedding. What's there to be nervous about."

Dean shrugged. "Expectations? We've built this up to be a huge thing, and now that it's almost here, I want to make sure it's absolutely perfect. No patients for me. No outlaws, terrorists, or rogue Unusuals for you. Just you and me as normal people."

"Like you and I will ever be normal."

Dean started to protest, and Jaz held up her hands in surrender. "I told you. I promise. I'll be just normal old Jaz, an ordinary girl from Elk City, Maryland. We'll be like every other tourist on vacation."

Dean laughed at the way she switched on her innocent, dumb blonde voice in the middle of what she said. He reached out and pulled her close, kissing her for what felt like the first time in days.

She melted into it and they stood there by the sink with the water running for a long time, enjoying each other's company.

When they finally parted, he felt a little flushed from the encounter. He was pleased to see it had the same effect on Jaz, too.

He decided to change the subject so they could both focus on cleaning up and packing for the trip in the morning. There'd be plenty of time on the trip for that kind of closeness.

"What are your meetings about in Dublin? Anything interesting?

"Not really. An old friend reached out to me recently and asked when I'd be over in Europe next. I told her I'd let her know. She's traveling down from somewhere to the north to meet me there tomorrow. The other meeting is just a quick check on my Irish operations team. I haven't stopped there to see them on site, they've always come and met me in some other European city. I thought it would be a good idea to check in with them and look over their offices and set up."

"A surprise inspection?"

"Not really. I told them this morning I was going to be dropping in tomorrow or the next day."

Dean laughed. "So they only have twenty-four hours to hide the bodies before you get there."

"They better have hidden any bodies long before that. They have had no active ops of their own for months. That's one of the reasons for the drop in. I want to make sure they're keeping their eyes open and covering our local clients appropriately."

"I love it when you go all boss-lady. You sound all tough."

"And I'm not tough other times?"

"Oh, no. I'm not falling for that one. You, my dear, are the epitome of a tough bad-ass Hunter every single day of the week."

Jaz flicked a wet tea-towel at him as he turned away. She snapped it with a pop so it stung him on the backside as he jumped out of the way.

"Hey! I'm unarmed here."

She dropped the towel and chased him down the hallway to their bedroom. Dean ran, laughing all the way and wondering if the honeymoon might start a little early. He decided, as Jaz tackled him onto their bed, he was a hundred percent okay with that.

Chapter 9

"YOU GOT EVERYTHING, DEAN?"

Dean checked the back of the SUV one last time and nodded at Jaz. "I have the suitcases, as well as my laptop bag. I loaded some new games to keep me busy while you're at your meetings tonight and tomorrow."

Jaz nodded and closed the driver's door, thumbing the key fob to lock the doors. She shouldered her own leather briefcase and followed him down the alley to the front entrance to the small Irish gift shop on a busy downtown street. Dougie O'Nolder, the leprechaun owner of the store, had told Dean in an email to park in the small lot behind the store and then come around front.

She checked her watch after Dean knocked on the front door for the second time. "What time did you tell him we'd be here? It doesn't look like anyone's inside to let us in."

"I said we drop by around nine-thirty. He opens at ten, but he said he'd be in early."

Jaz check her watch. "It's only a little after nine. We're early."

Dean gave his wife an awkward smile as they stood on the street with their two suitcases and shoulder bags. "I'm sure he just forgot we were coming. His car was there in the lot. It sat a few spaces from ours. Let me knock again."

He rapped on the glass door and leaned in close to the glass. He cupped his hands around his face to peer into the dark interior. The shelves of random Irish gifts packed the place and blocked most of his view to the back of the shop. He was about to pull out his phone and call the owner when he spotted some movement in the shadows.

"He's in there, I think. He must've been busy with something. Like you said, we are early."

Dougie moved out of the shadows inside and waved at Dean, holding up a finger to wait. Other figures moved about in the shadows, and Dean tried to see what was going on. Maybe he was doing inventory with his employees before they opened for the day.

A muscular form in a black T-shirt slid into view just inside the glass door. The guy was taller than Dean, and he had to tilt his head back a bit to see the face scowling down at him.

"What do you want? Shop's closed." The guy's thick Irish brogue was almost unintelligible.

"Dougie knows we're coming. I just saw him. He said to wait a minute. We're good unless you want to let us in so we don't have to stand outside with our luggage."

The man inside glanced around Dean and took in Jaz and the bags on the sidewalk. "Going somewhere?"

"Uh, yeah. Just a brief trip." Dean wasn't sure how much the guy inside knew about the owner's secret door to a pub in Dublin.

The guy inside made no move to open the door, and Dean's temper started rising. This guy was rude, especially since Dean had told the brute he knew the shop's owner.

Before he could say anything, Dougie showed up. The six-foot-tall leprechaun bustled over, nudging the bigger fellow out of the way. "Uh, Dean, I told you nine-thirty. You're early."

"Force of habit, I guess. Is it still okay we come in and use your little, uh—" Dean glanced at the big guy.

Dougie smiled. "Sure, sure. You're welcome to use the door. I just wasn't expecting you so early and I had some other business to attend to." He looked over his shoulder and seemed distracted by something going on in the back of the store.

Dean tried to move so he could see past Dougie, but the big, muscular guy slid over to stand in Dean's way. It irked Dean, but he didn't want to make a scene. He didn't need Jaz jumping in and putting this refugee from bouncer school in the hospital.

"Doug, if this is a bad time—"

"No, not at all. I think they're finished up with what we were packing away. Cyril, go back and make sure the storeroom door is closed."

Cyril scowled at the shop-owner, but he left and disappeared into the back of the store.

"Come with me and we'll get you two ready to go. You must both be excited to take this little excursion."

"We are. I really appreciate you letting us use the portal."

"Think nothing of it. It's the least I can do after all you did to save us all with that Armageddon mess."

Jaz smiled. "We're all very proud of him." The smile disappeared as quickly as it showed up. She nodded at the back of the store. "What was that all about? That Cyril guy seemed a little nervous to have us around."

"Jaz," Dean said. "Don't start interrogating Dougie. We are here on vacation. His business is his to deal with. We don't need to get involved."

His wife started to object, but he glared at her. To his surprise, she backed down.

Not wanting to give her any time to ask any more uncomfortable questions, Dean said, "Can we get going? We're kind of in a hurry to get on with our trip."

"Certainly, let's get the portal fired up and you can be on your way."

He led them back to the storeroom door Cyril had just closed. Dougie opened it and gestured for them to walk past him. Dean expected to see others in there, but whoever they were, they'd left with Cyril. The storeroom was empty.

Dougie pointed to a large steel door at the back of the storage area. "That's the back door. You're parked in the lot out back, right?"

Dean nodded.

"Good, then when you return after your trip, if the shop's closed, just go out that door and let it close behind you. It'll lock itself once you make sure it's latched."

Dean gave a thumbs-up. "Got it."

Dougie led them to the large green door set in the wall between tall floor-to-ceiling shelves. He unlocked it with a black iron key from his pocket. He tugged at the stout wooden door and the strange magic portal opened in the wall.

Dean grabbed his suitcases and nodded reassurance to Jaz as he stepped into the small room on the other side. The worn hardwood floor had the dark stained look of something ancient compared to anything he'd see in Elk City. Jaz followed him.

"Have fun," Dougie said. He winked, then shut the green door behind them.

"So what now?" Jaz asked.

"We go through that door and we're in Ireland."

"It's that simple?"

Dean nodded. "Come on. I'll show you."

He opened the door and led his wife into the common room of the Mulligan's Pub in downtown Dublin.

He noticed the difference from his last visit right away. It was nothing like the bustling, busy Irish pub he'd visited a few years before. For a moment, Dean thought they'd somehow ended up somewhere else. The dark hallway leading to the equally dark common room confused him.

Once he got his bearings, he realized they were in the right place. But it was empty. No people. Not a sound. As he walked around the common room and looked behind the bar, he corrected himself. This was the pub formerly known as Mulligan's. It appeared to have been closed for some time. Someone had stacked the chairs on the tables, and the shelves along the wall behind the bar were empty of the liquor bottles that had lined them the last time he was here.

"This isn't what I expected, Jaz. I didn't know the place was closed."

She tapped away on her phone for a few seconds. "It says here the owner, Jason Mulligan, died suddenly about six months ago. The pub closed down and an unknown investor bought it from the estate."

"That's a shame. The food and atmosphere here were great. I wonder why Dougie didn't tell us?"

Jaz glanced back at the door leading back to Elk City. "There was something strange going on back there in the Irish Shop. I couldn't put my finger on it, but now it makes sense."

"What? You think those other people must've come through ahead of us?" Dean looked around. "If they came back, they left already."

"Dean, I think your leprechaun friend is involved with some sort of smuggling operation." Jaz walked around, looking into the kitchen and returning to her husband. "It could be drugs or any other sort of contraband."

Dean didn't like her assumption but stopped. Dougie had acted distracted and a little annoyed they'd come early. Could he have been in the middle of a secret he didn't want Dean and Jaz to see?

"Jaz, is this something we need to get involved with? I mean, there's no actual evidence of a crime. We're just speculating. I think we should continue on with our plans."

From her hesitation to answer him right away, Dean could tell she wanted to push forward with an investigation. She gave a brief shake of her head. "You're right. I'll hold off, but I am going to put someone from the office on it and see what they uncover while we're here."

"Fair enough, as long as you keep your hands off. So, what now? We're not staying here for a bite as planned, so my itinerary is already out the window."

Jaz tapped on something on her phone and held it up to her ear. "I'll have someone from the Dublin office stop by and pick us up. They can take us to the hotel. We'll check in and I'll catch up with my first meeting a little early."

She opened her mouth to say more, but someone must have picked up on the other end of the line. Jaz held up a finger for Dean to hold on. "This is Jaz Errington. I need a car to come pick me up. I've pinged your system with my phone so you can get my location."

After a brief pause for the reply, she continued. "Good. See you in twenty minutes." She put the phone back in her pocket. "So, husband of mine, we have a few minutes to do some local sightseeing. What else is around here?"

Dean laughed. "I have no idea. We never left the pub. Let's go outside and find out."

With a nod, the two of them grabbed their bags went to the front door. It was locked but opened from the inside. A quick check showed the door would lock behind them. "Good thing you can pick locks, hon. Otherwise, we'd have to find another way home."

Jaz rolled her eyes. "Given how many things on this trip have already proven a little sketchy, I'm thinking I need a contingency plan. Maybe we should book a flight home."

"No, no, that's not necessary," Dean said with a groan. "I've got this all figured out. I promise. Everything else will go fine."

"If you say so, I'll hold you to it." Jaz pointed to a small independent bookseller across the street. "Come on, let's browse for a bit in that shop. I'd like to get a local guide to the city just in case you get us lost."

"Very funny." He lifted the suitcases off the curb and rolled them across the street. "It looks kind of cramped in there, especially if we take in our bags. I'll hang out here and wait for the car. You go and get your guidebook."

"I was just kidding. You're my guide for the trip." She glanced in the window for a few seconds. "I would like to go in and browse, though, if that's alright?"

"I'll be here. Go have fun."

Jaz entered the bookstore. Dean watched through the display window as she looked through a few books. The shopkeeper, a woman in a grey cardigan came over to help her and soon the two were deep in conversation. Now and then, one would look his way with a smile on her face. When both glanced at him and laughed at one point, he smiled back and waved. That only got them laughing even more.

A few minutes later, Jaz emerged, stuffing a *Guide to the Emerald Isle* in her shoulder bag. She glanced at her phone. "The car's almost here."

"Did you have fun making a new friend?"

"Oh, yes, Saoirse's very nice. She thought you and I make a cute couple. She also told me some more about the pub's sudden closing. The owner had complained to her that someone tried on many occasions to get him to sell the place. They'd put a lot of pressure on him, but he still said no. About a week after he told her this, he died."

"You see a mystery everywhere you look, don't you?"

"And you don't see potential illnesses with every person you meet."

Dean smiled. "Not all of them. I've never diagnosed you, though I do like to play doctor."

Jaz gave him a playful shove. "Save if for later, big boy. There's the car."

A black SUV pulled up and the passenger window, on the wrong side of the car, wound down. The woman behind the wheel leaned over and asked, "Ms. Errington?"

"Yes. You must be Niamh." Jaz said.

"Yes, Mum." The young blonde got out and walked around back. "If you and your husband will climb into the Range Rover, I'll get your things loaded into the back."

"Nonsense. Stay put. We can load our own bags."

Dean nodded, following Jaz to the rear of the vehicle. Niamh popped open the lift gate and they both slid their suitcases inside. Dean noticed a familiar black lockbox bolted in the back. He suspected it carried an array of weapons, just like the Errington Security vehicles back home.

Jaz got in the front passenger seat and Dean got in the seat behind hers. Having the boss sit up front flustered the driver a little, but she regained her composure and pulled out into traffic.

"You're new with the Dublin office, aren't you?" Jaz asked.

"Yes, Mum. My father recommended me for the position. He's a retired member of the Garda."

Jaz smiled. "You wanted police work, and he knew enough to find you a job that paid a lot better."

"Something like that. He also knew I loved reading all kinds of fantasy and mythology books growing up. I guess I've studied for this job all my life. He couldn't wait until my first day home from orientation to see my face."

Dean laughed. "I take it he was part of the Irish National Police version of our Unusual stations?"

Niamh nodded. "Yes, sir."

"No need calling me sir. I answer to Dean. You work for her, not me."

She glanced to her left, waiting for a slight nod from Jaz. "Yes, s —, I mean, Dean."

It was a minor victory, but he took it. He knew why Jaz had to maintain some distance and authority with her subordinates. That didn't extend to him, at least, not in his mind. Jaz might not agree, but on this Dean didn't care. He enjoyed being on a first name basis with folks.

Niamh talked about ongoing projects with Jaz for the rest of their brief trip, so Dean took in the sights as they drove through the city. In some ways it looked much like any other modern city, but now and then he got a sense of how old this country was compared to his home.

As they unloaded their luggage, Niamh pulled a folded black duffel back from a pocket in the rear compartment. She opened the locked security box with her thumbprint and a six-digit code. As expected, the armored box contained a variety of weapons, including handguns and a few blades.

"Do you have any particular preference, Mum?"

"The Glock and four spare magazines. I can't use a Katana. Too hard to hide here. I'll take the silver dagger, though."

Niamh glanced at Dean.

"Nothing for me, thanks. I'm a healer, not a fighter. Besides, we're on our honeymoon."

The woman shrugged and closed the box after transferring the pistol, a clip-on holster, magazines, and the dagger to the duffel bag. She zipped it closed and handed it to her boss.

Jaz slipped her arm through the duffel bag's handles and moved it up to carry over her shoulder. "I'll see you at the meeting tomorrow at our offices. It's a pleasure to meet you."

"You, too, Ms. Errington." She nodded at Dean and got in the Range Rover.

Dean extended the handles on both their suitcases and rolled them behind him as he followed Jaz into the hotel. It was very nice, as he expected. His wife didn't skimp when she traveled. She'd told him once that she spent far too much time sleeping on the ground in creepy old ruins not to take advantage of a good bed when she could. He didn't disagree with the practice. He liked staying somewhere posh, and she was paying for it, after all.

Ten minutes later, they were in their suite getting settled. Dean started unpacking his suitcase in the bedroom, putting his clothes away. Jaz turned her attention to the duffle bag. She fetched a towel from the bathroom and sat on the bed as she field-stripped the pistol, laying the pieces on the towel as she went. After she reassembled it and checked the magazines, Jaz pulled the dagger from its sheath and checked the edge before putting it away.

"Jaz, is there something you're not telling me? We don't need all the firepower for the trip I have planned."

"I've learned the hard way that it pays to be prepared for the worst. You know I feel naked when I'm unarmed."

"How's carrying that pistol even work over here. I know you can carry just about anywhere in the U.S., but things are different outside those borders, aren't they?"

"I've got a diplomatic waiver on my passport. As long as I don't flaunt that I'm armed, we shouldn't have problems. If we do, that waiver should cover us."

"If you say so. What's next on your agenda. You wanted to meet up with that friend of yours, didn't you?"

Jaz nodded and pulled out her phone. "Let me reach out and

tell her we're here." She tapped at the screen as she walked into the bathroom.

She hadn't told Dean much about this friend of hers, and the mystery intrigued him. He wanted to know who this person was. His wife's secretive nature about it had his imagination working overtime.

It turned out, Dean didn't need to be worried, at least not that first night. Jaz's friend had been delayed getting to town and that left the night open for just the two of them. As soon as he had the opening, Dean jumped into action and reached out to the front desk for a special dinner he had originally planned for a few nights from now. The manager was glad to bump up the reservation to that evening.

They spent the rest of the afternoon relaxing in the room together. As it got dark, they got dressed and went down to the lobby to meet the concierge. Soon Dean and Jaz sat in a private dining room while a personal chef prepared a fine dining experience for them in the small kitchen next door. Their dedicated server opened a bottle of champagne and served them their food as each course arrived.

Jaz lifted her glass to her husband in a toast. "This is nice. You pulled out all the stops. I like it."

"I stayed within the budget we discussed; I swear."

"I already told you that wasn't necessary."

"It's important that I cover half this trip with my city salary. I have to pull my weight in this relationship."

Jaz shook her head but said nothing. They'd hashed out this topic frequently, and both of them knew the other's position well enough.

She smiled and sipped at her bubbly. "Thank you for planning this. I appreciate how hard you work and how long you've saved for this trip."

"I want us to enjoy the night since we suddenly have nothing else planned. This way, when your friend shows up, we won't have to miss out on something else."

"I hope it works that way. She's seemed distracted in her messages and mentioned being in the middle of something."

"You still haven't told me much about her. Come on, who is she, some sort of 007 character?"

Jaz smiled. "She'd wipe the floor with Bond if they met in real life. No, she's someone I met on a demon hunt a few years ago and we hit it off. Since then, we've traded intel and helped each other when we could on various missions."

"That still doesn't tell me much."

Jaz shook her head. "Sorry. Anything else, she'll have to tell you herself if you get the chance to meet her."

Dean shrugged. Jaz's reluctance to share more irked him, but he figured the mystery would solve itself once this friend showed up.

The server came in carrying their next course, and soon their meal distracted them from talk of Jaz's friend. Dean settled into having a good night on vacation with his wife. So far, the trip was going pretty well.

Chapter 10

DEAN SPENT the next day hanging out in and around the hotel while Jaz attended to things with her Dublin office team. It was all an opportunity for Errington Security's Dublin crew to show the boss what they had going on. Jaz asked Dean if he wanted to come along to the office and join in the briefings and threat analysis.

He declined.

Jaz ended up having to add a second day of meetings when Elsa Behringer, the leader of European operations, came to Ireland to meet with her. The move to put her in a job previously only held by humans made Dean proud of how far his wife had come from the Hunter assassin he'd first met over a year before.

At the end of the second day, he gave in to another invitation and met up with Jaz and her employees at a restaurant. She was taking the whole Dublin team, along with Elsa, out to dinner to wrap up her official visit. They'd each be bringing along their significant other, and he figured he should be there, too. He could play the part of the dutiful husband. It turned out to be a lot of fun, and it gave him insights into why her teams respected her so much. Her two days here had been well spent, creating a synergy that would open lanes of communication from now on.

The easy-going conversations around their dinner table showed how well everyone got along, not just with Jaz, but also each other.

Afterwards, they all said their goodbyes. It was raining as they left the restaurant. Niamh and her girlfriend, Sasha, offered them a ride back to the hotel, which they accepted.

As they rode alone in the elevator up to the twelfth floor, Dean reached out and held Jaz's hand. He took in his wife as she stood beside him in dark gray slacks and a matching blazer. She looked every bit the successful corporate CEO.

"I'm proud of you."

She glanced up at him, a smile curling the corners of her mouth. "What brought that on?"

"I don't always get to see you as the big boss lady like that. They all look up to you. It's good to see you in that light. It suits you. Back home, I've gotten to know the gang at the office, and it feels much more relaxed. I see now that is something you take with you when you visit these places."

"You could see it more often if you wanted to."

Dean shook his head. "No, not right now. After everything that happened a few months ago, I need a return to normal."

Jaz tried to hide her disappointment, but he spotted it in her expression.

"A no right now isn't a no forever, Hon. I will get to the point someday where a desk job will appeal to me more than being on the street. Every paramedic hits that point where the hard work is better left to the younger crews. When that time comes, I'd much rather ride a desk as part of Errington than for the city."

She gave his hand a squeeze. "I guess that's a bit of a win."

"It is."

They'd reached their floor and Jaz fished their room keycard from her blazer jacket. She passed it over the reader on the door and pushed open the door to their suite.

Dean headed for their bedroom. "I'm going to see if I can dial up one of our streaming TV services on the flatscreen in the bedroom. We can settle in for some binge-watching in bed."

"I like the sound of that," she replied, veering off for the bathroom. "I'm going to wash up. It's been a long day."

Dean picked up the remote from the bed as he kicked off his shoes. He stopped as his socks soaked up water from the carpet and he stepped back away from where he'd been standing, trying to understand where the water had come from.

Their bedroom had a small balcony with a sliding door. It was open about a foot. The sheer curtain waved slightly as the rain blew in. Thinking the maid must've left it open, Dean walked over and closed it. That was when he noticed a puddle in the carpet by the door and over by the bed, but not in between. It was like something wet had dripped the water on that part of the carpet.

A chill ran down his spine. He stared around the room, searching each shadow for something or someone. There weren't many places to hide in here. He ducked and checked under the bed and then over in the closet.

Moving to the living room to check there, his sock squelched in another wet spot on the carpet. Whoever or whatever it was, they had passed this way.

Across the living room, Jaz came from the bathroom. Dean froze and caught her eyes with his. She took one look at his face and stiffened beside the floor to ceiling windows overlooking the street below.

"Dean, what?"

"Someone's here."

As soon as he said it, a shadow detached from drapes behind her.

"Jaz, watch out!"

Before he could get his warning all the way out, Jaz reacted. She dropped to the ground, swinging her left leg wide as she spun to face to the rear.

The spinning kick caught the attacker by surprise. The shadowed figure stumbled backward into the wall, barely blocking the heel of Jaz's foot as it swept past their head.

That was all the opening Jaz needed. She jumped up from her

crouch, leading with a double punching combination to the attacker's body.

The dark shadows in the living room kept Dean from seeing everything. Neither of them had turned on the lights beyond the foyer and he couldn't see in the dark the way Jaz could with her Hunter charm. He ran to the panel by the door and clicked on the overhead lights.

The recessed lighting in the ceiling revealed his wife and a dark-skinned woman in blue jeans and a black leather trench coat trading blows in a flurry of punches and kicks almost too fast to follow.

He thought Jaz had the advantage until the woman dodged a punch at her face, grabbing the extended wrist and twisting to the side.

The maneuver yanked Jaz off-balance, and she cried out in pain. The other woman pulled harder and threw her hip outward, catching Jaz's falling body and flipping her to the floor.

"Jaz!" Dean yelled as the intruder lifted her foot to stomp down at her prone target.

Jaz rolled out of the way at the last moment, but moved towards the other woman, not away. The evasive maneuver rolled her up against the other woman's planted ankle.

Reaching up, she hooked her fingers over the thick leather gun belt beneath the swirling trench coat. Jaz kicked upward with one foot at the same time she yanked down on the woman's waist.

Dean's alarm turned to a cheer as the kick launched the woman up and over the sofa to crash into the coffee table. The wooden table collapsed under the woman's weight.

Jaz had already regained her feet. She leaped over the table to land atop the attacker as she struggled to get up. Jaz delivered a rapid series of powerful punches to the woman's chest.

Ordinarily the attack would have been devastating to an opponent. Dean wasn't sure what effect it had, though. The other woman wore tight-fitting black body armor of some sort beneath her coat.

Jaz brushed aside the attempts to block her attacks until the woman let her hands relax to the floor beside her head.

The flurry of punches stopped. Jaz snarled, "Give up?"

The other woman stared up at Jaz with her stunning brown eyes. The two glared at each other for a few seconds, then the intruder nodded.

To Dean's surprise, both their faces broke into broad grins. Jaz leaned down to offer the other woman a hand up. The attacker took the offered help with another nod.

Once she stood, the newcomer leaned in and the two women exchanged an embrace that seemed almost—friendly?

"Jaz, what the heck is going on? Who is this woman?"

"Dean, I'd like you to meet Chief Inspector Hangbe Dahomey, though I'm pretty sure that's not her actual name. She's the friend I told you I had to meet up with while we were here."

Dean spluttered as he searched for an answer. He'd just witnessed one of the fiercest fights he'd ever seen. Neither of them had pulled any punches. "But, I mean, why all the—?"

Hangbe smiled. "Jaswinder and I like to test each other. We've always been sort of competitive." She had a slight British accent with a hint of something else in the background, maybe West African?

"You started it," Jaz responded. "You began that string of practical jokes while we investigated that demonic incursion in Nigeria."

"You can't really blame me. You were so shiny and new, you practically squeaked. Someone had to take the polish off you once you were out from under Daddy's watchful eye."

"Yeah, well, I'm not under anyone's eye, not anymore."

The inspector's eyes turned sad. "I'm sorry about that, Jaz. I was half-way around the world and the news was weeks old when I found out what happened to your family. If I was closer, I would have come to help you right away."

"I know. It turned out I did alright with the help I had. That's where I met Dean." She held up her hand, flashing her wedding ring. "I guess it was worth it."

Hangbe cast a doubtful glance at the bling. "I can't believe you've finally settled down."

Jaz shook her head. "No settling down here at all. If anything,

I'm busier than ever. We had to squeeze in our honeymoon on a business trip."

Hangbe looked from Jaz to Dean and back again. "Oh, so this is him? I thought I'd crashed another one of your infamous one-night-stands."

Dean looked from Jaz to Hangbe and back again. "What does she mean by that, exactly?"

Jaz laughed, but her expression wasn't all that joyful. She glared at her friend. "She's just stirring up crap. It's her favorite past-time." She kicked a piece of the table from in front of the couch. "Come and sit down. I had them make sure the mini-bar was fully stocked for you. Can I offer a drink?"

The taller woman sat down and shook her head. "Better just a sparkling water tonight. I've got some more leads to run down after this."

Dean waved off Jaz. He tried to forget the earlier comment as he said, "I'll get the drinks. You go sit and chat. Bubbly water for her and single malt scotch on the rocks for you, dear?"

"That would be perfect. I suppose you can have a beer if you want."

"Gee, thanks, honey."

Jaz laughed, sitting beside her friend.

Dean pulled open the cabinet hiding the minibar. He fetched the drinks and studied his wife and the other woman. It was clear they knew each other, probably pretty well from the way they riffed off each other. He listened to their conversation. He knew little about Jaz's early days before they met. This could be his way in to get some interesting stories about his wife's earlier exploits.

He grabbed a bottle of French soda water and two miniature bottles of scotch from the minibar. He dropped a few ice cubes from the tiny ice tray in the freezer into two glasses and carried them over to the sofa. Jaz and Hangbe took them, each offering a nod of thanks without breaking their conversation. They seemed to be catching up on the locations of a few mutual friends.

Dean went back and got himself a bottle of German lager from the fridge and sat down on the chair across from the broken coffee table. They didn't even glance at him as he sat back, watching them and sipping on his beer.

When a lull in the conversation finally presented itself, Dean asked, "Hangbe, what kind of investigation are you working on that has you out after you leave here. It's already late. It must be important."

Hangbe glanced at Jaz.

She nodded. "He's okay. I wouldn't have married him if he wasn't. Also, he's a half-Eldara, though he's all human in the ways that matter the most."

Hangbe cast a glance at him. He got the impression she had reappraised him instantly based on Jaz's comment. "Hopefully not *all* the ways."

Jaz blushed and Hangbe let out a loud burst of laughter.

Dean wasn't sure what she meant by that, but he let it slide. He could ask Jaz later.

"In response to your question, Dean, I'm heading out to interview some sex workers downtown. They were busy working earlier in the night and I don't want to interrupt their trade. Later on, after the traffic slows down, I'm hoping I can convince a few of them to talk with me."

"Are they in some sort of trouble?" Dean asked. "Shouldn't you involve the local authorities if they need help?"

"I will help them, if that's what they want. Right now, I'm trying to figure out how they all got here and who brought them. There's a huge trafficking ring based around here somewhere and following the money has proven difficult. The trail goes cold here in Dublin."

Jaz asked, "Is it just sex trafficking or are they smuggling all sorts of folks?"

"Lately, they've been dealing in various sorts of shifters, but the non-violent varieties."

Something tweaked Dean's memory. "You mean like Selkies?"

Hangbe shot him a look. "Exactly like Selkies. I've just come from a small village on the coast of Scotland. They cleaned the entire place out. One day the people were there and the next, someone drove into the village and everyone was gone."

"That's not good," Jaz said. "Any signs of killing or violence?"

"Sadly, yes." Hangbe fiddled with the beads on an ornate and colorful necklace she wore tight around her throat. "I used a bit of necromancy, though, and raised a recently dead Selkie gramfer. He couldn't tell me much. Dark figures burst into his home, rounded up his children and grandchildren. Then they dragged he and wife into a nearby cave with about a dozen other elderly villagers, able-bodied men and boys, and killed them."

"That's awful," Dean said. "If you could communicate with him, he must have been able to give you a description of who did it."

Hangbe shook her head. "They wore all black and were masked. They spoke in a language he didn't know. He thought it might be Spanish, but he wasn't sure."

"What about the others who went missing?" Jaz asked. "Do you have any idea where they were taken?"

"Traffic cameras picked up a rental truck that came over on a ferry from England. I tracked that down and it led me to here. Since then, I've been trying to track them down. I figure they've been put to work somewhere in the Republic, but I can't figure out where."

Dean had been listening, drawing lines and connections in his mind. More questions came before he could stop himself. "Was this the first such empty village full of Selkies who went missing?"

"No," Hangbe said. "There are four that I know of. The local police investigated but couldn't find evidence of who killed the ones they didn't take. They have swept it under the rug. They're telling the locals the small clans just moved on or left to go back to sea. They have closed the cases." Her voice turned hard as she said the last bit.

"You don't believe that." Jaz said.

"Of course not, but it's all the same. There's a lot of distrust for Selkies along the northern coastal areas and islands. They've been given a bad rap for things since the days of the Black Plague. People aren't sad to see them go, so the authorities won't dig into what might have happened. It's the perfect place to kidnap people."

Dean nodded. "What if they're not in Ireland at all?"

"Where else would they be? I've checked the sea and airports. There's no evidence they've left for anywhere else. If that was what they wanted, they could've smuggled them into container ships leaving from Liverpool. No need to shuttle them over here."

Dean glanced at Jaz. From the tilt of her head, he could tell she was thinking what he was.

"Hangbe, you and Dean are both right. They wouldn't have come here unless there was an easier way to transport people elsewhere here in Dublin."

"Jaz, if you know something, tell me. I've been on this case for months."

"Give Dean and I a few days to wrap up our honeymoon time. You keep tracking down the leads you have. Talk to your ladies on the street and see what you find out. We can meet back here at the hotel for breakfast when we return. While we're gone, I'll have my local team do some digging, too. We'll all share everything we've got and see if anything clicks."

"That should work." Hangbe downed the rest of her sparkling water and set the bottle down on the floor beside the broken table. She stood and stretched her arms over her head. "I should get going. Nice to meet you, Dean. It's good to see someone tamed that girl. I wouldn't have believed it had I not seen it myself."

"Careful how you put that, my friend," Jaz said. "Someone might tame you, too, someday."

"Not a chance. There isn't a man alive who can satisfy me long enough to make me want to stay."

"If you say so."

"I do." Hangbe headed for the door.

Dean pointed to the bedroom. "Don't you want to go out the way you came in?"

"Why? I don't need a key to get out."

She winked and left Dean and Jaz sitting alone in their suite.

As soon as the door shut, Jaz asked, "You think her case has something to do with what you uncovered in Elk City?"

"And you don't?"

Jaz paused, thinking for a few seconds. "There's something

bigger at play here. I need to have my people do some checking on who closed that pub down. Once we get that and Hangbe tracks down her leads, we can compare notes. Maybe we'll see the bigger connection once we have more pieces."

"And until then?" Dean asked.

Jaz pulled him close and whispered in his ear. "Until then, I'm on my honeymoon."

Chapter 11

DEAN AND JAZ slept in the next morning, enjoying the first official day of their delayed honeymoon. As they got up and packed for the next phase of the trip, Jaz found a text from Hangbe sent in the very early morning hours. A call had come in from police in Northern Ireland. There'd been more disappearances there, and she was already on the road to check them out. She'd reach out if she found anything useful.

Dean and Jaz filed the message away, determined to continue on with their much needed alone time together. Dean swallowed hard, trying to clear the anxiety that roiled his stomach. He'd selected a quaint bed-and-breakfast place on the coast. The two of them would have a personal cottage all to themselves. The owners had stocked the kitchen with a few requested items for them to have for lunch and dinner, and they would deliver breakfast each morning. It had looked perfect, but now he wondered if it was right or not. He put on a smile and pressed forward. Too late to change anything now.

Jaz had requisitioned one of the company Land Rovers and she got in to drive to their little retreat while Dean navigated while he took in the passing countryside. The rolling hills stretched to the horizon on either side. To Dean, it seemed a lot like some rural regions of Maryland back home. Using his phone's GPS, he guided them to the turn toward the cottage. Jaz steered the SUV down a long gravel lane.

The location was just like the pictures on the app Dean had used to book the place. It sat on a bluff looking out over the Atlantic Ocean. He'd called ahead when they were a half hour out and the caretaker named Clive waited for them with a key. He told them his wife, Bess, had left something special in the kitchen. He also said she would be back in the morning to cook them an authentic Irish country breakfast. He mentioned they would especially like her Irish soda bread. The thought of fresh-baked bread alone had Dean already looking forward to breakfast the next day.

After the old man left, they entered and unpacked their suitcases. They had left a vase with fresh flowers on the kitchen table with a bottle of Irish whiskey. The note wished them a happy honeymoon. Besides the kitchen, there was a bathroom, a small bedroom, and a living room. It was just the right size for the two of them.

After settling in and checking out the cottage itself, Dean and Jaz went for a walk outside to get the lay of the land. At the edge of the bluff overlooking the ocean, a path led down to the rocky shore below. Dean's eyes scanned the beach, enjoying the foamy surf crashing on the thin section of beach he could see from where he stood. As he turned away to follow Jaz back to the house, he had a nagging feeling he was missing something he should've seen there. He shrugged, chalking it up to just being tired. He decided it might be nice to head down there for a run along the beach before breakfast the next day.

He and Jaz headed back to the cottage hand in hand. Dean's usually taut EMS senses had settled to a gentle murmur in the back of his mind, leaving him to focus on his wife. It was something he hoped she felt as well. They both had jobs that kept them on some version of alert most of the time. This was a much-needed opportunity for some downtime.

Back in the cottage, they made themselves sandwiches with the sliced lamb roast left in the fridge. There was a nice wedge of a sharp farm cheese, too, along with bottles of local beer. Taking a bottle each along with their plates, Dean and Jaz headed out to sit outside on a blanket they spread on the grass in back of the home.

Dean finished his sandwich and leaned back on one elbow while he sipped at his beer. "This is exactly what I needed. How about you, hon?"

Jaz smiled. "Me, too. You were right. We both needed to get away from home for a few days. Even with the work stuff when I got here, I could feel the relief of not having to deal with every little detail back home."

"See, I have a good idea every once in a while."

"Okay, but that's your one for this year."

"Hey, that's not fair." Dean laughed and then leaned in to kiss Jaz. The scents from the wildflowers and the sea breeze coupled with his wife's favorite perfume made it the perfect moment.

When they parted a few seconds later, Dean said, "Maybe we should clean up and head inside."

"What, afraid the locals might see us naked?" She glanced over her shoulder at the distant ribbon of country lane. "We're far enough off the road."

"I don't think there's anything wrong with a little privacy. Besides, I have a few surprises for you."

Jaz's grin turned wicked. "Me, too." She grabbed her plate and utensils and headed for the cottage. "Don't take too long cleaning up the rest. I might just start without you."

Dean didn't need to be told twice. He scooped up the rest of their dinner remnants, grabbed the woolen blanket, and ran in after her. He wouldn't keep her waiting.

The afternoon turned to night and both Dean and Jaz slept well with the help of a few shots of the whiskey, another quick sandwich, and more time alone together. It was early the next morning, when the sunlight beamed in the bedroom window, that Dean finally awakened. He shielded his sleepy eyes with his hand as he sat up and walked over to pull the heavy curtains closed. The room darkened and Dean checked to make sure Jaz still slept. He decided not to wake her. He'd dreamt overnight of running on the beach like he'd planned. He decided to take some time for himself and get some exercise at the same time.

Dean glanced at the clock over the stove in the kitchen. The caretaker's wife wouldn't be here to make breakfast for at least a half hour. It gave him just enough time to hit the beach below and still make it back in time for breakfast with Jaz.

He sent his wife a quick text message telling her where he was and headed outside. Making his way to the bluff overlooking the beach, he started down the narrow track. The trail down the bluff was steeper than it looked from the top, but it wasn't too treacherous. He took his time and soon he reached the bottom.

Dean looked both ways up and down the coast. A gentle tug at his subconscious he barely noticed drew him to the north, and Dean shrugged. It was as good a choice as any. He jogged along the shore, enjoying the way the early morning mist still clung to the rocky beach in many places.

He'd gone about a mile north and was about to turn back when that strange tugging sensation made him stop. Earlier it had been barely a hint. Now it physically pulled him away from going back the way he came. When he tried to turn back, something wrenched his shoulders back around to face northward again.

Realizing he couldn't fight whatever supernatural event had ahold of him, Dean scanned the beach and the cliffs above. Something held him here. Maybe he could find it and whoever was behind it. Up on the cliffs above he spotted a large box truck parked halfway down a gravel lane that wound down towards the beach and stopped at the edge of the high tide line a quarter mile farther to the north. No one was around it, and he wondered why it was there.

He started towards it, but before he'd taken two steps, it started up and drove away up the lane and disappeared. He stared at the empty lane for a few long seconds, then started walking up to where it had parked. Reaching the tire imprints in the wet gravel, Dean stopped. He had the driving urge to do something, but he couldn't figure out what. The truck was gone. Was he supposed to follow it?

Not having a better idea, Dean started up the gravel lane. He hadn't gone fifty yards farther before he picked up the faint sound of someone crying. He stopped and looked around. With the crashing waves, it was hard to pick up exactly where the sound came from.

Dean spotted some rock outcroppings jutting up at the base of the bluff below where he stood halfway up the lane. Turning around, he returned to the beach and walked around to the rocks.

They were each taller than he was and in a way that forced him to walk through several knee-deep tidal pools before he rounded the last one. As he did, the sobbing grew louder.

There at the base of the rocks was the broad opening of a cave with a sandy floor. A girl of about thirteen with long red hair crouched behind the outcropping. She wore a blue-green dress and had no shoes on, despite the rocky shoreline. Two long green streaks colored her hair on either side. The strips ran from just in front of her ears and down the hair over her shoulder.

As soon as the girl spotted him, she stood and craned her neck back and forth in a frantic search for a way out past him.

"Hey, hold on. I'm not here to hurt you. I heard you crying and came to see what was up."

She stopped looking past him and shifted her surprised gaze to his face. "You're an American. Does that mean you're not with them?"

"With who? I'm on vacation with my wife at a cottage to the south. I'm alone otherwise."

The girl craned her neck, trying to see past Dean.

He twisted his head to see what she was looking at. There was no one there.

"We're alone. It's okay. Tell me what's wrong and maybe I can help you. I have a phone. We can call for the police."

As soon as he pulled out his phone, she got more agitated. She stepped forward, pulling at his hand to keep him from dialing it. "No, the local constable is with them. If you call, it'll tell them where I am. You can't let them take me, too."

The girl turned her head and he spotted thin lines down the side of her neck. The parallel lines rippled and opened, revealing pink membranes underneath. He nodded, realizing what he saw. She had gills. That meant she was some sort of Unusual.

She caught him staring at her and clapped a hand to her neck. When she took her hand away, the lines had disappeared, leaving smooth skin behind. Like most Unusuals, she could hide who she was from humans.

Taking a chance that she might trust him better if she knew he was aware of people like her, he held out his hand where he had the invisible tattoo only members of the supernatural community could see. It was a paramedic's star of life with a snake and staff cadeusus emblazoned on top of it.

Her eyes widened. "What is that?"

"It's a sign of who I am and what I do. I'm a special paramedic, a helper who has sworn to take care of people like you. You can trust me."

She hesitated, her eyes shifting every few seconds to scan all around for trouble.

He kept talking, keeping his voice calm and soft. "My name is Dean Flynn. What's yours?"

"Kaylee."

"Hi, Kaylee. Do you mind if I ask you a question? I noticed your neck. Were those gills?"

Kaylee's hand drifted back up to her neck for a second, then she nodded. "I guess I was nervous, and I started to shift."

"What kind of Unusual are you? I can tell a little about folks I meet, but not everything."

"I'm a Kelpie. We have a small community that comes ashore from time to time when we want to trade with the villagers."

"Where are the rest of your family? If you're lost, I can help you find them."

She shook her head. "The cat-men took them. I swam back out into the surf when they jumped out of the truck and started attacking the others. I don't think they saw me. I swam around here to hide in this cave. I watched them load my family and the other villagers into the back of their truck. They'd tied up everyone.

That's when I saw the constable. The leader of the cat men gave him an envelope and he drove away in his police van. I thought maybe I could set them free. But then the truck drove away."

"I saw the truck leave. It just drove inland."

Kaylee's shoulders dropped. "Then they're gone. I'll never find them."

"We don't know that. My wife is here with me and she's great at finding things, especially bad people like those cat-men."

Dean was pretty sure he knew who those men were, and why they were here. He wondered if there was time to track down the girl's family before the traffickers took them through the door to Elk City.

"Come with me back to the cottage. My wife is there, and she can help. We can get you some breakfast, too, and maybe some dry clothes, too."

Kaylee thought for a long while before she answered. She kept looking back out to the ocean waves crashing nearby.

Dean turned to look at the water. "Is there someone back there that can help you? I'll find a way to take you to them if that's what you need."

"No. There's no one there for me now. The entire village came ashore to trade."

"Then let's get started back to my wife. She's your best chance at finding your family again."

Dean backed up to give the girl room. He smiled as he moved to work his way back around the rocks. Kaylee followed along, hesitating a little at first, but then keeping up as Dean started back down the beach. The strange tugging sensation he'd felt before had disappeared. A feeling of accomplishment and satisfaction replaced it.

As they walked, he texted ahead to warn Jaz. She didn't like surprises like this, and he didn't want the caretaker's wife to see Kaylee. If some locals were in on this, there was no way to know who was safe and who wasn't. Luckily, Jaz was awake. She texted back that she'd come outside at the top of the bluff for him once the woman prepared breakfast and left them alone again.

When they reached the trail, Jaz stood along the path at the top.

He'd been afraid she'd dress in her Hunter gear, but she didn't. She wore a skirt and blouse and smiled as Dean and Kaylee approached.

"You must be Kaylee. I'm Jaz. My husband says you're having some sort of trouble."

"Yes, ma'am. They took my family from the beach and drove away in a truck."

Dean nodded. "It's okay. You can tell her everything you told me. She knows about the cat-men and about Kelpies." He pointed up at the cottage. "Maybe we can go inside and talk?" He glanced at Jaz. "Is it clear?"

"Bess is finishing breakfast. I told her I was meeting you out here and wanted some privacy. She said she'd leave everything on the table for us and leave out the front. I thought it best not to involve her with this until we knew what was going on."

Dean let out a long sigh. "Good thinking, hon. Let's remain out here for a bit until she leaves."

Jaz smiled and nodded. "Kaylee, tell me what happened and maybe we can help you."

Kaylee related the story she'd told Dean. When she mentioned the cat-men, Jaz shot Dean a look. She pulled out her phone and tapped in a message while the girl talked. As Kaylee talked, a small compact car drove away down the lane. That had to be Bess leaving. They could go inside.

Dean pointed up the hill. "Kaylee, come inside with us and we'll get you some food. Then you can tell us more of what you know. Any detail might be important."

Once inside, Kaylee spotted the breakfast laid out on the table and sat down, filling a plate with eggs and sausages. Dean sliced a thick piece of the steaming soda bread for her, too. Then he and Jaz watched as she ate for a few seconds. Seeing she was taken care of, the two of them sat and filled their own plates to join her. A few minutes later, Jaz's phone rang. She showed Dean the screen. It was Hangbe.

Jaz excused herself to step into the other room.

"Where did she go?"

"It's okay, Kaylee. My wife has a friend who is investigating people disappearing like your family. I think that's who she is talking with."

Jaz came back a few minutes later and sat down. Dean and Kaylee had continued, filling their plates with another helping of the warm Irish soda bread, smeared with chilled sweet cream butter, along with more of the sausages and eggs.

Dean waited until Jaz sat down then asked, "How'd the call go?"

Jaz finished her bite before responding. "She is heading back this way. She'll be here this afternoon. I also reached out to Niamh to look into any underworld werecat clans operating in the area."

Kaylee fixed Jaz with a hopeful gaze. "Does that mean you can find my family?"

Jaz reached out and laid her hand on the girl's arm. "I'm going to do whatever I can to help find them and bring them home. You're lucky you ran into my husband. We kind of specialize in this kind of thing."

"You do?"

Jaz nodded. "Finish your breakfast and then I want to have you talk to one of my friends back in Dublin. She has some questions for you. Tell her everything you know. The more she can find out, the better chance we have of catching the people who took your family."

Kaylee nodded and went back to eating. Dean and Jaz shared a glance and finished their meal in silence. He wondered if his wife felt the same way he did. Once again, events out of their control dashed their plans for a relaxing honeymoon.

Chapter 12

AFTER EATING, Jaz took Kaylee into the sitting room and set up a video call with Niamh to get more details about the people who took her family. The Dublin team had some facial recognition software that could approximate a sketch of the perpetrators, and Niamh wanted to try it with Kaylee. Any small bit of information could make a difference, and Jaz's Dublin team would make sure they got everything they could from the young Kelpie to help find her family.

After Jaz got the girl set up on the call, she came over to where Dean stood in the doorway. She stared at him for a long time, holding the silver Hunter charm around her neck between her thumb and forefinger. After a few long, uncomfortable seconds, she nodded and smiled.

"What?" Dean asked.

"The Geas seems to be gone. I think finding the girl was the event the Rakshini foretold in her viewing on you."

Dean glanced down at his body and ran his left hand down the front of his shirt. A chill passed down his spine as he thought about the spell's magic effects on him. Had it helped him find the Kelpie girl this morning? "Are you sure?"

Jaz nodded. "I can't sense it anymore. I think you fulfilled the quest or whatever it was."

"It's not done until we make sure she's safe. How long until Hangbe gets here?"

"It shouldn't be long. She said she'd hurry." Jaz glanced back over her shoulder to where Kaylee chatted with Niamh on the video call. "I should get back over there and supervise. This could be important."

Dean pulled out his phone while Jaz returned to sit beside the Kelpie girl. He leaned against the door and checked his Station U email account before sending in a series of emails to his colleagues to see if they had any more information about Verity or the trafficking ring. Barry replied right away, telling him to stop worrying about it and to relax and enjoy the honeymoon.

He appreciated his partner's concern. Barry knew how much this trip meant to him. However, now that he had a patient to take care of, all his thoughts for himself went out the window. There had to be a connection between this and Verity's situation in Elk City. He intended to find it and track it down to find the missing girl and maybe Kaylee's family, too.

After the video call ended, Kaylee settled on the small couch and watched some game show on the TV. Dean and Jaz left her alone while they stepped outside the front door to talk. It was time to go over their next steps.

They'd barely started going over their options when a speeding sports car turned down the long, gravel lane in their direction. It swerved so hard to make the turn, Dean feared it would overturn as it slid to the side. It regained traction at the last possible instant, straightening out and racing down the lane in their direction. The speed and apparent recklessness alarmed Dean.

As it got closer, he tried to make out the driver through the tinted windows. He couldn't see more than a shadowed figure behind the wheel. The silver coupe slid to a stop near the cottage's front door in a spray of gravel. The door popped open and Hangbe climbed out.

The inspector pointed to the cottage. "Is the girl in there?" The tension and hint of alarm in her voice made her urgency clear to both of them.

Jaz nodded. "Why, what's up?"

"The local police are on the way. I overheard a radio transmission about picking up some runaway. Somehow, they know she's here. We have to get her out of here."

Based on the yelp of fear from inside, the girl must've heard Hangbe. Kaylee ran from the house, trying to get by Jaz, who blocked her way. Her head jerked from side to side, her body poised to bolt in either direction. "They've found me. I have to go."

"Stop, Kaylee," Dean said. He kept his voice level and his tone friendly. "You're not in immediate danger. This is our friend, Hangbe. She's here to protect you, just like we are. No one will take you anywhere you don't want to go."

Jaz caught his eye and shook her head. He realized he'd broken a cardinal rule of earning a patient's trust. Don't promise something you can't deliver. If the proper authorities showed up to pick up a minor child, they'd have to turn her over.

He shrugged, glancing from Jaz to Hangbe. "What do we do?"

The Interpol agent pointed to the car. "Girl, if you want to avoid the people coming for you, you need to come with me, now."

"I don't know." Kaylee glanced from the car to the ocean beyond the bluffs. Dean knew she wanted to run; she just didn't know which way.

Hangbe turned to Jaz. "There's no time. Tell her. Once the local police get here, it'll be out of our hands. I can't overrule a local officer on something like this."

"She's right, Kaylee," Jaz said. "Go with our friend. She can take you to Dublin where Niamh is. We'll pack up our stuff and follow as soon as we can. We'll wait just long enough to point the police in the wrong direction. We can meet up with you both and continue the search for your family once we know you're safe."

The girl didn't seem sure what to do. She needed someone to decide. Dean took charge. He walked over and gently ushered her to the passenger side of the sports car. "Get in. Hangbe won't let anything happen to you. We'll see you later tonight."

"Promise?"

"If we're not there, it's because it's not safe for us to come to you. We'll catch up eventually, though. Trust Hangbe. Jaz and I will see you as soon as we can."

Kaylee sat down and buckled her seatbelt. Hangbe nodded and climbed back in the driver's seat. "I'll head to Dublin. I'll leave a message for you at the front desk of your hotel. Check there if you don't hear from me."

Jaz nodded. "Contact Niamh at my offices there. She'll have additional resources for you and maybe some information. She's already started on tracking the people who took Kaylee's family."

Hangbe answered with a grim smile and closed her door. The sports car drove away, kicking up a fresh a shower of gravel as it took off back down the lane.

The car got out and disappeared down the road just in time. She hadn't been gone for more than five minutes before a police van drove down the lane. A rotund police constable got out. A tall, powerfully built man in a black leather jacket climbed out of the passenger side.

The pair walked up to the house where Dean and Jaz stood. The constable said, "I'm Police Constable Kelly. I understand from Bess Byrne that you two found a missing girl down on the beach?"

"We did," Jaz said. "Why, is there something wrong?"

"She's a runaway. This gentleman here is her uncle. He and the rest of the family have been looking for her. She's a troubled girl and likes to get folks all worked up with wild stories."

"I see," Jaz replied. She shrugged. "That's a shame. We fed her breakfast. As soon as she finished, the girl told us she had to leave. We tried to stop her, but she got away from us and ran off down the beach. I do hope she's alright. She's not dangerous to us, is she?"

The tall man growled under his breath, saying, "Why didn't you go after her? You two appear more than capable of taking care of a young girl."

Dean held up his hands. "Hey, we're not the bad guys here. We didn't know who she was. We just tried to be nice. Once she ran off, she's someone else's problem. We're just visitors here. We didn't know."

The constable and the one pretending to be Kaylee's uncle exchanged glances. Constable Kelly stepped forward. "Can I see some identification? I'm going to need to write this up and I must know where you'll be staying."

"Oh, I hope this will not cause an issue for us," Jaz said. "We were thinking of heading back to Dublin tonight."

"As long as I know where you'll be staying and you don't leave the country, that will be fine. My superiors may want to question you further."

"About what?" Dean asked. "We told you what happened."

"You told us what you said happened," the tall man replied. "we must verify your statements to see if you're lying. There will be severe consequences if we find out you did. Where will you be staying?"

Jaz stepped forward, her hands on her hips. She stopped a few feet away and stared at the man. "I'm sorry, are you a distraught uncle or a police investigator? Which is it?"

Dean tensed. Jaz didn't back down from anyone. He prepared for trouble.

The constable let out a nervous laugh. "He's just concerned for his niece, miss. He meant nothing by it. Just let me jot down some information from your passports and you can go back to the city. I'm sure this will all work itself out. No need to make an international incident over it."

Dean went inside and fetched their passports, handing them to the constable.

He snapped a photo of their documents with his phone and handed them back. "Where did you say you'd be in the city?"

Jaz answered the Constable but kept her eyes leveled on the taller man. "You can reach me at my offices. Just contact Errington Security. They can tell you where we are."

At the mention of the company name, the tall man's body stiffened. He stared long and hard at Jaz, studying her while considering this new information. He'd fallen for the innocent tourist act until now. Dean wondered why Jaz had let out the information that way.

A second later, the uncle nodded. "I think we should leave these two alone and get back to searching for my niece, Constable. You have everything you need, correct?"

The constable nodded, confused by the sudden change in direction. He smiled and said goodbye.

The van drove off and Dean realized he'd been holding his breath. He was sure Jaz was going to end up fighting the uncle right there in the driveway.

"That was close. I was worried."

Jaz cocked her head to the side. "Why were you worried? I had everything under control."

"How? What if he had attacked you? Were you just going to shoot the guy?"

Jaz laughed. "You have no idea how much I wanted him to make a move. I'm almost positive he's the head of the werecat clan that took those people. I could smell the musty shifter odor coming from him."

"But you're unarmed. Your sword and guns are in the SUV."

Jaz leaned down and pulled up one side of her long skirt to reveal a small holster strapped to her leg, mid-thigh. She pulled out the pistol and checked the chamber before returning it to the holster.

"I'm never unarmed. You know that. Especially not when we have things like this going on around us. If he'd so much as twitched in our direction, I'd have filled him full of silver slugs before he'd taken two steps."

Dean knew she wasn't kidding. When he'd first met her, she was a shoot first, ask questions later kind of person. He thought she'd mellowed a little since they'd gotten together. Every now and then, though, she reminded him just how deadly she was.

"What should we do now? He's got to know we've hidden her somehow."

"We pack up and head back to the city. If he has taken those people and they're part of the same werepanther clan that you ran into back in the Maryland, then there's only one way for them to get those people to Elk City. If we hurry, we can stop them there."

"You think they're using the Irish Shop portal to transport their victims?"

"And you don't?" Jaz asked.

"I'm not sure. I guess I don't want to think that Dougie is mixed up in something like this."

"He might not be a willing participant. Remember how the local pub owner died mysteriously? They probably threatened the leprechaun, too."

Dean hoped that was the case. He went into the house and started packing up. So much for their spending a couple of relaxing days here with all the peace and quiet. The honeymoon was definitely over.

Chapter 13

ON THE DRIVE back to Dublin, Dean's mind kept going over how their nice belated honeymoon trip had gone off the rails. He wondered if there was any way to salvage something from the trip. In the end, he gave up on the idea. There were more important things going on and he felt selfish for focusing on his meager problems while others were dealing with kidnappings and family disappearances.

As he caught glimpses of the city in the distance, Dean broke the silence. "What are we going to do with Kaylee if the were-cats have already taken her family through the portal?"

"I've been trying to work through that problem. We can't take her through with us. She'd be just another illegal if she got into any trouble. I need to ask around and see if there's anywhere safe to put her here until we find her family."

"You know there's a chance we won't find her family, Jaz? It's hard to track down traffickers and their victims. If we don't intercept them here in Ireland and they get to the U.S., they could go almost anywhere."

She shrugged. "We'll find someone here who can take in a long-term guest until we either locate her family or find her next of kin. Let me call in to the office. They might be able to help."

Jaz tapped the phone icon on the dashboard screen and selected the number for the local Errington office.

Niamh answered. "Errington Security, Limited. Niamh speaking. How may I help you?"

"Niamh, it's Jaz. I'm on my way back into the city. I need you to arrange a room at the same hotel we stay at before. We should be there to check in within the hour. Meet us there."

"You cut your trip short, ma'am?"

"With everything that happened with the girl, we followed up ourselves. I'll get you more info once we get in. Tell the others in the office you're on detached special duty as of now under my direct orders."

"Yes, ma'am. I'll have everything set up when you arrive at the hotel. Should I prepare for anything special while on this duty with you, ma'am?"

"No, just requisition one of the SUVs with a standard load out. I'll explain more when you meet us at the hotel." Jaz hung up. She glanced at Dean. "That's one thing down. We can work out the rest of the details about this issue once we make sure Kaylee's safe."

Jaz had Dean send Hangbe a text to meet them at the hotel once she checked it out. The other woman replied with a simple thumbs up. Dean showed it to Jaz and settled back in his seat, wondering what Jaz had planned.

Niamh waited for them on the curb as they pulled into the hotel's driveway. Jaz and Dean climbed out as the porters removed their bags and the valet took the SUV to park it.

Niamh handed Jaz and Dean two keycards. "I got the same suite you had before, Ms. Errington. I hope that is acceptable."

"Perfect. Let's go up now. They've got our luggage loaded on the cart."

Once they arrived upstairs and the porter finished unloading their luggage, Jaz took charge and filled them in on what she had planned. She pointed to the chairs in the suite's living room. Niamh sat down on the couch while Dean took one of the matching chairs. Jaz remained on her feet.

"Niamh, I'm about to ask you some unusual questions. There's no wrong answer, and if you decide what I need you to do is too much, there will be no repercussions. Okay?"

"Yes, ma'am. I'm sure there won't be any problem with your request. What is it you need?"

Dean hid a smile. The whole clandestine nature of things had the girl leaning forward in her seat with anticipation. He feared she might topple to the floor.

"You live with your parents, right?"

"Yes, ma'am. It's me, and my ma and da. My two older sisters have their own families. They have homes not too far away."

"Is there room in your parent's home for a special houseguest? This is a person who needs protection from certain underworld groups. I need a place where they're unlikely to look for her."

"I suppose so, ma'am. I'd have to ask my parents to be sure, but I think they'd say yes. It's the girl, right?"

"I cannot tell you until your parents give you an answer. That is all I can say right now."

Niamh nodded and pulled out her phone. "Let me call them right now and I'll get an answer for you." She crossed to the far side of the living room to make her call. She kept her voice low as she talked to her parents, but Dean could still pick up on most of what she said. Whatever their response was, it didn't seem to upset the girl.

It didn't take long to get an answer. Niamh's father had been in the Garda and it seemed his background protecting Unusuals carried into his retirement. Both parents agreed to help without reservation.

Jaz nodded and Dean got the sense she'd known what the answer would be before she'd made the request. His wife had a good sense for the type of people she worked with. That included their family backgrounds. She liked to know she could count on the team members to have her back.

Once Niamh returned to her seat on the couch, Jaz filled her in on what was going on with Kaylee, especially the fact that they had reported her as a runaway and the authorities might be looking for her in addition to the traffickers. The instructions were simple. Keep the young Kelpie safe while Dean and Jaz searched for the family, probably somewhere in the U.S. It might be an extended stay, so Niamh would need to create new identification papers for the girl as a visiting cousin or something.

"How about an exchange student?" Dean suggested.

"That's a good idea. What do you think, Niamh?"

The girl nodded. "That would help with the questions my sisters will have. I can say they arranged it through my work with the company. They should accept that."

"Good. That's settled then." Jaz started to say something else but stopped when there was a rap on the door.

Dean checked the peephole. It was Hangbe and Kaylee.

He opened the door and let them in. Jaz filled the pair in on what they'd already planned. After making sure Kaylee seemed confident enough to go along with the plan, Niamh got the SUV keys from Jaz and left with her charge. The Errington employee was closer to Kaylee's age and knew how to chat about things to keep her mind off all that had changed in her life. The distraction helped calm her down, and she went along with no further delay.

With that taken care of, Jaz, Dean, and Hangbe sat down to work through the next steps dealing with the larger problem.

The Interpol agent jumped in with what she'd uncovered, or rather, failed to uncover. "I've found nothing. This group is very good at covering their tracks. I followed them to the city. I know they came here, but then they disappear. Either no one knows where they go, or they have enough clout to keep people from talking."

"Dean and I think we know something that might help explain their disappearance." Jaz explained about the portal back to the U.S. She described the strange encounter on their way here and her suspicions related to Dean's encounter with his patient the previous week.

Hangbe smiled. "That's good news. Plus, I haven't been to the States in a long time. It'll be fun to visit and follow this investigation over there." She paused and looked up at the ceiling as a potential problem came up. "I don't know my way around Elk City at all, though. I'll need someone there to help show me around, someone who knows the Unusual side of the city. Any ideas?"

Jaz scratched her head. "None of my local team are available right now." She looked at Dean.

He shrugged. "I can make a few calls. James might be able to free up someone from his organization. It's in his best interest to keep this sort of thing out of Elk City."

"Who's James?"

Jaz jumped in with an answer. "Vampire. He's the local lord. He's decent enough, but he has his own agenda."

"They all do. Maybe I should look into his business dealings while I'm there."

"No," Dean said. "If you're involving James to get his help, then do that, but don't double cross him. He's done a lot to help us both out. I don't know all of his business dealings, but I'm sure he's mostly legitimate."

Hangbe shrugged. "As long as he gives me someone competent, I'm sure it'll be fine. I am a sworn law officer, though. If I discover something untoward, I have to investigate."

"Fair enough. Let me see what I can do." Dean pulled out his phone and started tapping in a message to Brynne. She'd be able to get the help he needed.

It turned out James was traveling, along with Rudy and his primary security team for a few days. That meant James' assistant, Celeste Teal, was also unavailable, which was a shame. She would have been a perfect choice. Brynne said she'd try to come up with someone else, but she wasn't guaranteeing anything.

Dean slipped his phone back into his pocket and returned to sit next to Jaz.

"Well?" Jaz asked.

"We're working on getting someone. The people who would've been on the top of my list are not available, though. Brynne's trying to dig up someone else on short notice from James' organization, but I don't think she's too hopeful."

Dean went down the list of potential guides in his head. The paramedics he worked with would make excellent choices, but they couldn't afford to take off work for more than a day or two and there was no telling how long this might take.

After going through the list again, though, a sort of crazy idea popped into his thoughts. Jaz noticed the smile on his face.

"What? From the look on your face, you've thought of something. What's that crazy brain of yours come up with?"

"It's too early to tell. I don't know if it will work yet. Let me reach out and check on a few things first. When would we be heading back?"

Hangbe said, "Now. The trail has gone cold here. That means they're already gone. If they did what you think and took the portal to Elk City, we'll find evidence of their passage on the far side."

"Okay," Dean glanced at the time. It would be getting into the evening hours back home. The shop would be closed soon. That might be a good thing, though. He didn't want a confrontation with Dougie about the trafficking ring until he had time to dig up more information. He still couldn't believe the leprechaun was part of this mess.

Dean sent out two different messages and waited for replies. While he did that, Jaz and Hangbe completed their plans for when they got to the other side. He listened to their conversation as he checked his phone. There were still a few days left on his vacation. He might help out should the opportunity arise. Finding these missing people was on the top of his list.

Chapter 14

A FEW HOURS LATER, the three of them stood in the shadows across the street from the pub. The lights were out except for a single light Dean could make out through the front window. It shined over the bar, probably left on for security purposes.

"It looks empty," Dean said. "What are we waiting for?"

"It's possible they left a trap," Jaz replied. She had changed out of her pretty skirt and blouse. She wore her standard tactical outfit, black cargo pants, black T-shirt and a leather jacket. She'd included a single pistol rigged in a shoulder holster hidden by the coat.

Hangbe wore black jeans with molded black body armor with a pistol at her side hanging midway down her right thigh. In response to Jaz's warning, she said, "Let me check."

She reached up to her ornate multi-colored bead necklace and pinched a large red bead between her thumb and forefinger. She moved her fingers, rolling the bead back and forth while she stared at the pub.

After several seconds, she said, "There are no magical wards, though something must mask the portal. I can't sense it at all. Is it open all the time or is there something you need to do to operate it?"

Dean shrugged. "You open a door in one place and walk through a room to another door that leads to the next place. I don't think there's anything else, at least not that I saw."

Hangbe's eyes narrowed as she concentrated on what she saw. Her finger and thumb moved faster, rolling the red bead back and forth with increased speed. "Curious. I sense nothing to indicate something with that much power resided within."

"It's there, I promise," Dean said.

A grin creased her serious face for a moment as she glanced sideways at Dean. "I believe you, but I dislike mysteries I cannot explain."

"That must be hard in your line of work."

"A little."

Jaz said, "Let's get this over with. I'll go first, then Hangbe once I open the door. Dean, you come over once we're inside."

He nodded. He knew he came last in case there was trouble inside. Had he gone first, and they ran into trouble, he'd just be in the way. He wasn't a fighter. Dean felt no shame in admitting that. He was fine with his wife being the badass in the family. He kind of liked her that way.

Jaz checked the street one last time and stepped from the shadows. She darted across the street, crouching down by the pub's front door. She pulled lock picks from the pouch at her belt and worked at the door for ten long seconds.

For a moment, Dean thought she wouldn't get it, then she stood, flashing them a grin before she pushed open the door and went inside.

Hangbe ran across the street, following Jaz in before the door closed. Dean waited a few seconds, checking for any traffic, then followed them, hauling the luggage.

Inside, Jaz and Hangbe finished checking the side rooms and behind the bar.

"It's clear," Jaz said.

"Here, too," Hangbe added, coming from the kitchen.

"Good," Dean said. "Let's get home. All this sneaking around makes me nervous."

The two women exchanged grins. They followed him down the hallway to the plain wooden door at the end. Dean opened it and stepped into the small room. Jaz closed the door behind the three of them and Dean leaned forward, pulling the key from his pocket and opening the door leading back to Elk City.

It opened with ease and a few seconds later, they stood in the darkened Irish Shop, back in Elk City again. Dean closed the wooden door guarding the portal and returned the key to its hiding spot, as Dougie had told him.

Hangbe looked around, picking up a few random items from the shelves. "Who would buy this junk?"

Jaz chuckled, "You'd be surprised. A lot of people here have a thing for the Irish."

Dean gathered their suitcases and started towards the back door leading to the parking lot behind the building. "I'm taking these out to the SUV."

"Go ahead, we'll be right out," Jaz said.

Dean hauled the suitcases outside and smiled when he saw the beat up white van pulled in beside Jaz's company SUV. Gibbie climbed out of the van and walked over to help Dean with the bags.

"Hey, I got your message. What's the big secret you couldn't tell me in the text?"

"Jaz and I have a special guest who needs some help getting around the city for the next few days. I thought you might want some extra work, and it's for a good cause."

"And you thought of me? Dean, I'm honored. I won't let you down. What's it pay?"

"It's coming from Errington. It's a few hundred a day and if you keep track of your mileage, she'll reimburse you for that, too."

Gibbie rubbed his hands together, a huge grin on his face. "Just show me who this VIP is and I'll give him the full Gibbie tour."

"She's inside with Jaz. They'll be out in a sec."

"It's a girl?" Gibbie's eyes got wide. "Um, you know I'm not really all that comfortable around women, Dean. I don't think they like me all that much. Are you sure I'm the right person for this job?"

"You have to be. There's not anyone else I'd trust with this." Dean didn't add that James couldn't spare Rudy or any of his shifter security team right now. Gibbie was literally all that was left from Dean's initial list.

Gibbie's chest puffed out with pride. "I guess I have to do it then. I mean, how hard can it be to show someone around town. Who is she, anyway?"

Jaz and Hangbe came out of the store's back door right on cue. Dean said, "Gibbie, meet Hangbe, special agent for Interpol. Hangbe, meet Gibson Proctor. He's—"

"A vampire." Hangbe shot Jaz a hard glare. "You got me a vampire to tour the city with?"

Dean stepped in before Jaz could answer, anger rising in him. "Gibbie is the perfect person to show you around. He's connected with all the Unusual groups in the city. He knows the town like the back of his hand, and I'd trust him with my life. He's the best man for this job, hands down."

He gestured for Gibbie to step forward and stand next to him, but he held back. Dean turned to face a dumbstruck expression on the frumpy vampire's face. He didn't move. He just stared at Hangbe.

"Does he have a voice, or does he just stand around with a stupid expression on his face?"

"Of course he does," Dean said. "Gibbie, come forward and greet the inspector."

Gibbie shook himself, swiped his palms down the front of the grey hoodie he was wearing. "It's a pleasure to meet you, Inspector. I'm honored to be the one to show a person of such stature and grace around town."

Dean couldn't get over the goofy grin on Gibbie's face. Jaz had noticed it, too. She shot Dean a stern stare. He shrugged. They were committed now.

"Don't call me Inspector. I'm undercover. Hangbe will do just fine."

"Hangbe it is. Undercover is great. I'm all about low key. They call me low key Gibbie. Well, not really. But they could if there were a reason to. Like now." Gibbie cringed and tried to reset, the words pouring out in a rapid jumble of excited syllables. "Here, let me take your pack. I'll put it in the back of my van."

"I'll need a place to stay. Can you take care of that?"

Jaz said, "You can stay with me at the Errington headquarters."

Hangbe shook her head. "No, too much chance someone could see me come and go."

Gibbie cleared his throat. "I could get you a temporarily vacant apartment above a restaurant downtown."

Dean nodded. "Above Sabatani's?"

"Yeah, Kristof has a place between tenants. I'm sure he would let us use it for a while." Gibbie turned back to Hangbe. "It's already furnished, so it should be perfect and low key, since you're undercover and all. It can be your hide-out on the down low, you know, until you're ready to go all inspector lady on people."

"I suppose that will be acceptable," Hangbe said, her lips curling up in a slight smile. She looked Gibbie over from head to toe while he fidgeted with his car keys. "I guess you'll do. You certainly are amusing enough. Let's go take a look at this hide-out you've found me. If it doesn't work out, I'm sure we can find other accommodations."

"Of course," Gibbie replied. "I'm yours to command. Just say the word."

The smile broadened on the woman's face. Dean swore she did a quick check of Gibbie's butt as he walked by. She handed him the backpack. He took it from her, pausing to admire the ornate leather and wood scabbard strapped to the side. It was just over a yard long and had leather-wrapped hilt jutting up from it.

"That's marvelous work. Western Africa, if I recognize the design."

Hangbe nodded. "Very good. Few people recognize the origin of my blade."

"It's a hobby of mine. I've always been interested in the history of that region. Your necklace caught my eye as soon as I saw you. It's very old, but I don't recognize the specific country from which it comes."

"It's my homeland. It belonged to my grandmother."

The two of them kept talking all the way over to Gibbie's van. He pulled open he passenger door and quickly shoved some random papers off the seat to make room for his guest. Hangbe climbed in and waved back at Dean and Jaz. A few seconds later, the van pulled away into the night.

"I'm not going to lie," Dean said. "That went way better than I expected."

"I hope he doesn't screw this up. She'll probably kill him if he does."

"What?"

"Relax, I'm just kidding. Probably. Let's just get home. We're both tired, and I have to follow up with Niamh on how Kaylee's doing first thing tomorrow."

Dean climbed in the SUV's passenger side as Jaz got in and started the engine. She pulled out of the parking lot and drove off towards the Errington building. They were back home again, with another mystery on their hands.

Chapter 15

DEAN PAWED AT THE NIGHTSTAND, trying to silence the persistent buzzing of his phone. His searching fingers closed around the annoying device and he brought it over towards his pillow. Cracking open one eye, he spotted the number. It was Brynne.

Groaning, he swiped at the screen to pick up as he sat up on the edge of the bed. Jaz rolled over to check on him. He waved a hand to tell her he was fine.

"Brynne, what's up?"

"I heard you were back in town. I know you're supposed to be on vacation til tomorrow, but no one else is available."

Dean got up and hurried from the room, pulling the bedroom door shut as he entered the hallway.

"I was hoping for a few more days of a break."

"Bill was supposed to come in today to cover for Tammy. She's out with a sick kid. Somehow, Bill broke his ankle playing basketball last night. I just saw him in the ER. Lynne and Brook are out of town for training, and Barry's already maxed his overtime this week. I need someone to come in from the squad or I'll have to defer Station U calls to regular paramedic units from the city."

Dean looked back at the closed bedroom door. Jaz had already told him she was planning on working today. He could pick up an extra shift or two. "I guess I can come in. I reserve the vacation day to use later, though."

"No problem. See you in an hour."

Dean ran his fingers through his unruly hair. He needed a shower. That would wake him up. He stumbled towards the bathroom as he worked to wake up.

He made it into the station with twenty minutes to spare. The smell of Freddy's latest fresh breakfast cooking brought a smile to his face. He still had time to eat.

Brynne looked up from where she sat at the double workstation across the room. "You don't look too bad for coming in on short notice. Thanks for doing that."

"No problem. How's Bill?"

"He'll survive, but he's gonna be on desk duty for four to six weeks with that ankle fracture."

Dean winced. They didn't have that many medics trained to work on the Station U team. It would force the rest of them to pick up even more hours when they were already stretched thin. "Maybe it's time to bring on some new blood."

"Funny you should say that."

Dean frowned. "Uh-oh, I don't like the sound of that. What do you have planned for me today?"

"The academy just graduated a new class—"

"A probie? Brynne, you remember how green I was? You said you'd never bring a squeaky new medic in like that again."

"Let me finish. The new class includes a special candidate. She's an Unusual herself who wanted into the program. She's excelled at her classes, and she already has a degree from Elk U, in psychology. She's smart, talented, and motivated to do the job. All you have to do is keep her straight and show her the medical ropes. She's already got the Unusual stuff down."

Dean grumbled, "I should've stayed in bed."

"I heard that," Brynne said, tapping her ears. "Vampire hearing, remember?"

"I don't care. This is a hell of a thing to spring on me first thing like this."

"It wasn't something I planned. Tammy was supposed to be her training officer. Now it'll be you."

"Okay, Brynne. You win. Just remember, paybacks are hell."

A voice from the doorway behind Dean said, "I'm sorry, am I interrupting something?"

A woman in her early twenties, probably about Dean's age, stood in the doorway with a backpack over one shoulder. She wore the crisply pressed uniform of a brand-new paramedic.

"Not interrupting at all, Leah," Brynne said. "Come on in. This is Dean Flynn. He'll be taking you on during your probationary period with Station U."

The woman crossed to Dean, extending her hand. She shook his hand with a firm grip and smiled. "I'm Leah, Leah Casado. It's a pleasure to meet you. I've heard quite a bit about you, Dean."

Her confidence and easy-going manner brought a smile to his face despite his annoyance at having a new probie. "I'm sure only half of it is true. I'm just a medic like you, trying to save some lives and do right by people."

"I'm excited to get on the unit with you. I'm sure you've got a lot you can teach me. There's only so much I could do while in the academy sessions in the field."

Dean studied her face. He had no idea what kind of Unusual she was, and he couldn't pick up any clues from this initial encounter. He'd figure it out soon enough, or she'd volunteer it. Until then, she was just another squeaky new medic who needed some polish rubbed off so she could do her job.

"Rely on your training and listen carefully when I tell you something. If you do that, I'm sure you'll do fine."

Leah smiled and glanced around. "Is there somewhere I can put this?" She lifted her backpack off her shoulder.

Dean nodded. "Come with me and I'll give you the full tour." He led the way back to the men's and women's bunk rooms. There were lockers in there for each medic in the station. Once she stowed her gear, he showed her around the station, including the ambulance bay, empty now with the ambulance still out on a call. He finished up back in the squad room.

"What is that wonderful smell?" Leah asked.

"That is the best kept secret in the Elk City Fire Department."

On cue, Freddy stepped out from the small kitchen carrying in a tray filled with individual eggs Benedict servings, a plate of bacon and sausage, and freshly squeezed orange juice.

"Leah, meet Freddy, the famous zombie chef of Station U."

"He cooks breakfast for you?"

"And lunch and dinner, too," Freddy said. "If there's something special you like, you let me know and I'll see what I can whip up for you."

"That's great. I'll let you know."

"Sit down and grab a bite. I'll check the GPS tracker on the computer to see where the ambulance is. They should be back soon. Then we need to be ready to roll if a call comes in."

Leah nodded and sat down to breakfast. Dean logged in to one of the two desktop terminals connected to the city's dispatch and reporting system. According to the tracking system, the station's ambulance was on the way back now. Dean figured they'd have about five minutes to get breakfast down. He'd make it work. Eating fast and on the fly was in the paramedic's job description.

Barry and part-timer, Kisha, walked in a few minutes later after parking the ambulance in the garage.

"Hey, Dean. I thought you were off for a few more days?"

"Me, too. I got back early and Brynne found out, so here I am."

"Sucks to be you."

Dean shrugged. "I'll survive. Can't let you grab all the OT. I could use some, too."

"How was the honeymoon?"

"Cut short, but mostly pleasant."

Barry shook his head. "Trouble with the newlyweds already?"

"No, work stuff with Jaz. We had to come back sooner than expected. That's all."

Barry turned to Leah. "You must be the noob. I'm Barry. Keep an eye on Dean. He's a magnet for trouble. All the crazy calls come his way."

"At least my life isn't boring," Dean said. "Come on, Leah. Let's go over the checklist for the start of shift. Then we can talk about how we'll handle the patient care on calls to start."

Leah got up and followed Dean out to the ambulance bay where he took her through the ambulance from front to back, and top to bottom. He brought up the checklist on the tablet in the rear of the ambulance and watched as she went through it, checking the bags and cabinets to make sure they were fully stocked before the first emergency call came in.

About halfway through the process, Brynne poked her head into the back of the ambulance. "Hey, my ride is here, so I'm going to head out before the sun's all the way up. You two good?"

"All set here, boss," Dean said.

Leah nodded as she looked up from her work.

"Good, I'll be back this evening. Call if you need anything."

Brynne opened the bay's garage door so the driver James gave her could drive inside out of the sunlight. Brynne hopped in, disappearing behind the dark tinted windows as she closed the car door. It drove off and Dean walked over to close the garage door.

"What's it like having a vampire as your boss?" Leah asked.

"Not as weird as you'd think. I knew her before she was turned, so I'm actually glad to see her back on the job."

"Really, so she hasn't been undead that long?"

"Almost a year and a half now. Maybe if you work out for a few weeks, I'll even tell you the full story. Until then, just know she's about the best medic I've ever met."

"I'll keep that in mind. Sorry about prying."

"Don't worry about it. Everyone in the station has a story of one sort or another. You'll hear them all, eventually. Give it some time. For now, keep you mind focused on learning the ropes and taking care of patients.

As if the EMS gods had read his mind, the radio speakers in the bay squawked with the alert tones followed by the dispatcher's voice.

"Ambulance U-191, respond for a fire at 1516 Eastern Boulevard. Still awaiting confirmation about injuries."

"Jump in the passenger seat, Leah. Time to earn our keep."

Dean headed for the driver's side. As the new probie, Leah would take on primary patient care while Dean acted as an observer. He'd only step in if she had trouble or there was a second patient.

He clicked the button to raise the bay doors again and started up the ambulance. Thirty seconds later, Dean and Leah were speeding down the road, lights flashing and sirens blaring as they headed towards Leah's first official call.

Chapter 16

IT WASN'T hard to find the location of the fire. The column of black smoke led Dean right to it. Located in an older section of Elk City, the two- and three-story brick buildings on either side of the street were from a time when this was the bustling industrial district of the city. Now, at least half the buildings were empty or used simply as warehouse space by businesses with more modern buildings elsewhere.

The fire crews had put out the blaze by the time Dean pulled the ambulance in behind the last fire engine in the long line of vehicles. Fire crews milled around down the street on the sidewalk in front of the gutted brick building. The structure took up most of the block.

Despite the grim situation with the fire, Dean smiled. Time to break in the new kid and see what kind of grit she had inside. Burn victims were particularly challenging. "Call in to command on the side channel and see where they want us. This fire has been going on for a while so we can't be the first ambulance on the scene."

Leah hesitated a second before reaching out for the mic clipped to the dashboard. Her hand trembled a little as she brought it up to her mouth and keyed the button on the side. "Um, incident command, this is ambulance U-191. We're on location about a block away. Where would you like us to stage?"

The gruff male voice on the radio replied, "Don't stage anywhere. Get up here. We've got another patient for you."

"Uh, okay, U-191 received. Proceeding into the scene."

Dean nodded. "Good job. It'll get easier as you practice."

"He seemed a little annoyed over the radio. Did I mess up?"

"No, that's just Assistant Chief Jonas. He always sounds like he just finished chewing on broken glass while smoking two packs of cigarettes." Dean slipped the ambulance into gear and pulled back into the street. "Keep your eyes open on your side. Firefighters like to dart out into the street between the engines when they're fetching equipment. Let's try not to run over any of them."

He caught the hint of a smile from Leah out of the corner of his eye. It disappeared as she stared ahead at the street and the line of fire engines and trucks.

Dean concentrated on avoiding any of the fire hoses arching out from the engines before curving around towards the building. Ahead, one of the ladder trucks on the scene had extended its long ladder, so the nozzle mounted at the top could shoot down into the remnants of the building.

As he neared the spot where Chief Jonas had parked his command vehicle, the incident commander turned and pointed to a spot on the pavement just behind his vehicle. Dean nodded and pulled over, slowly pulling up over the curb until he had two wheels up on the sidewalk and had cleared the way for other vehicles to pass if needed.

"What should we grab?" Leah asked.

Dean looked around the command vehicle in front of them. He shrugged. "Not sure. I don't see a patient anywhere. Let's go ask the chief, then we'll know what we need."

The two paramedics got out of their ambulance and approached a short, squat figure that was Assistant Chief Jonas. His round figure barely fit into his turnout coat, but his white helmet fit atop his bald head just fine.

He spotted the two medics approaching. "Ah, Dean, I'm glad it's you. We had no idea this one involved any of your Unusual patients until we started overhauling the building after we knocked down most of the fire."

Dean's eyebrows raised in surprise, and he glanced at the building again. "Someone survived that?"

"We pulled two survivors from the basement. They'd broken their way through barred windows from the inside. They didn't speak English, and we couldn't figure out if they were the only ones in there. The fire was fully involved and there was no way to send any of us in safely, anyway. We had the medics on the scene load them up and take them in. We didn't know they were special patients until we saw the rest of the basement."

"What did you see?" Dean asked. He still didn't know what the patient mentioned earlier needed or where they were.

"It's better if I show you. Grab your gear. Your patient's on the far side of the building."

"What injuries are we talking about?" Dean asked.

The chief shook his head. "I know he's not too bad off, just some minor burns, and a possible broken leg. One of the engine crews on that side of the building has been treating him while the police monitor him."

"Police," Leah asked. "What for?"

"Like I said, come with me and I'll show you."

"Give us a second to grab what we need. We'll be right back."

The two paramedics returned to the ambulance. Dean glanced at his partner. "What do we need? This'll be your patient."

Leah ticked off on her fingers as she named the equipment to load on the stretcher. "Trauma bag, oxygen and airway kit, patient monitor, med bag for pain management. Anything else?"

"No, that sounds about right." He pulled the stretcher out from the back and extended the undercarriage while Leah grabbed all the gear.

Once they'd loaded up the stretcher, Dean nodded at the head for her to take the lead. From this point on, he was there to observe her handling of the situation.

They joined the chief at the command vehicle, and he led them down the street to the front of the building. "Park the stretcher here. I need to show you something before we go any farther."

Dean stepped on the pedals to lock the wheels on the stretcher and followed the chief and Leah over to the open doorway closest to them. This corner of the building wasn't burned as badly as the rest. The metal stairwell leading down was still in pretty good shape.

As soon as they reached the bottom, Dean caught the unmistakable whiff of burned flesh. That gave him a little warning of what he was about to see, though nothing prepared him for what greeted them inside.

The smell didn't alert his probie to anything special, though her wrinkled nose told Dean she thought the acrid odor was unpleasant.

Chief Jonas pointed at the double steel doors at the bottom. "These were chained closed when we finally got in here. If we had known what was down here, we would have come in this way first."

"Why?" Leah asked. "You said the building was a total loss by the time you got here."

The chief's grim expression turned sad as he said, "Because we might have been able to save a few of them."

As he said it, he yanked open one of the doors, warped by heat. Through the open doorway, he switched on the bright LED flashlight mounted on the side of his helmet. The light played across the floor near the doors. Charred bodies lined the floor, dozens of them, piled up by what had been a locked doorway. Dean picked up on the animal features of a few of them. At least some were shifters, though it would take a full autopsy to find out the particular variety.

"My God, Chief, how many?"

"We're up to thirty between here and near the barred windows where we rescued the two survivors. Some of them had shackles around their ankles, Dean. They were prisoners down here."

A low snarl put Dean on alert for trouble until he realized it came from Leah. She shifted her gaze from the floor to him, and he caught the flash of yellow in her eyes before her irises returned to those of a normal human. He could have sworn they had a feline cast to them before switching back.

Dean had seen enough. "Where's our other patient? Is it another survivor from down here?"

"Not exactly," the chief said. He had a slight growl to his voice now, too. "Come on. I'll take you to him."

The commander led them back up to the sidewalk and around to the far side of the building. Two firefighters crouched beside a man propped up against the rear of the fire engine, in the shade. They'd spread a tarp on the ground for the patient and they were splinting the leg using the basic trauma kit they carried on the fire engines.

Officer O'Malley stood a few feet away with a stern expression. He watched as the two firefighters treated the injured guy.

"Okay, Leah, this one's all yours. I'll be over by the police officer if you need anything. Don't worry, I'll be watching what you do."

Leah nodded and grabbed the monitor and oxygen bag from the stretcher. She moved to crouch with the firefighters beside the injured man. Dean had a better look at his injuries. Besides the broken leg, he had burns on his hands and forearms.

Chief Jonas joined Dean and the police officer as they watched the new paramedic get to work. The fire officer asked, "Has he given you any trouble?"

O'Malley shook his head. He took off his hat and ran his fingers through his greying brown hair. "No, he knows better than to mess with me. Besides, that break's pretty bad. Even if he can regenerate, it'll be a while before he's running anywhere."

Dean asked, "You know him, then?"

O'Malley eyebrows raised in surprise at Dean's question. "You don't recognize him? I heard from Brynne you and he had a run-in back at your station."

Dean's head spun towards the man on the ground, looking more carefully this time. He hadn't seen through the soot and grime from the fire at first, but now he did and recognized Manton, the werepanther.

"What's he doing here? I figured he left town after he attacked me, especially after taking Verity from the hospital."

O'Malley crossed his arms, saying, "He's in a lot worse trouble now. They found him just inside one entrance, trapped by a smoldering beam. He had a pair of heavy chains and two padlocks with him. They were just like the ones on the doors to the basement. Once the arson investigation is complete, I suspect he's going down for setting this fire and killing all the people trapped below. Two detectives are already waiting at the hospital to interview the two survivors."

Dean had heard enough. He crossed to kneel beside Manton and leaned in as Leah finished taking his blood pressure. "Where's Verity? You snatched her at the hospital. We know that. Where is she now?"

Manton's sneer and quick glance towards the burned out building was all he needed to see. Clenching his fists, Dean wrestled his anger under control. It sounded like O'Malley had him dead to rights on the fire and deaths here. He had to remember his place and job right now. It was hard to swallow his boiling rage, though.

Taking a few deep breaths, Dean asked, "Is he stable, Leah?"

"His vitals are a little high, but consistent with someone in considerable pain. No arrhythmias on the monitor. I was going to get an IV and start some morphine if that's okay?"

Dean wanted to tell her to hold off on the pain management, but he didn't. This was her patient, and she was right to treat him strictly according to protocol, despite what she had undoubtedly overheard.

"Good treatment plan. I'll get the stretcher ready. Once you've given the morphine, we'll load him up."

Manton sneered at Dean as he turned away. His burned hand clutched at the paramedic's arm. "You got no balls, Flynn. Here I am helpless as can be and you don't have the guts to do anything. Don't worry, though. I won't forget you. I'll heal fast enough. Once I'm out on bail, I'll come find you and we can finish our little tussle."

Dean wanted to threaten the man back, but he knew Manton would see anything like that as bluster.

To his surprise, Leah leaned in close. Her eyes had gone all cat-like and yellow again. She whispered something to Manton that made his eyes go wide for a second. After staring into her shifter gaze, he nodded and looked away, focusing on the ground beside him. His bluster and confidence drained completely.

Leah nodded with a grim smile on her face. Her eyes returned to normal and she went back to her work starting an IV and preparing the morphine dose.

Dean went to prep the stretcher, wondering what she'd told the werepanther that made him back down. What kind of Unusual was she that could have that effect on the outlaw cat shifter?

Chapter 17

MANTON DIDN'T SAY another word to anyone all the way to the hospital. He just lay there, casting a wary glance towards Leah occasionally, but otherwise staring straight ahead. O'Malley followed them to the hospital in his police SUV and escorted them into the ER. Dean checked the board by the nurses' station, hoping to see Ashley's name. He knew she could handle the werepanther if he made trouble.

The Eldara wasn't working, but O'Malley must have called ahead. Two uniformed security guards awaited them at the ER's entrance and stayed with Manton after they moved him to the hospital's cot. Leah gave her report to the nurse while Dean took the stretcher and put on a fresh set of sheets.

O'Malley came over as Dean worked. "What's with the new medic? She got that shifter to back down mighty quick."

"Yeah, I'm not really sure. She's a recent graduate from the academy. She seems to know her stuff well enough from a medical standpoint. I know little else about her."

"She's gotta be a shifter herself to get that kind of response. Only other shifters and maybe a vampire get that kind of response from people like him. It was broad daylight, so she isn't a bloodsucker."

"Hey, you know I don't like those kinds of terms. We need to treat them with some respect if we want them to trust us."

O'Malley held up his hands in apology. "Didn't mean to offend anyone. She did a good job from what I could see. I just wonder who or what she is."

He shut up and pretended to check his phone as she came over with the tablet computer after checking in the patient. From the glance she shot the police officer, she'd heard at least part of the conversation. She said nothing, though. She set the tablet on the stretcher and took her spot at the head.

"Ready to go, Boss?"

"Uh, yeah, sure. Did you want a water bottle or snack from the EMS ready room before we go? We get to grab stuff since they know we miss a lot of meals while running calls."

"No, I'm good. Still full from breakfast." Leah grabbed the bar at the head of the cot and tugged it towards the exit.

Dean shrugged and followed along, guiding the cot's back end out to the ambulance ramp. They loaded the stretcher and took a few minutes, throwing out some trash from their call and making sure everything was ready for the next call. Dean didn't have to tell Leah what to do, she seemed to know what he expected of her and jumped to it until the work was completed. He kind of wished he had her initiative and confidence when he got started.

Climbing back into the cab, Dean started the ambulance and started back towards Station U. "Put us back on the street, Leah."

She nodded, grabbing the microphone with more confidence the second time around. "Dispatch, this is U-191 clear and returning."

The radio reply from dispatch came right away. "Copy 191. Clear and returning to station."

They drove in silence for a few minutes while Dean tried to come up with a non-threatening way to ask her what she'd said to Manton. Finally, he decided she was his probie, and he didn't really need a reason when it concerned one of their patients.

"Leah, I have to ask you about what happened back at the scene. That guy and I have a history, as I guess you figured out. I was perfectly alright dealing with it. Then you said something to him, and he changed his demeanor completely. What did you do?"

Leah sighed and her shoulders sagged a little against the bucket seat. "No matter what I do, I'm never going to get away from him."

"Who, Manton? He's no danger to us. I didn't think you were afraid of him."

"Not him." She lowered her eyes, staring at the floorboard by her feet. "My father."

"What's your father got to do with all this? Are you in some kind of trouble? Believe me. I understand when your dad causes issues in your life."

"He has a certain amount of pull with the shifter cat community, that's all. I didn't like how that guy was throwing around threats at you so I told him my father wouldn't like it if something happened to you."

"Sounds like something out of *The Godfather*." Dean thrust out his jaw and tried a horrible Marlon Brando impersonation as he said, "I have an offer you can't refuse."

Leah shook her head and snapped, "I don't like to talk about it. I'm nothing like him and want nothing to do with him. I'm not part of that world anymore. Can we drop it?"

Dean realized he'd crossed some line with the reference to Don Corleone. "Hey, everyone has family they don't want to own up to. I completely understand that. Consider it dropped, okay?"

She gave him a curt nod but said nothing. Dean let the silence settle for a while as he headed back to the station. He'd let his curiosity get the better of him, and he needed to make up for that. Leah deserved his professionalism on the job, not his prying questions.

Back at the station, as he backed into the ambulance bay and parked the unit, Dean hooked a thumb at the rear of the ambulance. "I'll do the restock if you want to get started on your report in the squad room."

Leah shook her head and frowned a little. "No, I need to know how to do all this stuff. Show me what needs to be done. I can do it."

"Leah, I might be your training officer for the next little while, but that doesn't mean we aren't partners, too. You can help me. That'll get it done faster and I can show you where to get the fresh supplies from the cabinets in the garage bay."

Dean walked towards the row of storage cabinets along the wall, but Leah stopped him. "Dean, I'm not angry with you for asking about my dad. I guess I still have to get over my hang-ups. You did nothing wrong."

"Fair enough, but I could have kept my curiosity in check."

Leah laughed.

Dean cocked his head to one side in question. "What's so funny?"

"One of my academy instructors had a saying. She said, 'a paramedic who isn't curious, isn't much of a medic.' I guess that makes you pretty good at your job."

Dean laughed along with her this time. "I guess it does at that. Come on, we could get called out at any minute. Let's get this done and see what Freddy's making us for lunch later."

The rest of the day turned into a pretty routine day, at least where you could say such a thing where Station U was concerned. Dean observed Leah handle a patient with chest pain and some ventricular heart arrhythmias that needed some attention at the hospital. She took on a few respiratory distress calls, including a pediatric asthma patient in the Fairy community at the New Barrens. Overall, she proved to be both knowledgeable and compassionate, the two traits Dean most appreciated in other health care professionals.

As they backed in after the last call of the day, Dean was pretty confident Leah had the makings of a top-notch paramedic. He told her as much while they completed the end of shift checklist together and returned to the squad room. Brynne was there, as was Barry, Dean's former partner.

Barry pointed at Leah and shouted, "I knew it. I've joined the first wives' club. You've traded me in for a newer model."

Dean laughed. He was happy to see Leah smiled as well. "Leah, may I present my previous probie and partner, Barry Winston. He's the reason I learned to be such a hard-ass the first day."

Brynne asked Leah, "How did you do?"

The new medic shrugged. "Okay, I guess. I don't think Dean has too many complaints, right?"

Dean nodded as he took off his jacket and sat down to send off his last report of the day. "She's every bit as good as you said she was, Brynne. Whoever spotted her at the academy and pointed her this way, they should get a big high-five."

"It was me," Brynne said. "I ran into her about six months ago and she asked about the paramedic job. She jumped into the new accelerated program almost right away."

Dean clicked send on the last report and spun around in the chair. "Wow, Leah, she must've said something pretty impressive to get you to join up just like that. What was it?"

Leah blushed a little and shook her head. "I think I'll save that story for another time. My mother always raised me to keep a little mystery going with folks."

Brynne laughed and winked at Leah. "Well played. Your mother raised you right. Now Dean'll be wondering what got you into this field for weeks."

Dean waved Brynne's comment off with the wave of his hand. "I'm sure it'll come out in time. I can wait." He wouldn't let his innate curiosity show, not when they'd laid the mystery out there like a challenge.

Brynne caught Leah's eye and shook her head. "Don't you dare tell him until you make him squirm for a while first."

"Hey, you're the lieutenant. I have to follow your lead. Sorry, Dean, you'll have to wait until the boss lady gives the okay."

A rap at the door interrupted their conversation. Dean answered it, surprised to see a police officer when he opened the door. He couldn't remember the guy's name, but he was one O'Malley's colleagues in the police version of Station U.

"Hey, what's up?" Dean asked, stepping back to let the cop into the squad room.

"They sent me over to check on you folks. Everything okay here?"

Brynne nodded, concern creasing her brow. "What's the problem, Seth?"

"We had a prisoner escape from the hospital. You all transported him there after a fire this morning?"

Dean and Leah glanced in each other's direction. Dean took the lead. "I remember. I'd had a run in with him before and he said some things to me on scene that might be construed as threatening. We dealt with it and took him in without a problem."

"Well," Seth said. "He broke out of the prison ward when they took him down for some X-rays. He killed one of the security guards at the hospital and was last seen jumping into a dark SUV that sped away from the scene."

Brynne jumped in, saying, "Have you checked the area outside?"

Seth nodded. "I did. It seems clear, but the sarge told me to make sure you all got home safely since it was shift change time."

Dean hated this. He refused to let Manton and his threats scare him, no matter how easily the werepanther had beaten him before. "I don't think that will be necessary, Seth. I can get home fine on my own."

"What about your partner," Seth asked, glancing at Leah.

She shook her head, too. "He'd be a fool to come after me."

Brynne said, "Maybe we're better safe than sorry here. I think it would be a good idea for the nice officer here to shadow you both on the way home. Leah, your apartment downtown is on the way to Dean's place. He can follow you that far with Seth following in his squad car."

Dean knew better than to argue with Brynne. Her serious tone made it clear that this wasn't a request.

Leah, however, didn't recognize the signs, or she ignored them. "I said I don't need any special treatment. If this cat comes after me, it'll be the last thing he does. I can take care of myself."

Seth snorted a chuckle. "Look who thinks she's all badass. What are you, some sort of hunter-medic with a death wish?"

Leah's eyes narrowed, and her fists clenched. Before Dean knew what was happening, short orange fur had sprouted all up and down her exposed arms. Black and tan splotches appeared, dotting the orange fur until she'd assumed the coloring of a jungle cat of some sort. Dean thought it might be a variety of panther.

Seth held up his hands in surrender. "Hey, I'm sorry I said anything. I didn't know you were a shifter yourself."

Brynne stepped in front of Leah, blocking her from the police officer's view. "You know what? Why don't you tell your sergeant I'll take care of security tonight? If you could have a unit swing by here a couple of times later to check on the station while we're out on calls, that would be great."

"You sure?" Seth asked. "I don't know. The sarge was pretty clear."

Brynne nodded. "I'll call him for you. I'll let him know I'm taking responsibility. I've kicked this guy's butt once already. He won't want a repeat performance."

Seth took a few seconds and then nodded. "I guess with a vampire and a werejaguar in the house, you've got things well in hand. I'll do a last sweep around the building before I leave."

Barry called out from his seat behind one workstation, "Come in after your sweep and I'll have Freddy pack up some dinner for the road since you took the time to check up on us."

"I'll do that, but it'll have to be in an hour or two when I do the second check. I have to report in to the sarge first."

"Suit yourself. He's made lasagna and his homemade pasta is amazing."

"Don't worry, I will be back," Seth said. He waved one last time and headed out the door.

Dean shook his head. "Brynne, I'll be fine. I'm going straight home. Nobody'd be stupid enough to jump me at Errington's HQ."

It was Leah's turn to be surprised. "You live at Errington Security? I didn't know they rented apartments there."

Barry laughed. "The apartments are for family members only."

When Leah's confused expression continued, Barry added, "Dean's wife is Jaz Errington herself."

Leah's gaze took in Dean and seemed to appraise him in a different light.

He shook his head. "I just married into the family. I'm not a hunter. I'm here on this earth to heal and that's it."

She nodded and forced herself to smile. "I, of all people, shouldn't throw shade on others for their family connections. Brynne's right, though. The Errington building isn't all that far from my apartment complex. I could follow you there to make sure nothing happened and then head on home."

Brynne nodded. She answered before Dean could object. "Perfect. You do that. Maybe you can both follow each other in first thing tomorrow morning, too, just to be safe."

Leah nodded. Dean reluctantly followed suit.

"Let's go, then. My wife is expecting me home for dinner."

Leah nodded towards the kitchen. "What about that delicious food Freddy made?"

On cue, Freddy came from the kitchen with two large paper bags. "I overheard the discussion and made an executive decision. Here are double servings for each of you. I didn't know if you had anyone else at home, young lady, so I erred on the side of caution."

Leah smiled. "Nobody else at home on my end, but that means more leftovers for me." She took one bag and Dean took the other.

"Fine," Dean said. "Let's get this little safety caravan on the road. Brynne, you and Barry have a *quiet* night, okay?"

Barry and Brynne groaned in unison.

"Agh," Barry said. "The 'Q' word. I can't believe you'd do that to me. It's Brynne who pissed you off."

"Sorry, pal. Make her do all the dirty work."

As if on cue, the radio squawked with alert tones and Dean laughed as he and Leah left the station for the parking lot.

He got in his white pickup truck and waited until Leah pulled around in a beat-up Nissan. It had mismatched quarter panels making it look like it had been assembled from spare parts in a junkyard. Dean didn't judge, though. He knew what kind of money new paramedics made working for the city.

He waved at Leah and started home with her right behind him. He decided not to ·tell Jaz about the situation with the missing werepanther and the threats. She might decide to make him take a driver from her security detail, and he did not want that. For now, a mysterious werejaguar trailing him home was good enough.

Chapter 18

DEAN DROVE up in front of the gates and pulled out his keycard to access the lot beneath the Errington Security building. Leah waved from where she'd pulled up on the street behind him. She drove off as he pulled down the ramp to the underground garage.

Gibbie's beat-up white van sat in one of the visitor spaces by the elevator. Dean smiled. He wondered how the vampire had fared over the last twenty-four hours, chauffeuring the Interpol agent around town.

After parking in his assigned slot, Dean walked to the elevator. James, the guard on duty in the windowed office beside the elevator, waved at Dean as he walked up. It had taken some getting used to living in a place that seemed to have more security than the White House sometimes. It was why he chaffed at the need to have an escort outside of these walls.

He rode the elevator car up to the top floor, using his keycard to access the private level. The sound of laughter greeted him as soon as the doors opened on their dedicated floor. Dean dropped his keys in the bowl by the elevator and hung his duty jacket up in the closet.

"That you, Dean?" Jaz called.

"Like anyone else could get up here besides me without an alert coming over your phone?"

Dean walked into the living room.

Jaz smiled. "I know you like me to pretend we live a normal life in a normal house. I'm just playing the dutiful wife welcoming her husband home."

Gibbie, seated in a recliner in the corner, mimed gagging himself with a finger. Dean laughed out loud at the gesture.

Hangbe, seated in a plush straight-backed chair beside Gibbie, shook her head. "Don't let him domesticate you, girl. I spent too much time helping to foster your wild side."

"Don't worry, Hangbe," Dean said. "I don't think anything I do will ever get rid of that part of her. I wouldn't want to, anyway. It's part of what drew us together."

Jaz smiled. "Good answer, hubby. What's in the bag? I could smell it as soon as you came in."

"Freddy's lasagna, garlic bread, and probably a few cannolis, if I know how he thinks."

Hangbe leaned forward. "It smells delicious."

"It is, and lucky for you all, Freddy always packs extra. There should be enough for all three of us." Dean glanced at Gibbie. "Sorry, bud. No blood in the house for you."

"It okay, I ate earlier while milady was sleeping."

Hangbe shot him a mischievous grin. "What did I tell you about calling me that?"

"Well, you shouldn't have told me you're descended from royalty."

Dean hid a chuckle behind one hand at the byplay between the pair. Apparently, Gibbie had gotten over his nervousness around the African Amazon.

He caught the expression on Jaz's face, too. She hadn't missed the exchange, either.

"Hey, hon," Dean said, turning towards the kitchen. "Do you want to come help me get the plates together? Maybe you can crack a bottle of wine, too."

"Good idea. We'll be right back."

Jaz followed Dean into the kitchen. He started unpacking the bag while she got out plates for them and turned on the oven to heat the garlic bread. The two of them had a routine down for reheating their chef-quality meals from the Station U cook.

Dean glanced back around the corner into the living room. Gibbie and Hangbe were chatting about something.

He smiled, saying, "Hey, is it just me, or is there something going on between those two."

Jaz laughed. "Hangbe and Gibbie? Give me a break. He's not her kind, AT ALL."

"I don't know. I sense some kind of chemistry between the two of them."

Jaz gave him a playful whack to the back of his head. "Maybe that knocked some sense into you. There's no way she'd have anything to do with a vampire, especially not Gibbie."

Dean didn't belabor the point. He was usually pretty good at spotting things like this. Maybe she was right, though. She knew Hangbe better than he did. She could just be humoring the strangeness of her tour guide around the city.

He finished plating the food after zapping the larger container in the microwave to rewarm it. Then he and Jaz carried everything in and set their small, round dining room table.

"Food's ready," Dean called. "Gibbie, I poured you some wine. I hope that's okay."

"Perfect, Dean. Like I said, I'm full already."

Hangbe came in and sat beside Gibbie. Dean took his spot beside Jaz. Once they'd sat down, Jaz raised her wineglass. "To friends, old and new."

Everyone raised their glasses and gentle tapped them together before sipping at the nice red Jaz had selected.

Hangbe took a bite and said, "Dean, there was a fire downtown today involving some deaths. Did you happen to know anything about it?"

Dean nodded. "In fact, we got called in today to pick up a patient there. It wasn't a pretty scene. At least thirty dead, and it definitely had something to do with our trafficking ring."

"What makes you say that?" Jaz asked.

Dean filled her in on what the firefighters had found in the basement. He skipped over details about his patient. Despite that fact that Manton had threatened him, Dean wouldn't divulge confidential information. He settled for describing bystanders witnessing cat shifters locking up the building's exits before the fire broke out.

Gibbie's jaw dropped, and he shook his head as Dean finished his description of the scene. "That must have been awful for those poor people. Why would anyone do something like that?"

"Probably because they know someone is tracking them," Hangbe replied. "They have to know I'm on their trail by now. I should have made the connection and come here sooner. Those people died because I didn't get here to America in time."

Jaz shook her head. "Don't you dare. You had no way of knowing where they were taking people until you met with me and we both made the connection together. You taught me a long time ago that the bad guys are the ones responsible for what they do. We can only do so much."

Hangbe shook a finger at Jaz. "I taught you too much. Those rules were for you to learn. They were not for you to recite them back to me years later."

"What's good for the goose," Jaz began.

Dean asked, "What if that's the end of the trail? Do you think they'd pack up and move on to some other city?"

Hangbe shook her head. "No, I think they were tying up some loose ends. They are probably hiding somewhere in the city, hoping we'll believe they've moved on."

Jaz stared at Dean and pursed her lips like she was going to say something but changed her mind.

"What?" Dean asked.

"I was waiting to see if you mentioned the police dispatch to your station this evening about the time you got off work."

Dean resisted the urge to scowl at her. He'd forgotten that she had people monitoring the radio transmissions of the city agencies about Unusual activity.

"What do you want to know? It was a routine check based on an earlier event. It turned out to be nothing. End of story."

"Were you going to tell me a shifter on a call threatened you earlier today?" Jaz had stopped even pretending to hold back. She was full on pissed at this stage.

"Jaz, maybe we can have this conversation later, when we don't have company over."

Hangbe decided it was time to insert herself into the conversation. "If you tell me who this shifter is, I'll take care of it so you and Jaz can pretend it never happened."

Both of them said "NO!" at the same time to that suggestion.

Dean took a deep breath. He was going to have to tell her the whole story anyway at this point. "Look, it is the same jerk who jumped me in the parking lot a few weeks ago. He was injured at the scene of that fire."

Hangbe leaned in. "So, he was the shifter connection to trafficking you mentioned."

Dean sighed. "Yes. I avoided saying anything because he's technically a patient. I shouldn't tell you anything about my encounter with him."

Gibbie countered with, "I don't know, Dean. If someone attacks or threatens you, that probably voids the caregiver arrangement. It would for me."

"The vampire's right," Hangbe said. "So this Cretan was the one who had locked the people in the building?"

Dean nodded. "It looks that way. He was injured. We took him to the hospital until he could regenerate enough for them to take him to the Unusual unit at the jail. He escaped from custody and the police are looking for him."

Jaz asked, "Why do you think this isn't a big deal, then? What happened that makes you think he won't come after you?"

"Because the probie I worked with today scared him off."

Jaz laughed, "What new academy graduate paramedic could scare off a werepanther with a grudge?"

"That's what I wondered," Dean replied. "She said something

to him about her father, and he sort of shut up and stopped being so scary."

"Who's her father?" Hangbe asked.

Jaz shook her head and said, "Back up. What's this girl's name? Let's start there. What do you know about her?"

"She's a shifter of some sort herself, maybe a leopard or some other jungle cat with spots."

Hangbe glanced at Jaz and then said, "A jaguar, maybe?"

"Possibly, why?"

Jaz leaned back and shook her head. "What's her name?"

"Leah, Leah Casado. She just came through the new accelerated paramedic program. She's very good for her first day."

Gibbie shook his head. "It can't be the real Leah Casado. There's no way she'd work as a paramedic in our city. I'd heard rumors she was around here somewhere going to college, but I thought it was all just rumor."

Dean glanced around at the others. He leaned back in his chair and folded his arms. "Okay, now it's your turn to fill me in. What am I missing here?"

Jaz said, "Dean, if it's the same girl, and it sounds like it is, your new partner is the daughter of the leader of the underworld cartel called the Jaguars. They're criminal royalty of the highest order. Here in North and South America, jaguar shifters are very rare, and very powerful. They descend from the high Incan priests and gained their power through blood sacrifice and magic. That's how they've held onto their power all these years later."

"So, she's the daughter of a criminal kingpin?"

Gibbie shook his head and leaned in towards Dean. "No, she's the daughter of THE criminal kingpin, at least the biggest one in this hemisphere."

Dean thought they were pulling his leg. He glanced from Jaz, to Hangbe, to Gibbie, and back to Jaz. They all nodded.

"I still don't get why that's important. Based on the way she reacted to my questions about her background, she clearly wants nothing to do with her past, something which I totally get, by the way. Why else would she take a job like being a paramedic unless she had broken all ties?"

Jaz said, "Except she didn't. She still felt perfectly comfortable dropping daddy's name with that werepanther to make him settle down. It worked, too, based on what you said."

Hangbe said, "I must talk with this girl. She might have valuable information for this investigation."

"No," Dean said. "You will not."

"You can't tell me no. I can investigate whatever and whoever I want in order to close my case."

Dean shook his head. "Not this time. She's my probie. That means she's under my protection. If you want to talk with her, you ask me, and I'll see if she wants to talk to you. I don't think she knows anything about what's going on. She's been in the academy for the last six months studying. Believe me. She's had no time for socializing."

Hangbe protested, but Jaz held out a hand. "Hangbe, I have to back Dean on this one. He's on our side and he wants to break this ring as much as you and I do. If he thinks she has nothing to do with it, then that's probably correct."

"But——" Hangbe started.

Jaz shook her head. "Let Dean find out what she knows. If he thinks she can help us, he'll let us know. Right, hon?"

Dean nodded. "Believe me, Hangbe, I want these animals in jail as much as you do. I saw those bodies piled on top of each other, trying to claw their way out of that burning basement. So did Leah. If she can help, I'll let you know and have her tell you herself. She wants to be a paramedic, then she's going to own the full responsibility of what that means in my book."

The words hung in the air for a few seconds. The last few minutes had been tense and everyone in the room seemed lost when it came to what to do next.

Gibbie finally broke the silence saying, "Hey, I've some dice in my coat pocket. How about we play a round of Yahtzee?"

After an exchange of glances, everyone broke out laughing. Despite the laughs, it turned out Gibbie had the perfect solution to diffuse the tensions building between the four of them. They played a few rounds and kept the conversation to lighter subjects. When the topic returned to work at the end of the evening, everyone had relaxed and worked out a plan of action.

Walking Gibbie and Hangbe to the door with Jaz, Dean said, "So, tomorrow, after work, Jaz and I will head down to the Irish Shop and talk to Dougie about closing the portal. There has to be a way to shut it down temporarily. That will cut off the traffickers from their support network and source of victims."

Hangbe nodded. "Good. In the meantime, Gibbie and I will concentrate on tracking down these cat shifters and their contacts here in the city to narrow down who the boss is here in Elk City."

Gibbie gave a thumbs up. "I'm right there with you, Hangbe. This vampire will hook you up."

Hangbe shot Gibbie a strange look, then said, "We'll all check back in tomorrow night and see what the next steps will be."

Everyone agreed and the two guests headed back down to the garage while Dean and Jaz prepared for bed. The weight of the long day at work suddenly hit Dean, and all he wanted was to climb in the sack. He had to be back at work in time for the next shift in the morning with Leah.

Jaz smiled as he yawned while helping her clean up from their dinner. "You go to bed. I've got this. You're back in early tomorrow anyway."

"You sure?"

Jaz nodded. "Go. I won't be up long. I'm tired, too."

Dean smiled and headed back to their room for a much-needed night's sleep.

Chapter 19

GIBBIE PULLED the van onto the street from the Errington building's garage and turned south towards the apartment he'd arranged for Hangbe. She sat in the passenger seat checking email or something on her phone. After a few minutes, she looked up and scanned the darkened sidewalks outside as he drove.

"Where are we going?"

"I thought you'd want to get some rest. You only had that quick two-hour nap when we dropped off your bags at the apartment."

"No time for that. I found some information in the Interpol database that might link to Manton. There's a werepanther by the same name who's associated with a clan out of southern France."

Gibbie didn't know how she kept going like this. He didn't technically need rest, and he was tired after their day tracking leads and locations Gibbie had turned up. He hadn't even gotten out of the van on most of them since it was daylight out. She'd been up for at least two days based on what Dean had told him about their time in Ireland.

"I don't know any French shifters in town, if that's what you're asking."

"No, but there has to be a place, a local pub, or something

where we might get a lead on who picked up that guy when he broke out of the hospital. There aren't many who'd hide someone associated with killing a human in a public place like that."

She wasn't wrong about that. He didn't know anyone, even among his shadier contacts, who'd put up with that in the community. Still, if she wanted to find someone who did, that meant going to The Watering Hole. A werewolf family originally from the hills of western Maryland and West Virginia ran the bar. They had contacts that came there from all over the country. They'd been closed earlier in the day, so he hadn't taken Hangbe there.

"I know a place. I'm not sure if you'll be able to find what you're looking for there, though. Most people here in Elk City are decent folks."

"Just get me in the door. I'll take care of rooting out the scum."

The gleam in her eye sent a chill down Gibbie's spine. It was both terrifying and a bit of a turn on at the same time. He kept his focus on the road as he turned off the original path home and took her deep downtown. He stole a few glances in her direction while he drove. There was something about this woman that excited him more than just about any woman he'd ever met.

Maybe it was that she was so far out of his league, or that he knew she'd kill him out of hand if he crossed her. He'd dated dangerous girls before. More than a few had tried to kill him, mostly in a fit of anger at something he'd done to piss them off. Hangbe was different. If she decided to kill him, it wouldn't be because he said the wrong thing or winked at the wrong waitress. There was something refreshing in that.

A few minutes later, Gibbie pulled the van to the side of the street in an empty parking space. He hopped out and fed a few quarters into the meter and waited while Hangbe came over to join him.

He pointed up the street. "The Watering Hole is up there one block. If someone downtown knows where this guy is hiding, they'll be in there. Otherwise, all those involved are probably locked down."

"Do I need a password to get in?" she asked as she slipped a silver Kukri knife under her jacket where it fit into a sheath hidden there. He knew she had a pistol hidden in a shoulder holster on the other side.

"No, I'll go with you. I know the bartender there. Just remember, if you cause trouble there, I can never go back."

"If there's trouble, it's probably a good idea for you to find a new place, anyway. You're a decent enough guy for a vampire, Gibson. It'd be a shame for anything to happen to you."

She dropped a sly grin as she said it and started across the street. He jogged along to catch up with her stride, propelled by her exquisitely long legs. He caught up with her as she turned and angled up to the next block. He pointed at a nondescript gray door in between a locksmith shop and a dry cleaner.

Hangbe pulled open the door and walked down the stairs just inside. Gibbie pulled the door closed and followed her down just in time to stop her from taking out the bouncer.

The big werebear had a hand pressed against her chest, glaring at her and shaking his head. "Lady, I think you're in the wrong place. This is a private club."

Hurrying down the last few steps, Gibbie rushed up to stand beside Hangbe. "It's alright, Anson. She's with me."

"Another one of your human floozies, Gibbie? She's not like your usual type."

"Uh, yeah, well, I'm trying to turn over a new leaf. Can we come in?"

"You know the rules. You're responsible for her behavior while she's here. You okay with that. With that hidden body armor she's got on, it seems like she's looking for trouble."

"Oh, that, we were paint balling earlier. We just want a drink and a chance to relax, right, honey?" He snaked an arm out and around her waist, hoping she didn't lop off his arm for being so forward.

To his surprise, she leaned into his embrace and smiled. "This is all so exciting, Gibbie. I never even knew this place was here. I've walked past it dozens of times."

Choking a little in surprise, Gibbie recovered, saying, "Oh, yeah, sweetie. Just remember, you're my guest and you can't just waltz in here any time you want."

He glanced at Anson. The big shifter nodded and moved to one side to let the two of them through. The noise of the live metal band washed over them both as the door opened. Gibbie steered Hangbe over toward the bar where he saw a pair of open stools.

As they worked their way through the crowded underground club, she leaned in close and whispered in his ear. "If you ever touch me again without telling me first, it might be the last time you touch anything."

Gibbie almost tripped over his own feet at that moment, casting his eyes down to catch the wicked grin on her face. He gulped and said, "Understood. I just thought we needed to work up a cover story."

"It was good work, just don't make a habit of it."

Gibbie nodded and let out a sigh of relief. He let his hand drop from around her waist to show her he'd gotten the message. To his surprise, she reached down and pulled it back into place. He settled his hand over the curve of her hip where the waistband of her tight jeans rode just below the bottom of the thin layer of body armor covering her torso. He tried unsuccessfully to hide the goofy grin on his face at being so close to such a magnificent woman.

Breck, the bartender saw Gibbie and Hangbe sit at the end of the bar and came over to take their orders. Gibbie ordered his usual, a sangria with a wedge of orange. Hangbe ordered a double Scotch, neat.

As she went to make their drinks, Gibbie leaned in closer to Hangbe and whispered, "What's the plan?"

"I've got to identify who in here is related to our trafficking ring. Let's wait for the drinks to come back."

Gibbie had no idea what she was going to do, but she clearly had something in mind. Breck returned with their drinks. He picked up his as soon as it arrived and sipped at the tangy beverage.

Hangbe left her drink sitting on the bar. Her right hand rose instead to touch her fingertips against two of the beads in her ornate necklace. A gentle crooning came from her throat. He only heard it because he was so close to her. He doubted anyone else had any idea she was up to anything.

He opened his mouth to ask what she was up to, but clapped it shut as she raised the forefinger of her left hand. The tune wafting from her never stopped, even after she turned her head in a slow pass so she could scan the whole place. She twisted back and forth twice before settling back to stare across the room at a lone door in the far wall.

"There, that is where I'll get my answers."

"What's back there? What did your magic show you?"

"I don't know. I only know that the ones I seek are behind that door."

Gibbie scanned the area and spotted the hulking form of a guard standing in the shadows not too far away. "You'll never get in there unnoticed. There's a guy watching it, see."

Hangbe batted his arm down. "Don't point, you fool. I see him. Look, I'll get up and head to the women's room. The bathrooms are in the corner nearby. You get up and distract the guard."

"Me? What do you want me to do?"

"Just get his attention on you and not the door. You do that and I'll be able to get inside. Can you get it done or not?"

Gibbie saw her beautiful eyes staring back into his, and he didn't hesitate. "Of course. One distraction coming right up. Just be ready to go."

Hangbe stared at him for a second longer, then got up and wound her way through the crowd towards the restrooms. Gibbie watched her go and looked around the room for the best way to get the guard's attention. A crazy idea formed in his head. Sliding off his barstool, he paused long enough to down the rest of his drink and scribble something on the napkin beneath his glass before heading into the crowd to put his plan into action. It just might work in this bar full of shifter bikers and other rough sorts.

He made his way to the bandstand and leaned close to the spike-haired woman running the sound board. "I'll buy all the band's merch for sale on that table over there if you get them to play this song for me." He handed her the folded napkin.

She opened it and read the words there. Raising one eyebrow, she glanced up at him. "Really?"

Gibbie nodded. "All the merch, but you have to do it up right."

"Okay, it's your funeral. I'll be right back."

He waited while she made her way to the rear of the stage and waited for the band to finish the current song. She handed the napkin to the shirtless and tattooed drummer and pointed at Gibbie. The guy read the napkin and squinted through the lights. Gibbie raised a hand and waggled his fingers at the guy.

The reaction he got was not what he expected. The drummer's face split into a broad grin. He called over the rest of the band, who all clustered around his drum set. Realizing his plan was about to go into action, Gibbie swallowed hard. The song was only part of it. The next part was all him. It would succeed or fail based on what he did next.

The band members spread out back to their instruments. The lead singer on keyboard said, "We have a special request from one of our biggest fans and we couldn't say no. It's one of our favorites and I'm sure yours, too. Join in if you know the words."

Dropping his hands to the keys, the music started with a familiar trumpet fanfare and a driving disco beat. The bass and lead guitar joined in right away with the intro. Gibbie knew it was now or never, and he let out a yell and charged to the center of the now-empty dance floor. He reached the middle just as the singer started in on the song.

"Young man, there's no need to feel down…"

Gibbie threw his hands in the air as he let himself fall into the music so it carried him away. By the time they got to the chorus, the dance floor had filled to bursting and everyone joined in with voices and arm motions as they all spelled out Y.M.C.A.

While everyone danced around him, Gibbie craned his neck and spotted Hangbe slipping through the door to the back rooms of the bar. Smiling that his plan had worked, he continued leading the dance party, only partly worrying if he had enough room on his credit cards to pay for the pile of t-shirts and stuff the band had for sale. All that mattered was that his plan had worked.

Chapter 20

HANGBE STOOD by the women's room door as Gibbie approached the bandstand. She wondered what he was up to. She waited and worried the vampire wouldn't be up to the task she had set for him. She was about to break into an improvised Plan B to get into the back room when the music started up again.

Her jaw dropped as her ridiculous guide to Elk City began dancing and gyrating around the dance floor in front of the band. To her amazement, the crowd cheered and began singing along, joining in the dance. When the chorus came around, everyone in the room began spelling the letters with their bodies, shouting at the tops of their lungs.

Two female shifters came running over and tugged the guard away from his position by the door. He'd been dancing in place for the first verse and chorus and didn't resist when they pulled out to the dance floor. Shaking her head, Hangbe slid along the wall, catching Gibbie's eye as she opened the door and slipped inside. He actually winked at her, which she'd have to deal with later. For now, his ridiculous plan had worked. Now, she had a job to do.

Letting the door close behind her, muffling the noise from the bar on the other side, Hangbe let her eyes adjust to the even dimmer light on this side. A hallway with several doors stretched ahead of her. The only light came from the open door at the end. Her sensitive ears picked up at least two male voices and the sound of someone sobbing softly from that direction.

Touching her beads of seeking, as she had done earlier at the bar, she reached out to find the source of the presence she'd felt earlier. It was someone linked to one of the missing persons cases she'd followed to Elk City, though she couldn't be sure which disappearance they related to. It was the first solid lead she'd found in the several months she'd been tracking this case.

Her magical necklace connected to the presence right away, and she got a sense of proximity that meant whoever it had linked to. They were probably in one of these rooms off this hallway. The voices at the end of the hall got louder and a loud smack followed by a cry of pain echoed down the hallway.

The male voices laughed as the sobbing grew louder, following the cry for help. Hangbe moved down the hallway, checking the other two doors on the way to the one that was open. Both were locked. She continued on until she reached the end and peeked into the open room.

A metal desk occupied most of the room. Four hulking forms stood around a woman tied to a metal chair. One man with his back to Hangbe raised his hand to deliver a backhand blow and said, "Are you going to try to escape again, girl?"

The woman in the chair wore a torn dress with a plain blue print fabric that had seen better days. Her brown hair hung down around her face but didn't hide the bruised cheeks and the tears running down them. She lifted her head to answer but stopped as her piercing blue eyes met Hangbe's brown ones. The girl gasped in surprise and Hangbe cursed under her breath. There went her advantage.

Just like that, the four men turned to stare in her direction, their eyes narrowing in anger as they spotted her. The largest of them pointed at her. "What are you doing back here? This area is closed to patrons of the bar."

Thinking fast, Hangbe stood from her crouch and shrugged. "I'm sorry. I was told the bathroom was this way."

She knew right away they didn't buy her act. The werepanthers closest to the door reached for her and dragged her into the room. Damn, they were fast. Still, that worked to her advantage.

Letting her momentum towards them help propel her forward, Hangbe launched off her back foot, snapping a kick with her boot into the midsection of the nearest shifter. As he doubled over, she reached into her jacket for her pistol.

As her hand came free with the gun, a fist like steel cracked down on her wrist. The blow sent a jolt of pain up her arm and loosened her grip on the Glock. Cursing as it clattered to the floor, she ducked under the two pairs of arms reaching to pull her closer.

The closest of them had doubled over from the force of her kick and she rolled sideways, using his back as support to move her away from his partner. That brought her nearer to the boss man, but he hadn't expected the move, so she caught him by surprise.

His eyes widened as she slipped the Kukri free from inside her jacket and hacked the silver alloy blade down into the side of his neck. Blood spurted free, the razor-edge cutting vital vessels that would never regenerate. His hand came up and clapped against the spurting wound, gasping in pain. He fell backward and she turned to face the others. The leader would be dead in under a minute with that wound.

"Who's next?"

The one she'd kicked hugged his midsection as he stumbled towards the door, but the other two came at her, both shifting into their humanoid panther forms. Claws extended, they raked at her from both sides as she twisted to keep away from their grasping reach.

Her body armor took most of the damage and she was able to sneak in a hit on one of them with her Kukri that brought a yowl of pain as he yanked his injured paw back.

Hangbe tried to follow up on that strike but that exposed her back and she realized too late the other shifter had the reach to grab onto her shoulders. His iron grip pulled at her and slammed her to the floor hard enough to knock the wind from her.

Gasping and trying to recover, she realized she'd never get away in time to avoid the next attack. Reaching for her neck, Hangbe's questing fingers found the large glass bead just in time. Accessing the magic with her mind, she let the stored spell loose as the raking claws got too close.

A blinding flash of white energy pulsed out from the Amazon on the floor. Both attackers flailed at their eyes, trying to clear them.

Knowing she only had a second or two, Hangbe slashed at the ropes binding the girl to the chair and leaped over it, yanking the stunned prisoner to her feet.

"Follow me."

The girl nodded, stumbling after Hangbe into the hallway. The one she'd kicked had reached the door to the bar and stood talking to the guard who'd returned to his post.

As Hangbe and the girl entered the hallway and raced towards them, both men squared off to block her path. She reached for her pistol, forgetting for a second she'd left it on the floor in the room behind her. Cursing as her hands met an empty shoulder holster, Hangbe shifted gears.

She shouted at the girl, "Stay behind me and keep up."

Not waiting for an answer, Hangbe leaped forward, feinting left and then attacking to the right, leading with her blade. It worked, and she avoided the incoming attacks enough to slice across the torso of the one she'd belly kicked. He howled in pain and fell to the side, clutching at his slashed abdomen.

Ducking low and punching back to the left, the Amazon delivered a blow to the solar-plexus with a fist.

She didn't wait to follow up with a killing blow. She had to get the girl out of here to safety. Standing, Hangbe reached back for the girl's hand and tugged at her, pulling her into the crowded bar. The action at the doorway had drawn unwanted attention, though, and several werecats headed in her direction.

"Go, run for that door. There's an old white van parked down the street to the left. Meet me there." When the girl hesitated, her eyes wide with fear, Hangbe shoved her in the right direction with a hand between her shoulder blades. "Go!"

The girl stumbled in the right direction at least. Hangbe had hoped to hand her off to Gibbie, but the vampire was nowhere in sight. A pair of muscled, furred bodies blocked her view of the bar a second later just as more clawed hands grabbed for her from behind.

Spinning in place, she struck out with her blade, trying to drive the attackers backward. The silver alloy kept the attackers wary since the wounds wouldn't regenerate the way normal injuries would. There were too many of them, though. She got in a few hits, but then the claws pulled her to the floor.

Hangbe lay on her back, most of the attacks absorbed by her body armor, and reached for her necklace. There weren't any offensive spells there, but she could heal her injuries at least. Then she'd figure a way out of this.

A booted foot stomped down. Pinning her free hand to the floor before she could activate the healing bead. A black panther's face snarled down at her.

"Let's finish her. Hunters like her need to know where they can and can't interfere with us."

Yowls of agreement from the shifters all around her, holding her immobile to the floor. Hangbe gathered her strength, determined to make them pay before they killed her.

A wild scream unlike anything she'd heard before interrupted the incoming attacks. The shifter standing on her free hand flew backward as a shadowy blur pitched him into the wall. The blur continued around the circle, taking down each of the shifters. The final two let go of Hangbe and backed away, trying to defend themselves.

The blurred shadow solidified. It was Gibbie. "Hey, you need a hand up? We should probably leave now."

He reached down and Hangbe nodded, taking the help. Her wounds were more severe than she realized.

Gibbie turned and bared his fangs at the nearest cluster of

shifters, stomping his foot in their direction. They all backed away a step.

Now that they had some space and path to the door, Gibbie pulled Hangbe's arm across his shoulder and helped her run for the exit. They burst through and raced up the stairs, reaching the street a few seconds later.

Hangbe paused as her head swung back and forth, searching the sidewalk in both directions. "Where is she?"

"The girl you brought with you is already in the van. I took her out first, then came back for you."

Shouts from the open doorway behind them stopped the conversation. Hangbe nodded down the street. "Let's get out of here."

Gibbie once again assisted her as they half-limped, half-ran to the van. The girl huddled against the far corner of the bench seat behind the driver's seat. Hangbe nodded at her as she eased herself into the passenger seat.

The driver's door popped open and Gibbie hopped in. "Wow, that was exciting. I didn't know what you had planned when you went back there, so I kind of had to improvise. Sorry it took me so long to get back to help you."

"You did everything right. The girl was the one who needed saving." Hangbe paused, realizing how that sounded. "Uh, thank you for returning to check on me, though."

"Think nothing of it. After all, what kind of guide would I be if I abandoned you?"

Hangbe nodded and stole a glance at Gibbie, suddenly seeing the frumpy, unlikely partner in a new light. As the passing streetlights flashed overhead, they lit up his smiling face. A grin spread across hers as well.

She settled back and touched her healing bead, waiting for the healing warmth of the magic to wash over her. She swiped a hand across her forehead and shook her head. For some reason, she was already a little flushed before the spell started.

Chapter 21

DEAN'S ALARM startled him from a nightmare. He'd been trapped in a basement with fire all around him. He woke gasping for breath, surprised at first that he wasn't hacking from inhaling caustic smoke.

"You okay, hon?" Jaz asked, still half asleep beside him.

Dean ran his hand through his hair, scratching at his scalp to wake himself as he checked the clock. "Yeah, just a bad dream. I have to get ready for work. Go back to sleep. Sorry to wake you."

Jaz mumbled something he didn't quite get as she rolled over. He asked her to repeat it, then noticed she'd fallen back to sleep.

He gathered a fresh uniform shirt and pants from the closet and carried it all into the bathroom. He'd shower and get dressed in there so he didn't wake her again. She'd been up late working on some paperwork left over from the day in the office.

A half hour later, Dean rolled out of the parking lot. Leah had pulled up on the curb outside the ramp, waiting for him. He waved as he passed her. He'd forgotten about her driving in with him this morning.

She followed along behind and together they reached the station about twenty minutes later. Dean always enjoyed this time of the day. There weren't that many cars on the road yet, and it always made the city seem so peaceful.

Leah parked next to him and by the time he'd gathered his backpack with a spare change of clothes, she was waiting by the back bumper of his truck.

"You could've gone in. I'm fine."

Leah shook her head. "Nope, I'm not losing my job because my training officer died on my watch."

"Gee, thanks." They both chuckled at his response as they headed for the station.

Barry and Brynne sat at the table inside, already started on their breakfast. Barry worked on a stack of waffles and Brynne sipped some warmed blood from the stores Freddy kept on hand for her.

Dean smiled as he took in their relaxed state. "See, I didn't jinx you after all. Neither of you look any worse than you did last night when we left."

Barry's smile turned to a scowl. "Oh, the jinx was in full effect until about two hours ago. It finally settled down enough for us both to catch up on our reports. I just sat down to eat."

Brynne raised her mug and gestured to the ambulance bay door. "We left the rest of the shift checks for the two of you. A gift for your impertinence. We ended up dealing with the aftermath of a bar brawl at some shifter club downtown. Some pretty serious injuries, though no one was talking about how it started."

Dean laughed, and Leah joined in after a second. "All's fair where the jinx is concerned. Let us catch some breakfast and we'll take care of it so you two can get out of here."

As the four of them finished their breakfast, Dean asked, "Anything from last night we need to know about?"

Brynne thought for a moment and said, "No, not really. Nothing more on the trafficking thing and everything else was pretty normal, aside from the thing at the bar. Just back-to-back calls that kept us running all night."

Dean nodded and finished his waffles and sausage. He waited for Leah to finish then said, "Ready to get started?"

She nodded.

The two of them went to get the ambulance squared away for the day while the other two packed up their gear.

Brynne stuck her head into the ambulance bay to say goodbye before leaving. Then Dean and Leah were alone while they finished their checks on the equipment. They settled in after that to go over the in-house training on the computer network, since Leah was new to the system.

Their first call came in on the radio an hour into the shift, followed by a succession of routine medical emergencies, all excellent tests of Leah's skills.

Before he realized it, they'd finished their last run of the day and were headed back to the station. His stomach growled loud enough they both started laughing. They hadn't had a real lunch, only able to grab a few snacks from the supplies at the hospital between dropping patients off. He looked forward to whatever Freddy had for them when they got back.

Brynne and Barry had already arrived back for their next shift by the time they rolled back into the station. Dean plugged in the land line electric to the ambulance to keep everything charged and checked to make sure Leah was working on restocking from their last few calls.

"I'll fill in the log for the last two calls. How are you on your reports?"

Leah looked up from where she'd been digging in the med bag. "I'm in good shape. I probably have a half hour left to finish up."

"Okay, Brynne will check them over for you before you submit them. I have a meeting I have to get to."

"You sure?" Leah asked. "I figured I'd be following you home again."

"No need. No one's seen any sign of Manton since yesterday. I'm sure he's long gone."

Leah's doubtful expression lingered for a second, but she shrugged and went back to work.

Dean headed into the squad room and dug into his last few items to complete the shift. He let Brynne know about double checking Leah's reports and then he changed into his civilian clothes to meet Jaz.

Freddy had a sandwich ready made with the roasted chicken he'd made for dinner. He dropped it in the brown paper bag he held. "I made one for Jaz, too. That girl forgets to eat just like you."

"Thanks, she'll appreciate it. And you're right. She skips lunch most days. This'll hit the spot." He waved goodbye to the others and headed out to his truck. Checking his watch, he knew he'd have to make good time to meet Jaz when he told her he would.

She already had the black SUV fired up and ready to go when Dean pulled into the garage and parked his truck. He left his bag and EMS gear in his truck. It was safe enough in the pickup truck here beneath the Errington building.

"You're raring to go," Dean said as he climbed into the SUV.

Jaz leaned over for a kiss hello. "I've been out checking on some local clients today and just got back. I thought you might beat me here."

"Seems like perfect timing, then."

Jaz smiled and backed out of her spot. Dean buckled up and leaned back in his seat. It was time to have a talk with the resident leprechaun of Elk City about shutting the portal to Ireland. He wasn't looking forward to what they might learn when Jaz confronted Dougie about the trafficking ring.

To Dean's surprise, the shop's lights were turned off when they arrived outside. He checked his watch. "That's weird, I know he keeps the store open until at least eight most nights."

"Maybe he closed early tonight. Let's go around back and see if his car is here."

Jaz pulled the SUV into the alley that ran beside store and drove to the rear parking area. Only one of the parking spaces in the back was occupied. A green and white Mini Cooper sat in the spot right next to the shop's rear door.

"Is that his car?" Jaz asked.

Dean shrugged. "I've never seen what he drives. It could be his."

"Let's try the door. Maybe he's still here."

Jaz and Dean got out of the SUV. Jaz wore her usual low-key

tactical outfit of black military fatigue pants and a black T-shirt. Instead of her usual holstered Glock on her hip, she had a smaller semi-automatic tucked into a holster at the small of her back.

Dean got to the back door first. He was about to knock when he noticed it was partially ajar. "That's strange, this door has always been shut and locked when we've come here before."

"Step back, Dean. Let me go first." Jaz had drawn her pistol and approached the door from the side, opening it a few inches and checking the interior from beside the opening before pushing it open the rest of the way.

Dean followed her inside. He could see right away, there'd been a struggle of some sort. One of the free-standing shelves in the storeroom had tipped into the wall. Most of the shelf's contents had spilled to the floor. Several snow globes had broken, and water and green glitter covered a portion of the floor.

Jaz pointed at the puddle. "Careful, don't slip."

Dean stepped around the mess and looked around for any sign of Dougie. His mind turned to worry for his friend. This looked like it had happened within the last few hours based on how wet the floor was.

"Do you see him anywhere, Jaz?"

She'd moved into the next room and as soon as he asked her, she called out. "I found him. Dean, get the medic bag from the truck."

Dean resisted the urge to rush in to see what had happened. Jaz could handle any life-threatening situations as well as he could. If she thought they needed the first aid bag from the back of her SUV, he trusted her judgement.

By the time he got back with the med bag, Jaz had already pressed a wad of paper towels against a gash on the leprechaun's head. The big leprechaun looked up and Dean and gave a weak grin.

Dean set the bag down, happy to see Dougie was conscious. "Hey, what happened to you?"

"Oh, nothing really. I fell down. That's all."

"Bull," Jaz said. "I know a shakedown when I see one. What did they want?"

Dean added, "And who is it who did this to you?"

Dougie pushed Dean's hand away from his head, taking the gauze pads himself and pressing them against his scalp. "Really, my friends, I'm fine. Just patch me up and I'll go home."

Dean leaned in to get a better look and shook his head. "You're not going home. You need stitches for that laceration on your head at the very least, and the doc will want you to get a CT scan as well for the potential head injury."

When Dougie protested again, Jaz cut him off.

"Douglas O'Nolder, you listen to me. I need to know what happened and if this has anything to do with a group of werepanthers running trafficked women and men through your portal."

As Dean took more gauze and pressed them against the gash on Dougie's forehead, the leprechaun glanced at the floor to avoid the Hunter's glare. Jaz kept her gaze locked on him until he threw up his arms and gasped in exasperation.

"Fine, yes, it was the cat shifters. They found out about my portal about six months ago and offered to pay me to use it. In the beginning it was just to bring in some crates of Irish whiskey without paying the duties, but then they branched out into other types of smuggling. I tried to stay out of it, but something must have happened while you all were over in Ireland. They got furious about what you were doing sticking your nose into my business. They worried you'd found out what they were doing."

Jaz nodded. "They thought you told us. You're lucky they didn't just kill you outright. They've murdered others to cover up their trail."

Doug started sobbing and said, "They might as well have killed me. I told them if they killed me, the portal would close forever. Instead, they took me pot-o-gold. Now I've lost all me magic and they control the portal and my riches."

Dean's anger bubbled up. He wanted to yell at Dougie. The big lug had helped those who killed all the people in that basement. And who knew how many others they'd injured or killed over the course of six months. Instead of shouting at him, Dean swallowed his anger. He had to try to salvage something they could use to shut the operation down.

"Dougie, you can help us. How do we shut the portal, even temporarily?"

"You can't," Dougie blubbered as tears streamed down his cheeks. "Now that they have my gold, they control my magic. I'm just a poor shopkeeper now. I have nothing else to my name."

Jaz growled deep in her throat. "Cut the pity party. You bought yourself this trouble trying to add to your little pot of gold. If you'd wanted to stop them, you could have gone to the police, or even too Dean and me. You had options."

All the leprechaun did was continue wailing.

Hoping to salvage something from the encounter, Dean asked, "At least tell us where they're hiding out in the city. You must know that much. Who's their leader? How do you contact them?"

"I never met the boss. I know he's named Finn something or other. I know nothing else about him other than he's relatively new to Elk City."

Dean glanced at Jaz. She shook her head. The name meant nothing to her. He shrugged and went back to his care of Dougie's injuries. He'd quieted down to simple sobbing now.

Jaz took out her phone and called in to the direct line at Fire Headquarters, calling for an ambulance to take the shopkeeper in for an evaluation. It didn't take them long to get there. Brynne and Barry came in, loaded up the leprechaun, taking Dean's report as they did.

The two of them watched the ambulance leave, then locked up the shop and walked to their SUV. As they drove away, Dean asked, "How do we close the portal if we need the pot of gold to control it? We can't let them bring any more people through it."

"We don't have to close it. We just have to restrict access. Between my people and Rudy's security teams, we should be able to take care of it. We'll mount a large enough guard force on both sides of the portal to discourage them from using it for now."

"We're still not any closer to finding Kaylee's family or Verity. If they're still alive, we have to find out where they are."

Jaz nodded. "We will. There aren't that many places they can hide in the city. We can narrow things down by a process of elimination. Any chance that new girl working with you has a way of tracking them down? She has to have underworld connections with the werecats in the city."

"Why use her?" Dean asked, instantly on the defensive to protect his probie from anything that could affect her chance to become a full paramedic.

"I'm just asking. Her family has to know who's behind this, even if they're not part of it."

Dean stood his ground. "I'll mention what we're doing, but I won't directly ask her for help. It's unfair to get her involved if she doesn't want to get involved. There are other ways we can do this. What about Gibbie and Hangbe? They might be able to use what we've found out from Dougie."

Jaz thought about it for a few seconds and said, "They might at that. We'll leave your girl out of it for now, but it might end up she's our only way in."

Dean knew Jaz was right. He didn't have to worry about it right now, though. "Let's exhaust our other leads first, okay. Call your teams and I'll reach out to James and Rudy about getting his pack and their security squads on the case, too."

When they got home, Jaz pulled out her phone and started making some calls while Dean did the same. Within two hours they had guards on both sides of the portal. It wasn't what they'd wanted at the beginning of the night, but it was a start. He'd do some more work the next day since he switched to night shift with Leah that evening.

Chapter 22

AFTER ANOTHER FITFUL night filled with vivid nightmares of fighting to get out of a smoke-filled room, Dean spent the next day working through a haze of sleeplessness, helping Jaz schedule coverage on the Irish Shop and the pub in Dublin. She was so preoccupied with what she was doing; she didn't notice how tired he was. He didn't tell her about the nightmares, figuring they were just a remnant of post-traumatic stress from what he'd seen in the basement of that building days before.

Jaz tried several times throughout the day to contact Hangbe and Gibbie to pass along their information on the gang, but both had dropped out of sight. Dean had wanted to get some of the other CERT team members and go looking for them, but Jaz told him not to worry. It was typical for Hangbe to do this when on a case. It didn't ease Dean's worry over Gibbie, even though he should be safe with her by his side. The vampire had lived at least four hundred years on his own without anyone's help. Still, between his nightmares and everything else going on, Dean was more than a little on edge.

Luckily, his first night shift with Leah went well, with no particularly traumatic calls or tension. Dean even managed an hour and a half of nap time in the middle of the night when things settled down for a bit. Leah continued to show the knowledge and hard work that had put her at the top of her class. She handled each patient with confidence and poise. She only needed a few checks with Dean to make sure she was on track.

The second night rolled around and Dean got to work even more exhausted. The dream still bothered him, and he only managed a few hours of fitful rest that afternoon. He hoped Leah was up to her usual standards because he was dragging. He needed the evening to go as smoothly as the last had.

He spotted her in the parking lot as he pulled in at Station U. The industrial park's streetlights weren't the best, and he almost didn't see her standing by the back of her car. A jet-black Mercedes sedan had parked beside her. She seemed to be in the middle of an animated conversation with someone through the rear window of her car.

Dean climbed out of his pickup truck and craned his neck to see who she was talking to. The rear window on the Mercedes was down, but the dark interior kept him from making out who it might be. Thinking she might need his help, Dean walked over.

When she turned his way, he stopped. She glared at him, her eyes glowing yellow. "Go inside, Dean. I'm in the middle of something."

Dean held up his hands, palms out, and backed up a step. "Sorry, just checking on you. See you inside."

Whatever had her upset, he had to remember to maintain his distance and remember she was far more able to handle herself in a supernatural world than he was.

He pulled open the station door and entered. Brook and Tammi sat eating dinner at the table and Brynne stood nearby, peering out through the window. She used her hand to lift one of the plastic slats in the blinds to see better.

She glanced his way before turning back to look outside. "Is she still yelling at her father? I can't hear them anymore."

"That's her father? I couldn't see inside the car."

"Brook saw the Mercedes pull up and sit idling in the lot before

Leah got here. I ran the tags through O'Malley at the PD. It came back to a company owned by Leah's family. When she drove in and got out to talk to whoever it was, I figured it had to be her dad."

Dean walked over to look out the window with Brynne. "They weren't yelling when I saw them, but she was angry about something. It looked like she was ready to shift."

Brynne nodded. "Her father isn't happy with her career choice. I think he believes in the 'once in the Cartel, always in the Cartel' model of underworld gangs."

"Do you think she's in danger?"

"No, but we should keep an eye on her just in case. Maybe you can get her to talk about it later tonight on shift. I'd like to know what brought her father back to town."

Dean wondered, too. Maybe it had something to do with the werepanthers and the recent fires. Outside in the lot Leah took two quick steps backward, pointed her finger at the car while shouting something he couldn't make out. She spun around and stalked towards the station. Her eyes still glowed bright yellow as she approached the building.

Brynne and Dean scrambled to get away from the window. Brynne sat down behind one of the computers, and Dean hopped into a recliner and pretended to watch the news playing on the flatscreen.

Leah stepped inside and shut the door. She stood there, breathing hard with her eyes closed. Dean half expected her to change into her werejaguar form, but when she opened her eyes, they were their normal human brown color.

Dean tried to act normal and asked, "Hey, Leah. Everything alright?"

"How much did you see?" She asked, turning to Brynne first.

Brynne sat back in her chair. "Enough to know that your father is still trying to get you to quit. I thought you'd worked all this out with him while you were in the academy?"

"Me, too. Apparently, when I had words with one of his minions the other day, it gave him the idea that I wanted back into the Cartel."

Dean didn't know all the backstory like Brynne did, but he understood fathers who had trouble taking no for an answer. "Maybe he was hopeful you'd changed your mind."

"No, he was making sure I understood that I couldn't live in both worlds. I had to either be in or out. He didn't accept my excuse that protecting my colleagues was part of my new job."

Dean shook his head. "Hey, if that run in with Manton is the cause of this, you don't have to worry about me. My wife is more than capable of keeping track of me if there's any sort of trouble."

Leah rolled her eyes. "Your wife came up, too. He must have done some checking on the people I work with. He has informants everywhere. He's worried Ms. Errington will use me to get to him."

Dean looked away, remembering the conversation he'd had with Jaz a few days before.

His expression wasn't lost on Leah. She said, "I figured as much. Look, I'm an open book. I told Brynne and I'll tell you, I'm not in that world anymore. There's nothing I can tell you about anything that involves my family. All I want to be is just another medic."

Knowing it was up to him to mend this since she was his responsibility, Dean said, "You're a very good one. I have no reason to believe you'll have any issues staying in this job for a very long time. If I had any ideas about turning to you for help with anything, you've made your position clear. As far as I'm concerned, the matter is settled."

"Really? That's it?"

Dean nodded. "Discretion is part of our job here at Station U. Usually it has to do with our special patients and who they are, but there's no reason it shouldn't apply to you as well. Share as much or as little of your life as you want. We'll keep our noses out of it."

Leah seemed like she wanted to believe him. "What about your wife?"

"I've had to tell Jaz to back off before and I'll do it again if I need to. It won't stop her from investigating things she's hired to look into, but I won't let her leverage my relationship with you to get information." He held up his right hand and drew a cross on his chest with his other. "Promise."

Brynne stood. "I'm glad that's settled. Now you two need to get to work. The shift's started and you haven't begun any of your regular checks yet. Brook and Tammi finished theirs early. If you hurry, you might get dinner before Freddy cleans up."

Freddy called out from the kitchen. "Don't worry, Dean. I can reheat things if you get tied up."

Good old Freddy, Dean thought. He always looked out for the team and somehow always turned out superb meals, no matter what time it was.

"Come on, Leah. Brynne's right. We should get started."

Leah nodded and followed Dean into the ambulance bay to begin the shift checklist. By the time they returned to the squad room twenty minutes later, Brook and Tammy had left. Brynne still sat at the computer, looking over something. He was sure she heard them enter, but she kept working without looking up.

Dean pointed over at the table. "Leah, grab some food. It's always best to eat while you can. You never know when—"

Before he finished his sentence, the radio alert went off. They grabbed their coats for the first call of the night. They'd have to catch dinner later or grab a snack on the road. Duty called.

Chapter 23

GIBBIE PULLED into the alley and slid the gear lever into park. Hangbe unbuckled her seat belt and swung around to climb into the back of the van where she'd stashed her weapons. He swiped his sweaty palms against his shirt and turned to follow her. She'd found a short sword in the style of a Roman gladius for him. It hid nicely beneath his gray overcoat as he slid it into its sheath.

"Are we sure this is the place?" Hangbe asked, staring out through the back window at the building across the street.

"It's the only thing this size built of that glazed yellow brick Shayna mentioned. I checked with several sources earlier while you were resting. A guy I know at the building permits office talked my ear off about how rare that style was in this area."

When they had gotten back with Shayna, the girl Hangbe rescued from the shifter bar, it had taken them a day to get her to trust them enough to open up about where they'd held her and who'd captured her. She was a from a sea-side village in Cornwall in the U.K. As best she could tell, she'd been here for almost six months, but she couldn't be sure.

Once they gained her trust and got her some food and rest, she told them all about the clan of werepanthers who'd taken her. She mentioned meeting other people from villages like hers, most of them women and young girls. All had similar stories. She remembered three places where they'd kept her together with a group of others. One matched the description of the building across town that had burned down a week before. The other two were harder to nail down until Gibbie seized on the yellow bricks she mentioned.

They were still trying to track the third location, but the building across the street from the alley in which they hid had to be the second building Shayna remembered.

"What's the plan?" Gibbie asked. "You don't have a gun anymore. I still don't know why you didn't ask Jaz for another one."

"Because she'll be angry I lost the first one. The authorities can trace it back to me through my Interpol file. She won't want to loan me one they could trace back to her."

"But you won't lose another one. I mean, what are the odds?"

Hangbe shook her head. "Don't tempt the fates. Besides, I'm more than capable of handling these cats with just my blades." She brandished the yard of sharpened steel she held before sliding it into a sheath at her waist. "Plus, I have you now. You've proven a more than capable companion on this investigation. You've got my back, right?"

Gibbie bobbed his head with so much enthusiasm, he bumped his head on the van's roof. "You don't have to worry as long as I'm around. I'll be your bodyguard as long as you'll let me." He cringed a little as he said the last part. He caught the hint of a grin from her when he said it, and he chastised himself internally for talking like an idiot. This woman didn't need him to guard her back or the rest of her exquisite body.

When he realized he let his eyes linger on her a little too long, he flushed and turned around to fumble with his keys. "I'd better be sure the van's security system is armed before we leave. This neighborhood is pretty sketchy."

Hangbe snorted a laugh. "I don't think anyone will bother this heap, Gibson. Don't get me wrong, it's the perfect van for a stakeout. No one will pay any attention to it at all."

"No offense taken. I know it's a little beat up but me and this thing have been through a lot together." He patted the bench seat.

A flicker of movement caught his eye. He leaned towards the rear window, sliding past Hangbe in the open rear of the van. "Hey, that guy matches that photo of Manton Dean showed me. He's going into that side entrance. This has to be the right place."

"I agree. We'll wait a few minutes, then follow him in. Are you ready?"

Gibbie nodded and reached down and held on with a white-knuckled grip on the hilt of his short sword with one hand. Hangbe grinned and opened the rear of the van, jumping down to the pavement. He followed and shut the doors, toggling lock on the key fob before sliding it into his pocket.

They moved into the shadows near the mouth of the alley and checked the building's windows for any lookouts. The whole place looked vacant, despite the fact they'd seen Manton enter. No lights showed anywhere in the three-story structure.

"Where is he?" Gibbie asked. "We saw him go inside."

Hangbe searched the street in both directions and raised her arm. "There. That's him leaving from that door at the far end of the block."

"Should we go after him or find out why he was here?"

A muffled series of screams reached Gibbie's sensitive vampire hearing. Hangbe's head whipped around back to the building across from them in mid-answer. She'd heard it, too.

"Smell that?" She asked.

Gibbie sniffed the air. "Smoke." He pointed to the door Manton had entered across from them. "See it coming out around the doorjamb?"

Hangbe tapped a bead on her necklace and charged across the street without answering. She moved quickly; he could barely keep up with her. Gibbie reached deep, accessing his vampire speed and strength despite his reluctance to use it.

She reached the door just ahead of him and dashed inside. Thick smoke filled the entry hallway, causing them both to crouch low to see under it. Hangbe coughed and paused to catch her breath. The screams were louder here.

Gibbie turned and found the source. A stairwell leading up and down opened to the right. The smoke came from there, billowing up from the basement. He remembered the fire Dean had responded to last week. They were killing off more of the kidnapped people.

Hangbe had already reached the same conclusion. She bounded past him and down the stairs. Despite the flames from the packing crates stacked in front of the chained double doors below, Hangbe charged forward. Gibbie raced along right behind her.

She leaped over the flaming crates and pulled at the doors. They opened a little but stopped as soon as the chains pulled tight. "Help me!"

Gibbie was already jumping past the flames even as the walls and ceiling burned. The heat blistered his skin, but he pressed on, shouting, "Stand to the side."

Hangbe moved up to the wall, crouching low. She'd produced a scarf to cover her face and mouth. It couldn't be doing much, but it was better than nothing. Gibbie didn't need to breathe except to talk so the smoke had little effect on him. The heat and flames were another thing entirely, but he pushed aside his fear and slammed into the doors with all his vampire strength and speed.

The chains held, but the doors' metal handles pulled free of the steel frames as he burst through to the basement. A huddle of people in the against one wall by a barred window shrieked when he turned towards them. He'd forgotten he was in full vamp mode with his fangs and glowing red eyes.

Settling his face back to normal, Gibbie shouted. "Stay there while I clear the stairs. Get ready to run out to the street." A few nods were all the response he got.

Hangbe had crawled into the room behind him. She appeared weakened as she stood. "Is there another way out?"

"Not sure, but I can clear the stairs of those crates if you can get everyone to run out when I do. The ceiling and walls are on fire, but it's the only chance they have."

She offered a grim smile. "Be careful." She went over to the clustered people.

Gibbie rushed back to the stairs, returning to vamp mode to access his strength and grabbed at the nearest crate. His hands burned from the charred wood, but he ignored it as he threw the crate behind him against the far wall, away from the shrieking people.

Ten seconds later, all the crates now burned in a pile across the basement. The walls and stairway ceiling had caught fire all the way up to the first floor now, but there was a path up in the center of the stairs if they ran. They were shifters and would heal if they got through without dying. It was their only chance.

He waved at Hangbe, and she shouted at the clustered women and girls. They rushed past him as the Amazon led them up the stairs. Gibbie followed the last of them up, picking up the two stragglers under each arm and carrying them up and out of the building. He set them down on the sidewalk and peeled off his tan windbreaker. It smoked and threatened to catch fire until he stamped on it with his booted foot.

He searched for Hangbe and found her leaning up against the side of the building nearby, catching her breath. She stared at him, studying him in a way that made him a little queasy.

"Are you alright?" He asked.

"I am. We should get these people away from the building before it becomes fully aflame."

Sirens sounded in the distance as the two of them herded the people across the street and sat them down on the sidewalk. Gibbie tried providing care, running down his first aid training from his CERT classes.

Hangbe tugged at his arm. "Let the professionals tend to them. We should be gone when the officials arrive."

He didn't understand but followed along after being sure there were no serious injuries among the people. Catching up to her at the back of his van in the alley, Gibbie stopped as she turned on him and yanked the door open.

"Get in." A heat burned in her eyes.

The steady gaze she held on him stirred a host of emotions. He followed her instructions and climbed in the back, sitting on the cushions laid out behind the bench seat. He turned just in time to catch a broad smile on her face as she pulled the door shut.

"That's the second time you've saved me."

"I was just doing my job."

"Shut up." She pressed him back as his eyes widened in surprise. He never heard the air horn of the fire engine pulling up outside. It blocked the alley, hiding the van from the street.

Chapter 24

AS HE DROVE to the address on the screen between him and Leah, Dean waited for additional information to come in from dispatch. He stiffened when the radio announced another building fire downtown with injuries.

From the grim set of Leah's expression, she had the same worry about what they'd find when they arrived. Dean resisted the urge to drive any faster, though. He was already traveling as fast as was safe, and additional speed would only put the two of them in danger from an accident. Then no one at the fire would get their help.

The glow of the fully involved building fire lit the night sky over the city. This time, headquarters dispatched Dean and Leah with the initial response from the fire department units. He hoped that was a good sign and there would be live victims waiting for him.

As they approached, Dean searched for a location to pull over that wouldn't hinder the firefighting operations. Flames thrust high into the black night sky and the first few fire engines on location were still connecting to the hydrants to throw water on the blaze.

He spotted a spot ahead near an alley. A fire truck currently blocked the entrance, but he could get them to pull forward enough to get the ambulance through if he needed to leave in a hurry. A crowd of people sat on the sidewalk nearby, watching the blazing building as the firefighters battled the flames to keep it from setting fire to any of the neighboring buildings. A few fire fighters stood with the people on the sidewalk. They waved to him as he parked. They must have a patient for them over there.

"Get the cot out, Leah. Grab the monitor, oxygen, and airway kits. Anything else we'll leave here. We can bring patients back here for anything beyond that initial care."

She nodded and hopped out to get started.

Dean leaned over and grabbed the mic from the dash. "U-191 to Dispatch. On location and staging for patient care."

"Received U-191. Switch to operations channel two to connect with fireground command."

Dean switched the radio and grabbed his portable unit from the charger beside his seat. He made sure he dialed in the channel and slid the leather strap over his head so it rested diagonally across his chest.

By the time he got to the rear of the ambulance, Leah had everything loaded on the cot and ready to go. He nodded his approval and keyed the mic clipped to his shoulder strap. "Incident command, ambulance U-191 on location in the alley off Piedmont. Are there any patients?"

"U-191," The female voice, that of Deputy Chief Alyssa Rowe, said. "Rescue 11 has two patients with burns and respiratory distress. Take over patient care from them. They should be just down the street from you."

Leah looked over her shoulder and pointed at the ECFD rescue truck halfway down the block where they'd seen the cluster of people and the two firefighters. Dean nodded and grabbed the foot of the cot as Leah pulled the head end towards their patients.

"U-191 received. On the way to Rescue 11 now."

As they got closer, the light from the burning building revealed a pair of firefighters tending to two women seated on a tarp on the sidewalk. Other women and girls stood around, clustered in small groups of three and four, watching the firefighters caring for the patients.

Leah left Dean to manage the cot the rest of the way and moved forward to take over patient care from the two firefighters.

"Hello, gentlemen. What do you have?"

The first firefighter pointed at the pair on the ground beside him. "These two women were here with the others as we drove up. We got to them and started basic care. I'll let them explain the rest of it. We need to get back to our crew."

Leah nodded. "I've got this. Go ahead." She waited for the two firefighters to leave and approached the pair seated on the tarp. They both had oxygen masks over their mouths and noses. Soot covered their faces and tattered clothing. Some of it had burned away, leaving blistered flesh underneath in patches on both, mostly on their arms and hands. They were lucky if the fire was that close.

"Hi, I'm Leah." She let her eyes flash a quick yellow glow to tell them she was an Unusual. Dean showed his UV star of life tattoo, hidden from all but Unusual eyes.

Leah continued after the special identification. "My partner, Dean, and I are here to help you. Can you tell me your names?"

The taller of the two spoke first, the lilt of her Irish accent clear. "I'm Devon. This is Haley."

She gasped a little as she talked, making Dean wonder if Devon had inhaled hot smoke and had some airway burns. He was about to say something to Leah, but she beat him to it, asking the patient about her breathing and airway.

Realizing she had it in hand, Dean took over assisting her with getting vital signs on both patients while she continued getting their history and assessing their injuries. Once again, she impressed him with her cool confidence and poise.

They both had some significant second-degree burns that needed attention. Dean and Leah started applying clean dry dressings to keep them covered for now. The burn center at ECMC would see to further treatment.

As he was applying the bandages to Haley's burns, Dean remarked, "You two were lucky to get out when you did."

Haley shook her head and spit on the pavement beside her.

"None of us would have gotten out if those two hadn't come and broken the locks that held all of us in."

"All of us?" Leah asked, startled and twisting her head around to search others standing nearby. "You were all in there?"

Devon coughed when she tried to answer and waved at Haley who said, "The bastards had been holding us to work on various jobs to pay off our toll to come here. Then one of them showed up tonight. But instead of unlocking the doors to take us to work, he set a fire in the stairwell and took off. We would've died in there if not for that crazy vampire and the sorcerer woman he was with. Now that we're free, we aren't sure where to go next or if we're in some kind of trouble."

Dean caught Leah's eye and then said. "You're not in any trouble as far as we're concerned. We don't care how you got here. We just want to treat your injuries. Once that's finished, the docs at the hospital will let you walk out on your own."

"Hospital!" Devon said, bringing on another coughing fit. She tried to stand and pull off the oxygen mask. Leah placed her hand on the woman's shoulder, pushing her back onto the tarp.

She said, "If you don't want to go to the hospital, we can't make you. Merrow like yourselves will heal pretty quickly if you can get to a source of salt water, right?"

The two nodded, eyes shifting from side to side, uneasy with the situation. They sat as if they were ready to jump up and run at any moment. Dean knew Merrow were the source of the legends of mermaids. He'd have to ask Leah later how she identified them. That could wait, though. Dean hung back and watched how Leah handled this. She was, after all, an Unusual just like they were.

"Easy," Leah said, holding a hand out to settle them. She lowered her voice a little and softened the tone she'd been using. "We are here to help you. Dean and I will patch you up enough to get you moving and then you can seek a way to regenerate, okay?"

After a long pause, Devon nodded. "I guess that's fine."

Dean took a chance and asked, "You mentioned the vampire and the woman?"

Haley glanced at Devon, who gave a quick bob of her head.

Haley said, "It was strange. A black woman with incredible power and the oddest vampire I've ever seen showed up and broke the chains holding the doors closed. They helped us get free and then the pair took off in that direction, almost too fast to follow."

"Gibbie," Dean muttered. He caught Leah's eye. "I need to make a call. Keep monitoring them. I'll be right over here."

Her brow wrinkled, a little confused, but she nodded.

Dean moved a few steps away while he dialed Jaz.

"Hey, Dean," Jaz said. It sounded like she was hands free in her truck. "You're down at that fire, right?"

He knew she monitored his calls on her police and fire scanner. "Yeah, and you'll never guess who else was here?"

"Hangbe, right?"

"Bingo, along with her vampire shadow. It was a good thing. They freed the people trapped in the building before the fire trapped them."

Jaz cursed and said, "Put her on. She's not returning my calls."

"They're not here anymore. They must have taken off after the ones who set the fire as soon as they got everyone out. I have no idea where they went next."

Jaz was quiet for a second, then said, "I might have a way. Can you get away to help me?"

"I have to stay here and work with Leah."

"Call Brynne. Tell her I have a lead on something. See what she says."

Dean stopped, trying to decide what to do. He hated not sticking with a task. But they needed to reach out to Hangbe and Gibbie. He thought some more and decided Leah was good, solid enough to manage care for a bit on her own. Brynne could take over when she got here.

"I'll call her. How far away are you?"

"I'll be there in five minutes. Be ready to go when I get there."

Dean shook his head. "I think I'd better wait for Brynne. She shouldn't take too long."

Jaz didn't like his answer based on her tone, but she said, "I'll get started without you. See you in a bit."

Dean dialed Brynne's cell phone. She picked up right away.

"Hey, Dean. You two okay?"

"Yeah. Listen, I have a strange request. Jaz needs me to help follow a lead on the guys who set this fire. Leah is here with me handling two Merrow patients with burns and smoke inhalation."

Brynne interrupted him. "And you need me to come take the rest of your shift so you can go play with your wife?"

At first Dean didn't pick up on the fact that she was messing with him. He stammered a bit, searching for an appropriate answer to her question.

Brynne followed up with, "I guess you'll be asking for conjugal honeymoon visits next."

Realizing she was messing with him; he forced a laugh. "Alright, very funny. I'll assume that's a yes. How soon can you get here?"

"I'm already headed down to HQ to pick up supplies. I'll give you the list and you and Jaz can grab them while I take over with your probie."

"We can do that."

"Good, I'll be there shortly."

Dean hung up and returned to Leah. She had taken another round of vital signs. Dean joined in and helped so she could record everything from the monitor for her patient report later.

"Brynne's coming. She's going to finish the shift with you."

"What, so you can go chase the bad guys?" Leah asked, grinning up at him as she crouched by the heart monitor. "I hope you've got some help. It's almost certainly those rogue cats again."

Dean nodded. "I'll be fine. Jaz is coming. She thinks she can track either the ones who set the fire or at least the two who freed these people."

"Hunters hunting in the night. It's the kind of thing my mother used to tell me to scare me into staying in bed." Leah's tone had turned hard. He wondered if she'd had run-ins with other hunters out there."

"My wife only hunts the bad guys. There's no reason for her to go after anyone else. She's on our side in this."

Leah said nothing, turning back to her work monitoring the two women. It occurred to him she might have a different view of who the good guys and bad guys were given her family background. He wanted to tell her that Jaz would never hurt anyone she cared for, but that would be a lie. If her father was mixed up with this somehow, Jaz wouldn't hesitate to take him down.

Dean pushed the disturbing thought from his mind. No need to borrow trouble. As far as he knew, there was no connection to Leah's father. He had to talk to Jaz about this before an accidental encounter caused issues.

A fire department SUV pulled up across the street and Brynne hopped out. She put on her Lieutenant's helmet and crossed over to join them. Before she reached them, Jaz's black SUV parked right behind Brynne's vehicle.

Dean let Leah give a quick report as if she was handing over patient care. It was good practice for her.

Brynne listened until she finished and nodded. "Excellent work. I'll be right with you."

She followed Dean over as he headed for Jaz, who'd climbed out of her truck. She wore her usual tactical gear, though she'd added dual holsters, one on each hip. It looked like she expected trouble. He knew from experience her sword was in the SUV next to her seat, too.

Jaz smiled when she saw them coming her way. "Hey, Brynne. Thanks for letting me steal Dean from you for the rest of the night."

"As long as it's not just an excuse for a midnight booty call, I'm happy to help. I'd like to get rid of the scum setting these fires, too."

Jaz asked, "Has James or Rudy got any idea who's behind this trafficking ring?"

Brynne shrugged. "Until Dean stumbled upon the one girl a week ago, we didn't know they were operating here. I know both James and Rudy are turning over every rock to see how they operated this long with no one telling them."

Dean said, "There haven't been that many werecats around that I've seen since I've worked here. They have to be relatively new in town."

Brynne nodded. "There are a few who live locally, but you're right. I hope you two can track them down and stop them."

Jaz glanced at Dean. "You ready to go? I want to get on the trail so I can go stab someone."

He smiled. "How can I turn down an invitation like that? I hope it's not me."

"If I'm going to stab you, you'll know it, husband of mine."

Brynne laughed. "What you two do in your spare time is up to you, just don't call me to patch you up. I'll get back to helping Leah. Keep me in the loop if you find anything. I'd like to pass it along to James."

Jaz nodded and waited for Brynne to cross to the other side of the street before she said, "Dean, get in. I think I figured a way to track in on Gibbie's cell phone signal. It turns out he's been playing some game app with a few of my guys. When they told me, I followed a hunch and got a friend to hack into his phone using the app as a back door."

"Great," Dean said, climbing into the SUV. "Where is he?"

"According to the last message I got from my friend, less than a block from here."

She fired up the SUV and pulled out onto the street. She did a three-point turn to turn around and avoid going past the fire scene and then headed back up the road.

Jaz was right on the money. They followed the map of the screen in the SUV's dash. It led them around the block and into an alley leading back towards the fire scene. Dean spotted Gibbie's van parked between two brick apartment buildings halfway down. Jaz pulled over and the two of them got out to search around for their friends.

A scream from inside the van sent both of them racing to the rear doors.

Jaz pushed Dean aside, drew one of her pistols, and reached for the door handle. She yanked it open at the same time she switched on the tactical LED mounted beneath her pistol's barrel.

The beam of the light revealed two naked bodies. It took Dean a second to recognize Gibbie on his back with Hangbe right beside him.

Gibbie screamed again, trying to pull some of his scattered clothes closer to cover up.

Hangbe shook her head and cast a glance at them. "Jaz, hon, do you mind? I'm a little busy here."

Chapter 25

AN HOUR LATER, in a diner a few blocks away, a waitress set down the last plate from their orders and refreshed everyone's coffee before leaving them alone again.

Hangbe smiled and continued with her description of the evening's investigative activities. "After we rescued the people from the building, we knew it was too late to follow the trail of our friend Manton. We got a little distracted after all the excitement."

She cast a wicked grin in Gibbie's direction and added, "I guess Gibson and I let the moment get the better of us." She cast a wink at Jaz. "It's an excellent way to relieve stress. You should try it some-time. I certainly don't regret the brief moment of release. What about you, dear?"

Gibbie looked up from his coffee like a deer in the headlights of an oncoming car. "Oh, no, of course not. Always looking to lend a hand for a good cause."

Dean coughed as the coffee he was drinking threatened to come out through his nose.

Jaz covering for her husband's spluttering attempt at a response, said "Um, let's put that part of it aside. We haven't heard from the two of you since we brought you through the portal. You were supposed to coordinate with my teams on this."

"Sorry, Gibson had some excellent leads that took us deep into the criminal underworld of the Unusual community. We didn't really have the time to come up for air and check in. It's a good thing we did. That's how we discovered the location of the building tonight."

Dean had regained control of his voice by this point. "You could have called in a warning to me or Jaz, or even to the fire department. They put firefighters in danger starting this fire. It would have been nice to avoid all that, let alone the risk to the people who'd been trapped inside."

Hangbe leveled her stare at Dean. "I've been after this group for a long time. A lot of people have died and more will die if they're not stopped. Sometimes you have to cut corners to get the job done in a more expedited fashion."

Jaz jumped in before Dean could come back at Hangbe. "What Dean means is you came here to work with our team. We hooked you up with Gibbie to be your connection, not just to the city, but to our broader efforts to stop this ring here in Elk City. Can you at least fill us in on what you've found so far?"

Gibbie had recovered some of his composure and used this opportunity to share what he knew. "It's really fascinating to watch her work, guys. Hangbe used some sort of questioning charm on her necklace to interrogate a few of the people we located. Then we found and rescued one of the kidnapped women. That's how she uncovered as much as she did. Like we found out the gang out of Ireland is financed by a third party who helped them set up shop here."

"Who is it?" Jaz asked. "If they picked this place on purpose, they have to be from here."

Gibbie shook his head. "We're not sure. But, after we got the location from the girl, I figured there had to be a local connection. I tracked down a guy I knew who liked to set fires. It turned out he didn't set the ones in these buildings, but he remembers talking to a cat shifter who asked him a lot of questions about how to burn a building down the right way and the wrong way. That guy matched Manton's description perfectly."

Hangbe smiled as Gibbie got more and more excited by the story. "It really was a stroke of genius by Gibson to track down this fellow. He was quite useful. Now that we know who the arsonist is, we just have to track them back to the source and we can roll this whole thing up with a nice little bow on top."

Jaz glanced at Dean. He could tell she wasn't happy by the firm set of her lips. It was her non-expression that hid her true feelings, though it didn't work as well as she thought it did. Not only did Dean see through it, Hangbe did, too.

"Jaz, I appreciate your expectation for a certain level of cooperation from me, however, I don't have time to file reports with people until I'm finished. I have to follow the case wherever it leads me."

"Even to the back of Gibbie's van, apparently."

"I will not make excuses for my recreational tastes. Besides," Hangbe reached out and gave Gibbie's pale hand a squeeze. "He's so much more than he appears to be at first glance, especially if you've seen as much of him as I have."

Dean almost choked on his coffee again. Gibbie blushed a shade of crimson most would have thought impossible for a vampire. Dean set the coffee down, resigned to not drink anything for the rest of the meal.

Clearing his throat, Dean asked, "Now that we're all here together, what's your next step. Maybe if would be a good idea to work on this as a team from here on out."

"Dean's right," Jaz said. "The time for freelancing is over. We have to catch these guys before they do this again and leave town to set up somewhere else. Manton got away while you worked at rescuing the trapped Merrow."

Hangbe shrugged. "Our lead disappeared tonight, which is a shame. Unless you have a magical way to track them I don't know of, Gibson and I will have to go back into the dark underbelly of this city and rattle some cages until something shakes loose again."

Jaz paused and tapped her chin. "That's actually a great idea.

We might have a way to track them magically. I hadn't even thought about it until now."

"What?" Dean asked. "Is there a contact you have that can lead us to the rest of the victims before they're killed?"

Jaz smiled and fixed him with a steady gaze. At first, Dean didn't understand. Then it sunk in. "You mean me? How can I track them?"

"The Geas. The Yakshini woman laid that Geas on you. I had forgotten all about it, but it's how you stumbled upon Kaylee the way you did in Ireland. I think it's still working under the surface. It explains how you've ended up scheduled during the shifts when these fires have been set. You're the connection to all this."

"I thought you said it removed the Geas after we found Kaylee?"

"It appeared to be, but I think there may be some underlying effects still in place."

Dean considered the series of dreams over the last few weeks, all about being trapped and held without a way to escape. Could they be connected to the strange spell the Yakshini seer cast on him?

"I'm not saying you're wrong, Jaz, but if the charm had any power at all, it's not particularly effective. I found a girl wandering a beach. That was definitely magic at play. But the rest? I'm not so sure. So I ended up working extra shifts. I do that all the time. None of it has gotten us any closer to the source of the trafficking in Elk City." Dean shook his head. "Gibbie has gotten more done with Hangbe than I have. The two of them actually rescued some people."

Hangbe leaned forward, excitement twinkling in her eyes. "Yes, and it was your idea to connect Gibbie to me. Jaz might be on to something here. What kind of charm was it? He's absorbed it to the point that I can't sense it."

Jaz said, "I smelled it as soon as he got home from work that day. It had an old school feel to it, not like something a younger caster would come up with. They're always improvising to try to improve upon the classics."

"If that's the case, then there's a component of connection we're missing." Hangbe's hand touched her intricate, beaded necklace, tapping first one bead and then another, lost in thought. "Dean, what were you doing when you first discovered the trafficking ring?"

Dean related the initial encounter with Verity and the later attack by Manton at the station after work. "I think about her a lot, especially since she was scooped up as she left the ER and carried away. I feel like all my hard work was for nothing. I'm pretty sure she died in that first fire. They were almost all Selkies according to the coroner's report."

Gibbie smiled, "It's almost like her ghost is calling you."

"That's it," Hangbe said.

Gibbie laughed. "I was right? Dean's being haunted by a Selkie ghost?"

"No, if she was dead, the Geas linked to her would have dissipated. I think she's still alive. I think she is the connection to the charm."

Jaz nodded. "It makes sense. Dean close your eyes and concentrate on trying to see Verity where she is right now."

Dean doubted this was the right solution, but he played along. He leaned back in the diner booth and closed his eyes, tilting his head back a little as he did. He thought about Verity as he'd seen her in the apartment when he'd first encountered her. It wasn't easy, other thoughts and memories kept drifting in and messing up his concentration. After a minute of trying, he opened his eyes.

Everyone at the table stared at him, waiting for some sign it worked.

"Well?" Gibbie asked, losing patience.

"It's no good. I can't seem to concentrate on her. All I can think about lately are the nightmares I've been having."

"What kind of nightmares?" Jaz asked. "You haven't mentioned them to me."

"It's nothing. Hazards of the job, that's all, honey. I keep seeing people trapped in a dark concrete room. I'm pretty sure it's related to some post-traumatic stress from the encounter at the first fire where all those people died. I probably need to talk to the department's counselor about it."

Hangbe laid a finger on one of the thicker beads in her necklace. The midnight blue painted bead had a streak of white across the center. She closed her eyes and muttered something to herself. With her one hand still touching the bead, she reached across the table and placed her index finger in the middle of Dean's forehead, all with her eyes still closed.

He held still, not sure what she was doing. He waited for her to open her eyes, which took about thirty long, awkward seconds.

When the Amazon's eyes opened, they bored into Dean's as if they pierced all the way to his soul. Her lips curled into a grin. "The nightmares are related to that incident, but only because the Geas heightened your fears they've killed Verity. The dreams are a connection to her in your subconscious. It links you to her and almost ensures she still lives. Describe what you see. Leave nothing out."

Dean closed his eyes again, trying to relax and let the disturbing dream thoughts in, rather than dismiss them. At first they resisted his attempts to focus on them. As he worked at it, though, more details filtered to the top of his mind.

"It's got to be another basement. The cinderblocks look stained in lines at various heights along the walls. People are chained up together, huddled in the cold and damp to stay warm. Their fear permeates everything about what I see."

"The walls aren't stone?" Jaz asked. She'd pulled out her phone and was scrolling through something on it, glancing up at him. "You're sure they're cinder block?"

Dean nodded.

She turned her phone around and showed him a photo from the first fire scene. It showed the scorched walls of the basement where the people had been trapped. The older building had a stone masonry foundation made from blocks of large cut stones held together by a layer of cement. None of the photos she showed him had cinder block walls.

"These are the crime scene photos from the first fire. See, not cinderblock."

"So it's not the fire basement I've been dreaming about."

183

Jaz shook her head. "Nope. You're dreaming about something that's happening now, not a past vision."

"Then Verity is still alive?"

Hangbe nodded. "Your connection links her to the Geas set upon you. That has to hold the clues needed to find her."

Dean didn't understand how that was going to help. "I can't tell you anything more about what is there but what I can see. It's always the same. The same stained cinder block walls. The same huddled figures, chained in the dark."

Gibbie held up a finger to say something, then changed his mind.

Hangbe glanced at the Vampire. "If you have an idea, my love, share it."

Gibbie blushed again at the Amazon's words. "Uh, yeah, so can you describe the stains on the walls again? You said they form lines. Are they horizontal or vertical?"

"Horizontal, but not straight. They're kind of wavy."

Gibbie smiled. "Of course they are. They'd have to be wavy, wouldn't they?"

Jaz groaned. "Gibbie, you're not making any sense. What do the stains have to do with anything?"

"They're important because they tell me exactly where to look for our missing victims, including Verity."

Chapter 26

DEAN LOOKED out over the waterfront by the Elk River where it led into the Chesapeake Bay. Warehouses and businesses lined the street in front of him. Nothing stood out as a potential place to start.

He shook his head. "Tell me again why you think this is the place to look for our victims?"

Gibbie pointed at the river. "Back in the late 1990s, I was stuck down here during a hurricane. It was during the day and I had to hide down in a basement. That ended up being a bad idea because the storm drove a surge of water up the bay and into the river. This entire area flooded. I was wet and miserable until the water level went down and night fell."

"I don't see your point. What does a flood decades ago have to do with our problem?"

"It hasn't just flooded that one time. This area floods whenever a big enough storm hits. That's every ten to twenty years. I noticed while I watched the water rise in the basement that previous floods had left similar lines as the ones you describe. There can't be another part of the city that has numerous floods in its history."

Jaz smiled. "Excellent work, Gibbie. I think your idea matches up with Dean's description perfectly."

"I guess so," Dean said. "There wasn't any water in my dream."

Gibbie shook his head. "No, Dean, the basements are dry the rest of the time, but you mentioned it was damp. That's what clued me in to how the water left a trace of their passage with each flood."

Hangbe nodded at the buildings down the hill from where they'd parked. "I can accept your explanation. How does that help us figure out which one they're in? We can't go along and break into each one. There are dozens of them."

The vampire frowned. "Now, that I don't know. I was hoping one of you would come up with a way to zero in on it. Can't Dean use the spell cast on him to locate them?"

Dean shrugged. "I guess it can't hurt to try." He closed his eyes and tried to relax, focusing on anything that pulled him one way or another. After a minute of trying to feel the connection, he opened his eyes and tried scanning the buildings, looking for some sign that would trigger the Geas and lead him to the ones he was supposed to help.

After the third time he swept the waterfront with his eye, Dean frowned. "I don't get anything. I have no idea how this works."

"Don't beat yourself up, Dean." Jaz laid her hand on his shoulder. "It was worth a try. Maybe you need to be closer to trigger a reaction."

Hangbe tapped the side of her head twirled one of the long braids hanging down around her finger. "If the building they're in has a cinder block foundation, then we should be able to narrow it down to newer construction. We're also looking for a building without too much foot traffic passing by. They wouldn't want anyone accidentally seeing something and calling police. It's got to be a building that's vacant or looks like it in a section away from well-traveled streets."

Gibbie snapped his fingers and pointed. Dean followed the arm to an area off to the right, away from the restaurants and waterfront shops. There were some businesses scattered around there, but not too many. Most of the buildings looked sort of run down.

"That looks right for what we're looking for, Gibbie," Dean said.

"Let's go down there and walk around some. I need to see if I can sense anything."

Jaz shook her head. "We'll drive down. I want my SUV close enough I can get to it for more firepower if we need it."

"Two guns and a sword aren't enough, honey?" Dean asked. Jaz's Katana hung across her back, and she had twin semi-automatic pistols in holsters on each hip.

"Werecats are fast and crafty, Dean. Even with all four of us, it wouldn't take too many to overwhelm us if they caught us by surprise."

"They won't," Hangbe said.

Gibbie cocked his head to one side. "Won't what?"

"Catch us by surprise. I have a spell bead that should protect us from any sneak attacks." She reached up and tapped a red and gold striped oblong stone threaded on her necklace.

"How do you keep all of them straight?" Gibbie asked. "I'd forget which one did what."

"I remember because I earned each one of them in the ceremonies and tests of my birthright as a Dahomey Amazon. They're a part of me now."

Hangbe gave the area one last look and spun around, following Jaz back to where they'd parked their vehicles.

Gibbie tugged at Dean's sleeve as they followed the women. "Isn't she wonderful? I can't believe how lucky I am to have found her. I want you to be my best man, okay?"

"Easy, buddy. You just met her. How do you even know she feels the same way?"

An expression of wide-eyed horror crossed Gibbie's face. "Oh no, what has she told you? I probably came on too strong." He started pounding his clenched fists into his thighs as they walked. "I'm so stupid."

Dean reached out and gripped his friend's nearest wrist. "Calm down. Nobody said anything. She likes you enough to sleep with you, but that doesn't mean she wants to marry you. Take is slow. Enjoy things as they are right now. She's a busy woman and settling down might not be in the cards for her right now."

"Good idea. She's a modern career woman. I've got to respect that. I can wait for her to propose."

Dean shook his head. Gibbie's history with women was questionable at best. This whole thing had a new level of improbability, though.

"You guys coming?" Jaz called. We only have a few hours until the sun rises. "We need to be done searching by then so Gibbie can get under cover."

"Yeah," Dean said. "Be right there. Gibbie has something in his eye."

Gibbie took a deep breath and let it out slowly. "Take it slow. Got it. I can be like molasses slow. From now on, it's all about the Gibbie slow burn. Women can't resist that."

Dean rolled his eyes. "Come on, Casanova. If we don't hurry up, she'll move on without us."

They rejoined the women and loaded into their vehicles. Gibbie led the way in his van until they'd pulled onto a street with a few run-down shops and some vacant commercial buildings. They parked and the four of them met up once again on the sidewalk.

Jaz pointed to the far side of the street. "Dean and I will go up that side. Check the foundations and identify which ones have cinderblock if you can. If we don't find anything definitive in the ones that do, we'll meet back here."

Hangbe and Gibbie nodded and set out up the street. Dean crossed to the other side with Jaz and checked the first building. It was an older one. They made the foundation from quarried stone. He and Jaz moved on to check the next while he kept his mind open to any sensation that might tell him he was close to Verity and the others.

He and Jaz reached the last building on their side of the street. It resembled a big grey barn because of the old, faded wood siding. It appeared to have once been an operation that sold and serviced outboard motors for boats in the marinas nearby. From the padlock on the front door and the empty showroom behind the large plate-glass window, it had been out of business for some time.

Dean knelt down and checked the thin strip of foundation

visible between the sidewalk and the lower edge of the siding. Jaz glanced down at him and he shook his head. The foundation was the rough, unbroken grey of poured concrete.

Jaz said, "We'll wait here for Gibbie and Hangbe to finish their side. Maybe they'll find something."

Dean stood, grumbling his frustration. "I feel helpless stumbling around like this. There's got to be a better way to search for them."

He turned and kicked the strip of solid concrete he'd checked moments before. The concrete cracked beneath the steel toe of his duty boot. On a sudden impulse to further vent his anger, he kicked it twice more in rapid succession. The cracks widened, and then the thin layer of concrete veneer fell away to reveal the top of a row of cinder blocks.

As he knelt down to check the patch of missing concrete, Dean reached out and traced the masonry joint now visible between two cinder blocks. A flash of imagery surged into his mine the moment his fingers touched the exposed blocks. This time, the shadowy figures in the dark had more definition, and as he scanned the faces, he recognized one in the group. Verity, her cheeks lined where her tears had left a track through the grime and dirt on her face.

"Jaz, they're here. We found them."

"Are you sure?"

"Look. The cinderblock wall was just covered up for cosmetic purposes, I guess. I got a quick vision of them, just like in my dream. They're here. I know it."

Hangbe and Gibbie jogged over from across the street.

"What's up? Did you find something?"

Jaz slipped the pistol from her left holster. "Dean says they're in this building."

Hangbe reached beneath her jacket and pulled out a short, broad-bladed sword. "Did you see any guards? We need to know how many people from the gang are here."

Dean shook his head. "All I can see is what I saw earlier in my dreams, just with more clarity and definition. The first floor looks deserted."

"If there are people held here, there are guards to watch over them," Hangbe said. "This building takes up the whole block. Let's circle around and see if there's another entrance they have used recently."

She tugged at the sleeve of Gibbie's windbreaker and the two of them started off up to the nearest corner. Dean followed Jaz in the opposite direction. He pulled out his phone and sent a quick message to Brynne to come with the ambulance to this location and stage nearby. There might be a need for medical care once they found the missing people.

The two of them turned the corner and proceeded along the side of the building towards the rear. A chain-link fence blocked off a section of the parking lot behind the building. A pair of newer model sports cars, a black Mercedes sedan, and a large white passenger van were parked inside the locked parking area.

"Someone's here," Jaz said. "They wouldn't leave nice cars like that parked at an abandoned building. Stay behind me. If trouble pops up, take cover."

"Gotcha."

They circled the enclosed parking area and got a closer look at the vehicles. The Mercedes sedan looked familiar. He stared at it, trying to remember where he'd seen it. Then he saw it. The license plate read, "W-CAT1."

"Jaz, I think Leah's father is in there."

"Really? I knew he had to be mixed up in all this."

"I'm not sure, but that Mercedes is the same one parked at the station earlier tonight. It's got to be him."

Jaz glanced around. "Where are Hangbe and Gibbie?"

Dean looked to the far corner of the building. "They should have gotten here by now. Maybe they found a way inside."

"If she did, it would be just like her to barge in without waiting for backup. Let's go check."

Jaz moved up to the corner of the building with Dean close behind. Sure enough, there was a single, windowless steel door in the wall about midway to the front of the building.

Staying a few feet back, Dean followed up to the doorway. Jaz reached out with her right hand and tried the knob. She grinned as it turned in her hand and she pulled the door open enough to peer inside.

Dean wanted to ask what she could see, but he knew better than to make a noise right now. If there were werepanthers inside, they would surely hear him, even if he whispered.

Jaz pulled the door open far enough to slip in sideways and then held it for Dean to follow her. A short hallway extended away from them with a few doors on either side and one at the end.

They checked each door as they moved towards the one at the end. Each was a storeroom that looked like it hadn't been opened in a while. Dust and mold covered the floors inside.

Jaz reached the last door at the end of the corridor. She pressed her ear to the wood for a few seconds and then tried the door. It swung out into a large open warehouse.

In the center of the room, Hangbe and Gibbie knelt with their hands on their heads. A cluster of men and women stood around them. They had pistols trained on the pair. Dean recognized Manton among them, which meant the others were all werepanthers like him.

Jaz had her pistol up and Dean knew she was trying to decide whether to try a rescue or back up.

The decision was made for them when the door behind them leading outside opened. Six armed men entered and stopped leveling their pistols at the two of them.

A familiar voice from inside called out. "Ms. Errington, Mr. Flynn, why don't you come in and join us. I wouldn't want you to miss all the fun."

Jaz paused for only a split second before she relaxed and held up both hands. Dean did the same as the shifters behind them came forward. They grabbed Dean's arms and pulled them down, wrenching his shoulder as they secured them behind his back with plastic zip ties. Another pair disarmed Jaz and secured her arms behind her as well.

Their captors led them into the center of the warehouse and forced to their knees beside Hangbe and Gibbie. Jaz glared at the Interpol agent, who shrugged in reply. Dean scanned the room, trying to see anything that might be a way to escape. He stopped when he reached a tall figure standing in the shadows nearby.

The figure walked forward. At first Dean thought it might be Leah's father, but as the light fell across the face, he gasped.

"Hello, Dean," Artur said. "I told you I'd be back."

Fury filled Dean. This man had caused so much pain and suffering for Dean and his patients, all he wanted to do was start shouting.

Jaz lifted her head and glared at the ancient vampire, dressed in a crisp charcoal business suit. "It's a good thing you have me tied up. I didn't get the chance to finish you the last time we met. Are you up to a rematch?"

"I rarely like to get my hands dirty, girl. I won't give you the satisfaction of dying with a blade in your hand."

Dean looked around behind Artur. "Where's Mr. Casado? I assume you and he were behind the whole thing from the beginning."

Artur grinned. He shook his head. "No, his arrival in town was merely a fortunate accident. I don't like to partner up with others. I prefer to keep the spoils for myself. Besides, my feline friends here were looking for a new leader. I was happy to offer my support for their endeavor."

The response confused Dean. He knew Leah's father had some sort of underworld connection and money. It only made sense that he'd have been involved with this somehow. Why would Artur deny it?

Artur grinned. "I'm sure you have more questions. I will answer all soon enough, including my desire to end your meddling in my affairs once and for all." He nodded at the shifters surrounding them. "Put those two with the others, then finish preparing the building."

Chapter 27

LEAH LEANED FORWARD, searching the street for the address Dean had given them. The GPS in the ambulance had gotten them close, but she and Brynne had to stop and look for numbers on the buildings.

Brynne pointed ahead. "There's Gibbie's van. They're down that way."

Leah searched the sidewalks and buildings as Brynne pulled up behind the van. "I don't see them."

Brynne handed her a handheld radio with a shoulder strap. "Take the ambulance's portable. I'll use my own. Let's get out and have a look around."

Leah took the radio and got out. The pair split up and searched both sides of the street a few hundred feet in each direction. They returned to the ambulance after their search failed to turn up their friends.

Brynne took out her phone. "I'm calling James. We need help. I get the feeling there's some sort of trouble."

Leah cocked her head to one side and sniffed. The faintest whiff of smoke wafted past her. "Do you smell that? Something's burning nearby."

Brynne shook her head. "No, but your senses are better than mine. Which way?"

Leah sniffed again and pointed to the end of the street. She didn't see any flames, but the smell of smoke seemed to get stronger as she and Brynn jogged up the street to the large wooden warehouse at the end.

"It's coming from inside. Look." The inside of the former marine engine repair shop had filled with the haze of smoke. A flash of flame in the back corner broke through the thick smoke for a few seconds.

Brynne raised her mic and pointed to the nearest corner. "I'll call this in. See if you can find a way in at the rear that isn't filled with smoke. Don't enter. Just contact me with what you find."

Leah nodded and took off around to the back of the warehouse. She made it halfway around the fenced in parking area to the rear before she noticed her father's car. It sat alone in the small lot next to a loading dock and door. The gates to the fence were open, so she ran up to the door and started to open it but stopped herself just before she touched the metal knob.

Remembering her fire academy training, she held the back of her hand up near the metal door and knob about a half inch away. When she felt no heat coming off it, she gripped the knob and pulled. When it didn't open, Leah groaned. She had to get inside, and she dreaded what she had to do next.

Releasing a bit of the iron grip she held over her jaguar self, she let the out some of the power instilled in her family by the blood rites of Incan high priests millennia before.

Her eyes shifted first, giving her the ability to see into spectrums no human eyes could see. Tawny fur sprouted on her arms and face, dotted with black and tan spots. Stopping the transformation there, Leah gripped the doorknob again and yanked with all her might while twisting the knob.

A squeal of twisting metal preceded the door popping open as the deadbolt broke off inside the metal door jamb. Smoke poured out through the top of the door.

Leah ducked beneath the smoke so she could both breathe and

see, racing inside to begin her search. The open floor of the warehouse area had a few boxes and crates scattered about, but no sign of her father or the others she sought.

The heat and smoke grew as she continued deeper inside. She realized this was like the other fires, and that meant they had to be in the basement.

At this point Leah had to crawl to stay below the smoke. She looked for any sign of a door chained shut from this side.

Her radio squawked. "Leah, where the hell are you."

She kept crawling as she reached up with one hand and keyed the mic clipped to her shoulder strap. "I'm looking for survivors inside. I think I'm close."

"Negative." Brynne's voice cracked with anger. "That's a job for the fire crews. Exit the way you entered. Right now."

Leah knew if she left now, it was as good as condemning anyone trapped inside to death. She reached down and turned down her radio's volume to drown out her lieutenant's voice.

Coughing, Leah continued on and was just about to turn around when she spotted the locked basement door. The chains hung down enough that she spotted them beneath the thick layer of smoke filling the upper part of the hallway.

She banged on the door. <Cough> "Is anyone in there?" <Cough, cough>

Muffled voices from the other side reached her enhance hearing.

Turning around, Leah planted her feet against the frame on either side of the basement door and gripped the padlock and chain with her clawed hand. Sweat poured down her face and her glowing yellow eyes stung from the smoke. She ignored all of it, focusing all her considerable strength on pulling the chains free of the eyebolts, securing them to the wall on either side of the door.

Realizing she had no time for a second try at this, Leah released the last bit of barrier between herself and the wild jaguar inside her. Snarling through the long teeth of a jungle cat, she pulled at the chains. She gave all her strength to it; her rippling feline muscles popping the seams of her uniform shirt at the shoulders.

Letting out a final roar of defiance, she pushed with her

powerful legs as she pulled with her arms. The chains finally pulled free and she dove forward to pull open the door.

Her shifted feline visage came face to face with a young woman with long red hair. The woman screamed and recoiled back, almost falling back down the stairs. Leah yelled for her to stop, but all that came out was a long string of ripping snarls.

Cursing in her mind, she wrestled her inner jag back under control enough that she could talk like a person again. "It's okay, I'm not with the others. I'm a paramedic. Hurry up and come out."

"Leah, is that you?" Dean called from inside. "I need help. I can't get them out by myself."

A few timid men and women started up the stairs. Leah pointed back down the hallway. "Go that way and turn right. The door out will be straight ahead. Stay low out of the smoke."

They darted past her and crouched low as they ran back the way she'd come.

Leah bounded down the steps two at a time with her uncanny feline balance keeping her from tumbling to the bottom. Dean waited for her. Bruises covered his face. Whoever had beaten him had ripped his uniform shirt open. Ragged tears in the skin on his chest oozed blood past edges already crusting with scabs.

"What happened? Did my father do this?"

Dean seemed shocked at her question, but then pointed behind him. Two shirtless figures slumped bound to a metal support column with woven silver cable. The restraints left angry red welts against their exposed torsos, sapping their strength so they couldn't escape.

One was her father, beaten into unconsciousness. The other was the portly vampire friend of Dean's. He gazed through listless, pain-filled eyes back at her.

Leah rushed over and reached out to free them, pulling back at the last second. The silver would injure her as easily as it did the two of them.

"I can't free them, Dean. I can't touch the silver, either."

"They stripped me of my gear. Do you have a pair of trauma shears on you?"

Leah's confusion at the request kept her from complying right away.

"Leah, yes or no. Do you have them? We don't have much time. It might already be too late." He glanced up at the floorboards covering the basement rafters overhead. Flickering firelight played through the cracks. It wouldn't be long until the fire burned through to the basement.

Shaking herself from the fog of indecision, she dug in the cargo pocket of her uniform pants and handed Dean her hardened steel trauma shears.

He snatched them and grabbed at the cable, twisted around Gibbie first. Leah winced at first expecting the silver alloy to burn him. She relaxed when nothing happened. She'd forgotten he was human.

Dean gripped the shears and opened them wide as he slid the thin braided cable back as close to the joint where the two blades hinged.

"You'll never cut that," she said.

"An old EMT once bet me he couldn't cut a penny in half with a pair of these shears." Dean grimaced as he used two hands to squeeze the handles together. "I lost that bet."

With a sudden snap, the trauma shears cut through the first cable.

Leah jumped forward. "Give me the shears. I'm stronger than you are. Hold the cable out so I don't have to touch it."

Dean pulled at the bindings and selected the next cable in the line. Leah, in her werejaguar form, powered through all the restraints in less than thirty seconds.

Together she and Dean pulled Gibbie and her father to the foot of the stairs. Flames filled the doorway above.

"We're not getting out that way," Dean said. "Give me your radio. Is Brynne out there?"

Leah nodded and handed Dean her handset and mic.

"Paramedic Dean Flynn to Lieutenant U-1. Need RIT team to basement for rescue of four individuals."

"Dean," Brynne responded. "There's a window on the northwest corner of the basement. Fire crews just arrived. I'll have the rescue teams meet you there."

"Northwest corner. Copy."

Dean oriented himself but had some trouble figuring out which way was correct. Leah pointed to the farthest corner of the cluttered basement. He grimaced. It was a long way, and embers already fell from the floor above. The ceiling could collapse on them at any time.

"My father's lighter than Gibbie. You take him. I'll take the fat vampire."

"Hey," Gibbie's limp protest might have been funny at another time. This time Leah ignored it. If she hurt his feelings, she could apologize later. Her inner jaguar had rougher edges than her human self.

Dean winced as he tugged at Leah's father, pulling him up into a firefighter's carry. He stumbled a little but stayed on his feet as he lurched towards the far side. Leah lifted Gibbie with ease over one shoulder and followed.

They made it to the far side just in time. The ceiling behind them collapsed into the basement as the fire consumed the floor above. Smoke started filling the space around them.

Dean reached out to Leah. "I'll boost you up to the window. Break out the glass so the rapid intervention team knows where we are."

Leah calmed herself enough to shift back to human form, though she held onto some of her shifter strength. She didn't want to alarm the human firefighters outside.

She stepped into the stirrup Dean made with his hands and pulled out the small metal flashlight from her belt. The window was small, only about three feet across and maybe two feet high. Gripping the flashlight in her fist, she hammered the butt against the window until the glass shattered outward.

Gloved hands reached in to pull her to safety. She batted them away. "There are others injured in here. I'll lift them up to you."

The nearest firefighter, wearing a lieutenant's helmet, nodded. He started calling out orders to his team while she climbed down.

"Dean, help me lift Gibbie up first. Then we'll get my father out."

With her partner's help, they lifted their two patients to safety. As soon as the firefighters pulled her father up through the window, Dean crouched down to boost her up.

Leah shook her head. "You're injured. You go first. I can leap up and pull myself out with no trouble."

Dean objected, but only for a second. He nodded and let her boost him up instead. The smoke had become so thick at this point that she had trouble breathing. Coughing, she mustered her remaining strength and leaped up to the waiting hands, letting them pull her to safety.

Chapter 28

DEAN, Gibbie, and Leah's father, Carlos, sat in the back of the Station U ambulance. Dean sat on the bench seat beside Gibbie while the older werejaguar lay propped up on the stretcher. Leah had wrapped the blood pressure cuff around her father's arm and pressed the button on the monitor to start the reading.

"I don't need all this, I'm already healing."

"You're in my world, now, Papa. You'll do as I say. You're not some young cub who got in a scrape."

The elder Casado grumbled a little, but let his daughter continue checking him.

Brynne crouched by Dean, tending to his cuts. He batted her hands away. "Enough. I'll live. I may not regenerate, but I've been through this before. We have to find Jaz and Hangbe."

Waiting until he finished talking, Brynne said, "You done? I've got O'Malley and the rest of the PD combing area businesses for surveillance video. I've called James and Rudy to get them on it as well. Now let me tend to these injuries or I'll strap you down and take you in to ECMC myself."

Gibbie snorted a laugh as he sipped on the bag of blood from the small refrigerator in the ambulance. His injuries had already mostly healed. "She's right, Dean. There's no way you're up to dealing with those werepanther creeps. And Artur is a force to be reckoned with all by himself."

"If we don't hurry, they'll kill them both. That has to be why Artur took them for himself." Dean hissed in pain and pulled away as Brynne dabbed at his cuts, trying to clean them.

"I will deal with this," Carlos announced. "The vampire is problematic, but the werepanthers are in my domain and we must make an example."

Dean glanced outside. "We can't stay here too much longer. It's almost dawn. Gibbie and Brynne need to get inside and under cover."

"I'm as good as new," Gibbie announced, leaning over and dropping the empty blood bag in the wire trash can filled with a red medical waste bag. "I'll get my van. I have a few ideas on where to look around town."

"Gibbie," Dean said. "If this whole situation has proven anything, you're not equipped to handle this alone."

"I won't sit by and do nothing. You've lost your wife. I've lost something, too. She's the one, Dean. Hangbe is the girl I've been waiting for. I won't lose her this way."

Brynne rolled her eyes. Dean understood, though. Gibbie had been through one girlfriend after another in the few short years Dean had known him. Each one treated Gibbie like trash, and the relationship usually ended badly. Despite that, the frumpy vampire never gave up on finding someone. If he thought Hangbe was a chance at that, who was Dean to discount it. He and Jaz hadn't looked like a perfect match in the beginning either.

Dean said, "Okay, Gibbie. Go. But check in with Brynne or I before you do anything. We're going to need extra help on this. Artur will find out soon enough we survived, and he'll know we're coming for him."

Carlos reached over and ripped the velcro free on the blood pressure cuff. "I can help, too. I don't have the resources here I would have at home, but under the right circumstances, I can handle a few werepanthers."

Leah's eyes flashed yellow. "Not alone you won't."

Carlos smiled. "Deciding to join the family enterprise after all, Mija?"

"No, this is a rescue operation, and I'm a paramedic. I can use my Unusual skills to help save the others and keep you from getting yourself killed in the process."

Leah's father didn't hide his disappointment, but he said nothing, only nodded.

Dean stood. "Good, then let's split up. Gibbie, you head out and see what you can uncover. If Artur is back in town and staying somewhere, there has to be a trail. He's not shy about killing or hurting his food source. I'd start there."

Gibbie nodded and jumped out of the ambulance. He gave Dean a thumbs up and left to get his van.

"The rest of us can head back to the station."

Carlos said, "I have a car here. I'll stay."

Brynne shook her head. "If it's that fancy Mercedes parked out back, it caught fire when the building collapsed on it."

Carlos deflated a bit.

Dean said, "Leah can give you a ride once we get back."

Brynne pushed Dean back down to his seat with one hand. "You sit down. I'll drive back. Leah can ride up front with me. You're still injured."

Dean knew better than to argue with her. "Yes, oh wise and ancient one."

"You'll pay for that later once we've rescued the others. Buckle up. I have to get back before daybreak."

Dean did as he was told and settled in with Carlos for a ride back across town to Station U.

James and Rudy waited in the Station U squad room when they got back. Tammy and Brook came into the ambulance bay as soon as Brynne backed the unit into place.

Tammy popped open the ambulance's rear doors. "Damn, Dean, are you alright? I heard you'd been injured, but you look like crap."

"I'll survive. I have no choice until I find Jaz." Dean climbed out, looking around the garage bay while his mind swam with random ideas of what he needed to do. Jaz could already be dead for all he knew.

Brynne walked back from the front of the ambulance. She gripped Dean's arm, spinning him around. "Dean, I see you panicking. Take a deep breath. I called ahead for help. Tammy and Brook came in early to take over."

"What if we're already too late?"

James Lee, vampire lord of Elk City, said from the squad room doorway, "Artur likes to play with his captives. He won't rush this and that gives us time."

Rudy, his werewolf security chief, nodded from behind him. "I've got the entire pack mobilized this time, Dean. I'm also coordinating with the Errington teams. We'll find him and get her back."

Dean struggled to pull himself together, trying to steer his racing thoughts in a coherent direction. Leah stood off to one side, talking with her father in hushed tones. After a few words exchanged back and forth, the elder Casado approached James.

"I wanted to apologize for not notifying you I was back in town. I assure you; I didn't return for business. I came back to deal with a family matter." He glanced back at his daughter before returning his attention to James.

The vampire nodded. "We had an agreement, Carlos. Family or not, you're in this now. What kind of connection do you have with the werecats we're dealing with?"

"As I said, I had no idea this was going on until I was contacted by someone who let me know my daughter had a run-in with the local werepanthers. I came to assure she was staying on the right side of our agreement. That is all. They approached me to parlay with the others, and I tried to make an arrangement with them. In the end, I'm as much a victim here as our paramedic friend and his loved ones are."

Brynne stepped in to break the tension. "His story checks out, James. They trapped him in the fire with Dean and Gibbie. They wanted him as dead as the others they held there."

"This has got to stop. Artur has meddled for the last time in my affairs."

Dean paced as an idea drifted into his mind. James and the others had tried and failed to catch Artur before. He had to have a contingency plan in place to deal with things this time, too. The only solution Dean could come up with was to bring overwhelming force and firepower along when they finally tracked him down.

"I think we need more than the ones we've assembled to track Artur down and catch him. We have to bring in some big guns."

James, Brynne, and Carlos all asked the same question in unison. "Who?"

"There are two women who've been after Artur for a long time. I think they'd be upset if we didn't include them in the search and rescue operation. They'll add some extra firepower and ability to the mix."

Brynne smiled. "I know where Ashley is. Do you have a line on Ingrid?"

Dean nodded. "She's been here the whole time since we closed the gates between the planes, just like Ashley." He checked his watch. It was almost six and then official end of his shift. "In fact, she should be starting an early class right about now."

James and Rudy exchanged a glance before James said, "I don't mind Ashley. She has a sense of self-control. Ingrid is a wildcard I'd rather not cut loose in my city."

Dean shrugged. "She's already here. She never left. I can assure you, if we ask Ashley for help, Ingrid will get wind of it and show up when you least expect it. Wouldn't it be better to include her in the plan from the beginning so you have some level of control?"

Rudy nodded. "He has a point, James. Plus, she brings a certain level of chaotic carnage to the table we might need."

"Fine, see if they're on board, Dean. Rudy, Brynne and I will go back to the Nightwing building and work on finding where Artur is hiding."

Dean glanced at Leah. "What about you two?"

Carlos said, "I have a hotel room downtown. Leah can take me there. I'll reach out to the people I know. Maybe they will have some ideas of where these rogue cats are hiding."

"All right," Dean said. "James, can you have Celeste field calls and coordinate things on that end? I'll fill Gibbie in so he knows, too."

James nodded and pulled out his phone. "I'll send each of you her number. Send anything you get to her and she'll get it out to the rest of the team. If nothing else comes up, we can meet in my apartment in the Nightwing building later and decide on our next moves."

Everyone seemed in agreement and started for the parking lot. The sun was just brightening the horizon to the east as Dean jumped in his pickup truck. He had a lot to do to find Jaz and Hangbe. He bit back the primal scream that kept trying to escape his chest. It held the fear they were already too late to save them. He refused to give it a voice. Hope was all he had left.

Chapter 29

HANGBE ROLLED over on the floor and tried to get some sense of where she was. The pitch blackness of the room in which she found herself didn't help at all.

A gasp from someone nearby in the dark froze her in place as she tried to determine if they were friend or foe. Dammit, she needed to see. They'd disarmed her when the vampire and the shifters took her. They had not removed her most potent weapon. The problem at hand was how to access it with her hands secured behind her back.

The other person in the room gasped again, this time giving voice to their groans. "Who's there? I hear you moving."

Hangbe relaxed. "It's me, Jaz. Looks like they locked us up here together."

"Where's here? I can't see a thing. One of the werepanthers took my Hunter necklace. He said he wanted a souvenir."

"Lucky for us, they didn't take a fancy to mine. I guess antique African beads aren't worth anything to these thugs."

"Wait, does that mean…"

"Maybe. I'm trying to figure that out now."

Hangbe shrugged her shoulders, trying to slide the ropes around her chest up so she could extend her wrists past her butt to bring them around to the front. After working at it for several minutes, she gave up. The ones who'd tied them up had known what they were doing. Time to try something else.

"I don't suppose you have a blade hidden in your boot or something?"

Jaz sighed. "No, they found the small folding knife I keep inside my combat boot. I've got nothing sharp on me."

"Alright, let me think." Hangbe worked through her options. The necklace she wore had belonged to her grandmother. Over the years after her initiation, she'd added to its beads as she'd found additional spells she could store in them. It still held at its core the beads the original Dahomey Amazons had given to each of their number during training. In the past, Hangbe had always had to activate them by touch. But was there another way?

The dark-vision charm was a large black and white bead just to the left of center in the first row of the necklace's ornate pattern. Hangbe tilted her neck, bringing her chin down so it rested on the necklace. She moved her neck and jaw around to figure out which row of beads she was touching. It wouldn't do to release a fireball in this enclosed space by accident.

Sliding her chin to the left and right, she finally thought she had the right bead identified. The dark-vision bead was one of the larger ones in the pattern. The magic it held was long lasting. Spell duration or power seemed to relate to the size of the individual beads making up the collection.

"Cross your fingers, Jaz. I'm going to try something."

"That's about all I can do right now."

Hangbe pressed down with the tip of her chin and summoned the power in the bead beneath it. At first nothing happened. She could feel a distant stirring of power, but it stayed just out of reach.

She redoubled her efforts, focusing her concentration on exactly what she wanted to achieve. After pressing on the bead long and hard enough to bruise the end of her chin, a flash of light almost blinded her.

Hangbe squeezed her eyes shut, fearing the worst. When nothing exploded, she opened them.

She could see.

A blue-green haze tinted everything, but there was enough light to make out where she was.

"We're in some kind of security vault."

"What, like a bank?"

"Yes, exactly that. The metal walls on three sides are covered in small locked doors of various sizes. The fourth wall looks like the interior of the vault door."

"Are there words that tell us which bank it is? Any sort of identification?"

Hangbe craned her neck, scanning the entire room. "No. Just some numbers on each door. You know this city better than I do. Where would there be an empty vault like this that Artur and those werepanthers could hide us?"

"I have no idea. Maybe there's an old abandoned bank somewhere in town. He has a thing for abandoned buildings. Hey, anyway you can help me see better?"

"Not with what I have. I might be able to get us free, though." Hangbe kept looking around. Their captors had secured their wrists and ankles with plastic cable ties. There were also ropes around their chests and knees, further hindering escape. The only thing in the room other than themselves was a small folding card table and an old metal desk chair on wheels.

"I think there's a way to cut the plastic ties. It's going to take a while, though."

Jaz laughed. "For now, time is the only thing we have."

"Agreed. Let me try something." She rolled across the hard metal floor towards the card table. Desperate times called for desperate measures. At least no one would hear her cry out if she cut herself by accident. With a grimace, she gritted her teeth and set to work.

Chapter 30

DEAN STOOD outside the martial arts studio, watching the class inside go through their routines under the watchful eyes of their instructor. They practiced two-handed sword combat with bamboo mockups of the real thing.

As each pairing took their turn, the instructor circled them, watching as they sparred, calling out suggestions, and occasionally stepping in to adjust a student's stance and position. Dean continued to watch for fifteen more minutes until the class ended and the students stopped, bowing at their teacher before heading into the locker rooms.

The instructor, a tall brunette with long braids on either side, glanced out the window at Dean and motioned for him to come inside. Dean nodded and headed in.

"Were you just in the neighborhood, or is the world ending again?" Ingrid asked.

Dean shrugged, worry coloring his expression. "Neither, I guess, though it feels like the world is ending to me."

The valkyrie stopped picking up the few towels on the benches. "It's not like you to mope around. What's happened?"

"It's Jaz. She's been taken and I need help."

"The last time I helped you, I ended up grounded and stuck on earth for who knows how long."

Dean winced at the venom in her tone. He'd been afraid this might be her reaction.

"Artur is back in town. He has her. I thought you'd want to know."

Ingrid resumed picking up towels. "You think dropping that scumbag's name is enough to bring me out of my early retirement? Go see my sister. She enjoys living here. Maybe she'll help you."

"She's my next stop. We need you both."

Picking up the laundry hamper, Ingrid headed for the door behind the counter. "Not my problem anymore. I take my orders from on high and, thanks to you, they aren't talking to me anymore."

Dean hesitated for a second before dodging behind the counter and into the back room. Ingrid finished filling the washing machine and started it.

"You're not allowed back here."

"Ingrid, it's Artur. This is your chance to stop him. You've been after him for centuries."

She stopped folding towels, putting her hands on her hips. "Look at me, Dean. I wasn't meant to teach bored suburbanites how to look cool on their dating profile. I'm a warrior for the light. You did this to me, so explain to me why I should care what happens to your wife?"

Dean stared at her, struggling to find an answer that might motivate her. He'd led with the one thing he was sure would have her drop everything and join the fight.

When he didn't answer her after a few seconds. Ingrid returned to the laundry. "Exactly. Now, if you'll excuse me, I have another class starting in ten minutes and they expect fresh towels or they complain to my boss."

Dean shook his head. "Not so much of a badass now, are you, now that your wings are clipped."

"Watch your tone, medic boy. You know I could kick your ass from here to Sunday if I wanted." When Dean still didn't leave, she cocked her head to one side and said, "I'll tell you what. Ask Gabe. If he's in, I'm in."

"I'm not talking to my father right now. He tried to end the world, remember?"

"I guess your wife's not so important to you after all."

Dean clenched his fists, grinding his teeth together.

Ingrid laughed. "Ooo, that got under your skin. Good, you deserve it. Now get out of here. If my boss shows up and finds you back here, he'll dock my pay and I can barely afford my apartment as it is. Come back if you get Gabe on board."

Dean bit back the insult on the tip of his tongue. He needed her. He couldn't afford to burn any bridges right now.

By the time he got to the parking lot, he'd got his temper under control again. Sliding into his truck, Dean checked his phone. It was almost lunchtime. If he hurried, he might catch Gabe on a break between lessons.

He didn't know what he could say that would make a fallen archangel like Gabriel help him out. It wasn't like their father-son bond was all that tight. Still, he needed Ingrid and her sword. If that meant he had to bring Gabe into this as well, then he'd figure it out.

Dean pulled out of the strip mall parking lot and headed for the highway to take him across town. He checked the clock on the dashboard and pressed on the accelerator, praying he didn't pass any cops. He couldn't afford any delays.

Chapter 31

THE ROBERT JONAS ELEMENTARY SCHOOL parking lot's visitor spaces were full, so Dean pulled into one of the empty staff slots. He hoped they didn't tow him while he was inside.

At the front door, he rang the buzzer and waited for someone to answer in the office.

"Can I help you?" The bored female voice said over the intercom.

Dean smiled into the camera mounted over the door. "I'm Dean Flynn. I'm a paramedic with the city." He held up his station ID in front of the camera. "I needed to talk with someone who works here about something private."

There was a pause. "Come on back to the office."

Dean waited for the door's lock to click and went inside. Back in the office, a woman with curly red hair sat behind a tall counter.

"I need to see that ID again, please."

Dean handed her his fire department photo ID.

She glanced at it and handed it back to him. "Who did you need to see?"

"I think he teaches trumpet here on Wednesdays?"

"Oh, Gabe. Yes, he's got the third graders right now. He should be done in a few minutes." She leaned forward and whispered. "Can you tell me what this is all about? I won't tell anyone, I swear. Gabe's so mysterious about his background. The others in the office here have all sorts of ideas but nothing we're sure of."

Dean schooled his face to remain calm and dispassionate. "I'm sorry, ma'am. I'm unable to say because of confidentiality rules. You understand." He glanced around. "I don't suppose you have somewhere I can speak with him alone. What I have to ask him is a bit, uh, delicate."

The woman's eyes lit up at Dean's words. "Really? Well, the principal is at meetings at the Board of Education all day. I suppose you could meet in her office. It's right over there. Go on in and I'll send him in as soon as he dismisses the class."

Dean smiled, nodding. She picked up the phone and tapped in a few numbers.

"Mr. Angel? Yes, there's someone here to see you. I've put him in the principal's office to wait for you." A brief pause and she hung up the phone. She smiled at Dean. "He'll be up in a few minutes. They're almost finished."

Dean walked back to the office she'd indicated. He spent some time reading a few of the plaques on the walls while he waited.

A few minutes later, a voice from the doorway said, "Oh, it's you."

Dean tried to hide his surprise as he turned around. Gabe, his biological father, was not the man he'd been a few months before. Since Dean had last seen him, his father had put on at least twenty pounds, hadn't shaved in a few days, and his khakis and light blue oxford shirt looked like the last time they'd seen an iron had been during the previous presidential administration.

Working to cover his shock, Dean said, "Hello, Father."

"Hello? That's all you have to say to me after what you did? What brings you out to the burbs? Did you want to get a look at the carnage your selfish choices made in my life?"

"My choices? I..." Dean choked off the rest of his reply. He wouldn't get anywhere attacking Gabe. As much as he hated being here, Jaz needed his help. Dean could suck down a lot of crap to save his wife.

He waved his hand, trying to cancel what he'd said. "Look, Gabe, I came down here because I have something to ask you."

"Ah, here it comes." He set down the black trumpet case on the small couch against the wall. "What is it you need, Dean? Parental validation? It's a little late for that, don't you think?"

"No, there's a problem and I think it might need your unique skills to deal with it." His eyes fell on the paunch sticking out around the belt of Gabe's Khakis. It was hard to believe this was the fabled Archangel Gabriel, the trumpet-bearer, destined to call upon the armies of the Lord for the last battle. Now he looked every bit the part of an elementary school music teacher.

"I'm sorry, I no longer have to deal with all that stuff. Ever since you cut off the bridge between this world and the other planes, I'm kind of stuck just being another human meat sack."

"Stop feeling sorry for yourself. Billions of people would have died if I hadn't done what I did. And you're far from helpless, despite what you look like."

Gabe shot him a hard glare, and Dean was afraid he'd gone too far. Then his father looked away, reaching down to adjust his belt.

"Look, Gabe. Maybe there's something I can do to help your situation. I need your help with something. What can I help you with in return?" Dean didn't want to owe this man anything, but Jaz needed this.

Gabe's frown turned upward. He tilted his head to one side as he raised a finger to point at his son. "You're really in trouble, aren't you? And it's something you have to have me along to deal with, too. Well, isn't this an interesting conundrum?"

Dean started to speak, but Gabe held up his hand to stop him.

"Don't tell me I'm wrong. Tell me what you need me to do and I'll tell you what I will want in return."

Dean sighed. He began at the beginning, trying to paint his efforts as noble, helping the trafficked people in the city find freedom. He got to the part about Artur and Gabe's grin widened. By the time he finished telling everything, his father exuded the typical

Eldara confidence and power he hadn't shown when he first walked into the office.

"So, you need the help of the Eldara, despite what you did to strand us here on Earth all those months ago?"

Dean nodded.

Gabe began pacing, his head tilted back as he walked, staring at the ceiling. After almost a minute he stopped, saying. "I'll help you and convince Ingrid to come along, too."

The wicked grin that followed the statement gave Dean chills. "What is it you want in return?"

"Oh, not so much. I just want you to open up the gates between the planes again, that's all."

"I have no idea how I'm supposed to do that, and I'm not sure it would be a good idea to do it even if I did."

Gabe put an arm around Dean's shoulders. "That's not something we have to worry about right now. I have some ideas we can try after we save your pretty little wife and her friend."

Dean resisted the urge to shrug off his father's arm. It was anything but comforting. He needed his help, though. Jaz needed it. Realizing he could doom the earth to eternal darkness just to save his wife, Dean nodded. "If you'll help, I'll do what you ask."

Gabe grinned, picking up his trumpet case and heading out the door.

"Where are you going?"

"I have the fifth grade trumpet students in a few minutes. Don't worry. Leave a message with Adele out front on where you want to meet up for whatever you have planned. I'll meet you after work and I'll bring Ingrid along, too."

"Have you been in touch with Ashley? She hasn't replied to my message yet."

Gabe chuckled, "I'll bring both the sisters. I know how to reach her wherever she is." He waved over his shoulder, walking away with a spring in his step that hadn't been there before.

Dean shook his head, dreading what might be in store for him once all this was finished. He pulled out his phone and looked up the address for the Nightwing Building downtown. He wrote it down on a slip of paper from the principal's desk and left the message with Adele on his way out.

He hoped they were having success in their efforts to locate Artur. He could bring all the help in the world to this thing, but it wouldn't do any good if they didn't know where Artur held Jaz and Hangbe.

Chapter 32

HANGBE PULLED the ropes from around Jaz's hands and stood. "Can you get the ropes around your feet?"

"Yeah, I think so. I can't see a damned thing in here. When I catch that shifter who stole my Hunter necklace, I'm going to take a little extra time on him."

Jaz's ever-present confidence and adrenaline always brought a smile to Hangbe's lips. She'd enjoyed mentoring the young Hunter when they'd first met a few years back. The girl picked up everything you taught her on the first go around, and she'd turned into just the sort of person you wanted at your back in a situation like this.

"As long as you leave that vampire to me, you can do whatever you want to the werepanther."

Jaz chuckled. "You might have to get in line on that one. He killed my family, has been on the hit list of a pair of particularly dangerous Eldara twins, and I'm sure there are others around who want a piece of him, too."

"I guess we'll see who gets to him first." Hangbe had moved to the inside of the vault door. She traced the mechanism visible behind the glass that covered the interior surface. "I'm not sure we have a way out of here yet, so it may not matter."

"What makes you say that?"

Hangbe twisted her head towards Jaz. She was still working at the knots that bound her ankles. "The inside of the door is covered in what I'm sure is bullet-proof glass. We can't get at the tumblers that would let us open it from the inside."

"Where there's a will, there's a way, Hangbe. You broke apart that card table easily enough to get the metal to cut through your bonds. That glass isn't unbreakable. Hit it enough times with something hard enough and it'll shatter."

The remains of the card table lay in the corner. Hangbe stared at the pieces and considered what her companion had said. It might work. There was one problem with the plan. "They'll likely hear us banging repeatedly on the door if they've got anyone close by."

"Good, then they'll be stupid enough to open the door and check on us."

Hangbe shrugged. That was a possibility. It would give them one last hurrah together before the werepanthers and the vampire overwhelmed them. There were too many for the pair of them to handle all at once. Their only chance lay in sneaking out and dealing with them piecemeal.

Jaz stood; her hands outstretched in the darkness as she stepped towards the broken table. She reached the spot and bent down, retrieving two of the metal tubes that used to be the folding legs. She stood and clacked them together a few times.

"These seem solid enough to do some damage. If they want to come in here after us, I'll be ready to greet them. I've got some payback to deal for killing my husband."

"You don't know he's dead. He's more resourceful than you give him credit for based on what I've seen. Gibson speaks very highly of him."

"Maybe they're both alive then."

Hangbe's eyes narrowed. "They'd better be. I've taken a liking to that particular vampire."

Jaz laughed. "I don't know what you see in him. He's a bit of a goofball. He's had his moments when he's lent a hand, but if you knew what he was like when Dean first met him, you might change your mind."

Hangbe shook her head. "There's something about him. He's…" she paused as she searched for the word. "…comfortable is probably the best word for him. Plus, he's got the stamina to keep up with me. I haven't met too many men who do."

Jaz shook her head. She'd moved over to the sound of Hangbe's voice until she stood next to her friend. "I really don't want that image of Gibbie and you. But hey, you do you, right?"

Hangbe put an arm around her protege. She returned her attention to the interior side of the door. Reaching up, she traced the metal frame holding the sheet of glass in place. Her fingers met the occasional bumps of the screws holding it all in place. Her smile broadened. There might be a quiet way out after all. Now all they needed was for Gibbie to use the special bonding spell she'd laid on him. With luck, the cavalry should arrive about the same time they got out of here.

Chapter 33

DEAN PACED in front of the broad stretch of floor-to-ceiling windows, staring out at the darkened skyline.

"Dean, you're going to wear out that carpet if you keep that up," James said. "Come sit down. I'll get you a stiff drink to settle your nerves."

"I can't drink at a time like this. I need to be at my best for what we have to do."

Brynne smiled. "Dean, he's right. We don't even have a location for them yet."

"Exactly, and every passing minute could be a minute too long."

James and Brynne exchanged glances as Dean returned to his pacing. He didn't care what they thought. Jaz was out there somewhere, and Artur had tried to kill her once already. There was nothing to keep him from doing it for real this time.

The elevator out in the penthouse's entry hall pinged. Dean craned his neck to see who it was. Rudy entered, accompanied by Carlos and Leah Casado. Seeing the pack leader and security expert coming in with the two werejaguars seemed strange. He was pretty certain werewolves and cat shifters didn't get along.

James crossed the room and shook Carlos's hand in greeting. He glanced at Rudy. "Any luck on your end?"

Rudy shook his head. "I've got the pack out looking for any sign of Jaz and her friend. I thought we might catch a break since a lot of them know Jaz and could pick up her scent. There's nothing so far."

Dean threw his head back and stared at the ceiling in a silent scream.

Rudy frowned. "Sorry, Dean. We're trying everything we can think of. Something will turn up. It has to."

Dean lowered his head. "What about you, Carlos? These werepanthers are supposed to be under your control. Surely you have some idea where they hide out here in Elk City?"

Carlos's eyes darkened and flashed yellow.

Leah laid a hand on her father's arm, settling him. "I've impressed upon my father the importance of this to me. He's doubly motivated because these rogue cats sully his reputation. He wants them and their vampire leader as much as the rest of you do."

"More. Much more, Mija." Carlos said. "James and I had an agreement in place, limiting the scope of my operations here. I honor my word and they have broken that promise. In my line of work, honor is everything. Others must know what befalls those who step in my way."

Dean snorted a laugh. "Pardon me if I don't get all shaky at the mention of your criminal empire. It is that criminal empire that started all of this to begin with. Even if it was a group of rogue cats, they were still yours to begin with. If they hadn't been here, my wife would be safe."

Brynne stood, walking to stand in Dean's eye line to Carlos. "This bickering isn't getting us anywhere. Stop it right now. That's an order, Dean. Let's go through what we know now that we're all here."

"Not all of us," Dean said. "What about Gibbie?"

James frowned, but said nothing. Dean knew the vampire lord didn't think much of the frumpy member of his undead community. Brynne jumped in, saying, "Maybe you should call him. He might have fallen asleep or something."

"That's not fair," Dean replied. "He's a lot better than you all give him credit for. He may not look like much, but I've learned I can count on him in tough situations. I only hope he didn't go after them alone."

The elevator pinged. Everyone's head turned to see who it was.

Gibbie charged from the elevator and raced into the room. "I found them. At least I'm pretty sure I did. I was just driving around town, moping mostly. Then I remembered this thing that Hangbe did to me when were together the first time. She's got some awesome magic, among other talents. She used one of her spells to…" He skidded to a stop when he realized how many people were in the room. Everyone had stopped and now stared at him.

Dean broke the awkward silence. "What did she do, Gibbie? How do you know where they are?"

"Oh, yeah, well, I tried to think about what I could do to contribute to finding Hangbe and Jaz. There wasn't much that came to mind. Then I remembered what Hangbe did to me in bed that first night."

"Gibbie," Brynne said. "Focus. Stay on target. Are you sure this is relevant?"

"I am. I wasn't going to mention the sex. I mean, it was A-mazing, of course. Oh, yeah, where was I? Um, okay, so that first time she traced a sigil on my forehead and over my heart. She repeated the move three times and then said something in a language I didn't recognize. I asked her what it was, and she said it marked us for each other."

When no one said anything or showed they understood, Gibbie said, "Yeah, well, I didn't know what she meant either. She told me it was so she'd always know where I was and how to find me if she was nearby. So I wondered if I could do it in reverse. I went down to that old Rakshini you took care of, Dean. I told her about the spell and she took a pinch of powder, blowing it in my face until I sneezed. Some powder fell on my chest and it made the sigil glow so I could see it."

Carlos asked, "I'm sorry, Mr. Gibson, is this going somewhere?"

"Yeah, it is. I left there and started driving around downtown. I used the standard square search grid system you and Brynne taught me in CERT class. Anyway, that's how I found them. I think."

James let out an exasperated gasp. "Where did you find them, Gibbie?"

"Oh, I think they're hiding out in the old Gnome's lair a few blocks from here. Once I knew what to look for and got close enough for our bond to light up, I spotted the werepanthers hiding out, watching the place as if they were guarding whoever was inside. It has to be the right place."

James nodded. "Alfonse left the place vacant when things turned bad during the pending apocalypse. He hasn't returned that I know of. If there's activity there, it's not him."

Rudy pulled out his phone. "If there are lookouts, we'll need more people." He turned away as he started tapping out a message on it.

Dean remembered the gnome's hideout. "That place is an underground fortress. I'm not sure we could get in there with an entire army behind us."

A voice from behind Dean startled everyone.

"You don't need an army if you have us along," Gabe said.

Dean spun around. Gabe, Ashley, and Ingrid stood in the doorway to the balcony. They each had flown in with wings now folded against their backs. Then the wings disappeared into whatever inter-dimensional hiding spot that hid them as the trio walked into the room.

"You came," Dean said.

"I said I would," Gabe said, displeasure tinted his tone. "Don't you forget you owe me for coming."

Ashley stepped forward and pulled Dean close. "You don't owe me anything. I remember how you came to find me when I needed it most."

Ingrid snorted, saying, "Yeah, yeah, everything is always kittens and rainbows where my sister is concerned. Gabe said you could open up the gates to Valhalla again, so I suppose I can help to get things back to normal."

Both Brynne and James shot Dean a startled look at the revelation of what he'd promised Gabe. Neither of them said anything, though. Dean shrugged as he caught their stares. They'd been there when the demons had tried to come through the open portal to Hell. They had the same questions as he did.

Ingrid, wearing her gleaming silver chainmail and winged helmet, crossed to the liquor cabinet against the far wall and poured herself a tumbler full of James's best Scotch. "So, is this a war council or what? You all sounded like you were in the middle of planning this little rescue mission. Carry on."

Dean said, "Gabe, you mentioned the Eldara could help us get inside without having to fight through every fortified inch to get to the central part of the lair."

Gabe smiled. He sauntered over to Ingrid and took the bottle from her, pouring a glass for himself. He wore a golden breastplate and a helmet of Spartan design. He pulled off the helmet and tucked it under one arm as he sipped at the liquor.

"The Eldara cannot be banned from any place on earth. It's part of our charge as messengers of the gods. We wouldn't be very good at it if we couldn't deliver the messages."

Ashley said, "What he means is that we can get at least part of the way inside. That should cause enough of a distraction to allow the rest of you to come in the front entrance." Ashley had a chainmail shirt like her sister's. Instead of a helmet, she had a silver chain woven through her dark hair and across her forehead. A triangular silver rune hung down against the skin between her eyebrows.

James clapped his hands together. "Sounds like we have the beginnings of the plan. Gibbie, you and Dean sound like you've been inside. Come over and draw out a map of what you remember and let's work out the rest. Time is of the essence now that darkness has fallen. Artur is a traditionalist and sleeps during daylight hours. He will have risen by now."

Dean and the others moved over to the large dining table nearby. James's assistant, Celeste, appeared with a large sheet of grid paper and Gibbie and Dean sketched out a rough diagram of the layout. Within a few minutes, they had a plan for how to get inside.

Chapter 34

DEAN GLANCED out the passenger window as Gibbie pulled his van over to the curb. Behind the van, two black SUV's stopped as well. Behind Dean sat Leah Casado and her father. Dean tried to ignore the rumpled covers on the mattress behind the seat. Every time he thought about it, the image of Gibbie and Hangbe tangled in the sheets kept creeping into his mind.

Gibbie twisted and rested his arm on the back of his seat so he could see all of them. "Okay, this is as close as I want to get with the security cars behind me. You three duck down in case anyone is looking this way. I don't think the werecats will recognize the van, so I should be able to get in with my keycard from when Alfonse used to live down there."

Carlos cleared his throat, "I don't like that we're leaving a lot of our muscle outside, even if they are just wolf-kind."

Dean said, "Stick to the plan. You two are here to do whatever mojo you can do on the werepanthers at the entrance. Then we can let the others in without sounding the alarm."

"Don't worry. Leah and I know what we have to do. We have a score to settle as well. I still don't understand why you're along. You have no abilities that I can sense. Surely someone else can alert the Eldara when we are ready."

"Ashley said it had to be me. Something to do with our history together." Dean let it drop at that. He really didn't want to go into their past as a romantic couple.

Gibbie pointed out the rear window as lights flashed behind them. "That's the signal. They're all set. That means the Errington team is in place to cover the exit after everyone goes in." He settled back behind the wheel and pulled back out into the street. "You all hide. We can't let anyone see I'm not alone in the van."

Dean ducked into the back. He and the two werejaguars pulled a quilt from behind the center seat and ducked under it. It was musty beneath the covering; with just a hint of funkiness he didn't want to identify. He was glad he didn't have the sensitive noses of the two werecats, judging from the wrinkled noses and expressions on their faces.

The van continued on, then stopped. The driver's window hummed as it opened.

A gruff male voice said, "Hey, where do you think you're going?"

"My girlfriend lives here. She gave me this keycard. I'm just here to pick her up and then we're leaving. What's with all the security. I've never seen two guards out here before."

"Just something new the building management is providing. Hurry back out. Don't make us come in there looking for you."

"Yes, sir." Gibbie replied. The van lurched forward and then tilted down as it started into the garage.

After a few seconds, Gibbie put up the window. "There are two up at the entrance and two more just inside. Are you sure both of you can take them out without raising the alarm?"

"You'll see," Carlos said, lifting the blanket away and shoving it behind him. "There's a reason the other jungle cats fear us."

Once again, his eyes lit up with a fierce yellow color. Leah's flashed as well, though she shifted uncomfortably when she caught Dean watching her.

Gibbie pulled the van over once it was down to the second level, out of sight from the entrance. As he stopped and waited, three figures stepped out of thin air into the beams of the headlights.

Dean started to call out a warning until he realized it was Gabe, Ashley, and Ingrid.

Ashley walked over to Gibbie's window. "We are here. We will breach the entrance down on the lower level. If Artur has any vampire or werepanther guards just inside, we will deal with them for you."

Dean nodded. "We should be down with the rest of the team shortly. Once we're in, you three will hold the entrance so no one escapes past us, especially Artur."

"Don't worry. If he tries, we'll take care of him." Ashley returned to the other two Eldara. They all turned and stepped out of the headlight beams, winking out of sight in the blink of an eye."

"Neat trick," Carlos said. "I wonder what it would take to hire one of their kind. They'd make a very effective assassin."

Dean shook his head. "I don't think they'd be all that interested. They're helping us because it furthers their own agenda, otherwise, they'd stay out of such matters."

Carlos snorted as if he didn't accept the answer.

Gibbie said, "Maybe you can ask them about it once we're finished today. Right now it's time for you two to go to work."

Leah nudged her father. Both Casados, dressed in tight-fitting black athletic wear, stepped from the van and closed the sliding door. They were out of sight for only a few seconds, but when they moved around to the front of the van, the headlights showed two heavily muscled werejaguars. One was shorter than the other, but both looked fierce and powerful. They loped on two legs into the darkened garage, heading back up towards the entrance.

"I hope this works," Dean muttered.

"Don't worry, Dean. We'll get Hangbe and Jaz back. Knowing them, they're already halfway out with an escape plan of their own."

Chapter 35

HANGBE SLAMMED the metal table leg twice against the temple of the werepanther coming at her. On the second hit, his eyes rolled up in his head and he slumped to the floor. He'd still raked at her side with his claws, tearing open the body armor at its thinnest point.

Pressing a hand against the wound, she glanced to the side. Jaz had dispatched the final one of the group they'd encountered. The pair had stumbled into the four guards as they'd run from their last encounter outside the vault.

"You okay?" Jaz asked, nodding at the blood seeping through Hangbe's fingers.

"I'll live. We need to get away. The noise from this fight will draw more down here."

Jaz nodded at the two possible exits from the room. "The question is, which is the best option? We don't even know where here is."

"Pick one, we know we can't go back the way we came."

The Hunter shrugged and started down the concrete corridor on the right. Hangbe followed. Unlike the rest of the rooms and hallways they'd seen so far, this one had no decor or fancy carpets covering the drab concrete walls. Maybe that was a good sign. It could mean this led to an exit.

Shouts sounded behind them a few minutes later. She glanced back to check the twisting passage behind. No sign of pursuit, but they'd be coming.

Ahead of her, Jaz picked up speed to a loping jog. Hangbe tried to match it but fell behind almost immediately. Fatigue and shortness of breath had set in, setting off alarm bells in her mind. The bleeding had slowed, but the way she felt almost assuredly indicated an internal injury of some sort.

"Jaz, slow down."

Jaz stopped. When she saw Hangbe lagging, ran back to her. "I knew we should have stopped and treated that injury sooner."

"Whatever's going on," Hangbe gasped, trying to catch her breath, "it's internal. I think I might have a punctured lung."

Jaz pointed in the direction they were heading. "It looks like it opens into a room down this way where the passage turns. I'll help you down there. Then we can see about treating this wound."

Pulling Hangbe's arm over her shoulder, Jaz lifted her friend up and together they staggered to the corridor's end. It opened into a small storage room lined with metal shelves. Judging from the dust and the old civil defense markings on the containers and boxes, this was part of an old nuclear bunker.

Jaz lowered Hangbe to the floor in the corner, propping her up against one of the shelves. "Let me take a look at that."

She pulled Hangbe's bloody hand away, revealing a deep gash in the skin. It looked deep and bubbled a little when she took a breath.

"You're developing a pneumothorax. That's why you can't catch your breath. Here, press your hand back against the wound. Try to press hard enough to seal it and keep air from leaking out."

Jaz started rummaging through the shelves, pulling boxes down and examining the labels.

"What are you looking for?"

"There has to be a first aid kit stored down here with all the survival crackers and expired meal kits. I need to find something to decompress your chest. Air is escaping your lungs and filling the chest cavity. If I can release that pressure so I can control it, it should ease your breathing. If Dean were here, he'd probably improvise something from what he had in his pockets."

Hangbe smiled. "Being married to that medic has rubbed off on you."

"I've picked up a few things. He's taught a few classes to a few Errington assault teams. Nothing too advanced, just basic combat and tactical first aid."

Jaz kept looking and then let out a quiet "yes" as she pulled down a cardboard box with a red cross on the side. She unsealed the tape around the lid and opened it. After digging through the contents, she smiled and held up a syringe. It was an old model, made before disposable plastics with a metal frame around a glass tube leading to a long stainless steel needle.

"This will do nicely. Here, hold this. I need to find some plastic to seal that wound in your side before I do the decompression."

Jaz searched through the room and came back with a roll of aluminum foil.

"What's that for?"

"Not plastic, but this should do the trick. We have to seal the wound off, and this will stay airtight if you hold still."

She tore off a piece of foil and folded it into a twelve-inch square. Pulling a roll of adhesive tape from the first aid kit, she taped the foil patch in place, leaving one side open.

"Exhale as hard as you can."

Hangbe did as she was told. Frothy, bloody bubbles oozed out from the open side of the foil patch. Jaz wiped the blood away, pressing on the seal to hold it in place before Hangbe took another breath. She taped off the last side as best she could and then wrapped several rolls of gauze around Hangbe's waist to hold it all in place and help the tape hold a seal.

Hangbe glanced down and nodded. Pretty good work for a makeshift occlusive dressing. Her breathing was a little easier now.

Jaz asked, "How do you feel?"

"A little better."

"Good, then I'll hold off on using the needle until you need decompressing again."

A shout from the corridor had them both start to get up. Jaz pressed Hangbe back down.

"You stay put. I think it's just a few of them. Are you sure, Gibbie is close by?"

"I am. Hopefully, he brought help. We just have to hold on a little longer."

Jaz nodded. She started pulling boxes from one shelf by the doorway. Once it was empty, she moved it into the doorway and refilled the shelves. Then she started on another. By the time the shouts grew louder, she'd blocked off the doorway with shelving and boxes.

"It won't hold them long, but it's all I can do." Jaz hefted the two metal table legs and moved over to the doorway. "I can at least make it painful to break down the barricade."

Hangbe closed her eyes and reached out with her mind, calling to Gibson. She could feel him, closer now than before. She tried to urge him to hurry, but she wasn't sure if that worked or not. Darkness closed in as unconsciousness took her.

Chapter 36

DEAN HUNG BACK and watched their backs as Carlos, Leah, and Gibbie fought their way through the werepanthers in front of them. As they took the final two down, he raced past them and squeezed through the partially opened vault door.

He skidded to a stop staring at the broken table in the corner and the two piles of ropes and broken plastic cable ties on the floor. His fists clenched as he looked around for some sign of where Jaz and Hangbe were.

Gibbie joined him, drawing in a deep breath, nostrils flared. "She was definitely here."

"Artur must have taken them. He's going to kill them and get away."

Gibbie pointed to the floor. "I don't think so. If he'd taken them, why untie them? And look, some ropes have been cut free. I think they got free on their own."

"Your mojo with Hangbe brought you here. Where are they now?"

Gibbie walked around the room. He returned to the door, tracing the large plate of glass leaning against the wall, then looking at the exposed locking mechanism. He nodded and squeezed out through the doorway to return to the outer room.

Dean followed. Leah stood to one side, wrapping her father's arm with a bandage. Both werejaguars had injuries, but Carlos's were more severe.

Realizing he'd dropped the ball on his duties on this rescue mission, Dean retrieved his trauma bag from beside Leah and dug through it to pull out a ten-pack of four by four-inch gauze pads. He started applying a dressing to a slashing wound on Leah's shoulder.

"Sorry, I thought we'd found them."

Leah smiled. "I understand. It's not that bad. Check on Gibbie. He's pretty beat up, too. He and my father took the brunt of the last fight."

Carlos shook his head. "I do not understand how it is they will not submit to our wills, Leah. Our power over other werecats should exert control over them. They shouldn't be fighting us. They should be surrendering and begging for mercy."

"Something has broken the control passed to our line," Leah said. "I felt the difference with the first contact we had outside. Somehow they've overcome it."

Carlos flexed his cat fingers, exposing his claws and then retracting them. "I first felt it back in that warehouse when they captured me. I had hoped it was isolated to proximity to the ancient vampire."

Dean finished dressing Leah's shoulder. "They're fighting like they've got no choice. None of them has tried to escape."

Carlos smiled, but it was the sort of smile that chilled the blood. "They know the only way they survive the encounter is by defeating us. If they run after being part of this, they know we will hunt them down and make an example of them. My daughter and I cannot let this affront stand."

"Speak for yourself, Papa. I'm here to help my friend recover his wife. I will not be a part of your vendetta against these others."

Dean moved over and dabbed at the wounds on Gibbie's chest with a dampened piece of gauze. He pretended not to overhear the confrontation brewing between father and daughter behind him. The vampire's wounds were superficial and needed only a little cleansing. They would heal on their own the next time he fed. Despite that, Dean stayed where he was, keeping busy until Leah and her father worked out their differences.

Carlos had had enough. He crossed over to the vault and glanced inside. Then he paced around the room, checking the exits.

Unsure what he searched for, Dean joined him. "Maybe we should reconnect with the other two teams and spread out from here?"

James and Rudy each headed up a separate team from the local werewolf pack. They'd taken two other side passages on the way here after werepanthers ambushed the group from inside one of them.

"We don't need the dogs to help us. The vampire can locate the women, can't you?"

Gibbie let Dean finish and then started pacing around the room. He stopped at each of the three exits twice as he circled. After the second pass, he backed up and stopped at the second doorway. It opened to a long, carpeted hallway with several pairs of doors opening from it.

"This way."

The two werejaguars joined him at the corridor entrance. Leah stopped and glanced back. "I smell death."

Dean's heart skipped a beat. Did she mean a dead human?

Gibbie interpreted it in a much more positive light. "Of course you do. Those two women aren't going to just waltz out of here without a fight. They've got payback on the mind."

He shouldered past the two werecats and started jogging down the hallway, checking the doors to either side as he reached them. Gibbie left the doors open as he continued on. Dean glanced inside as he passed. They appeared to be sparsely furnished guest bedrooms, which struck Dean as odd. Alfonse the gnome had seemed like a solitary individual on the one occasion Dean had met him. Maybe the rooms predated him.

Gibbie passed the last of the rooms and picked up speed. The Casados started speeding up as well. Soon Dean was jogging along alone, shouldering the trauma medical bag over one arm as he tried to keep up with them. He hoped the increased speed meant they weren't too late.

Chapter 37

JAZ BATTED AT THE ARM, forcing its way past the stacked barricade of shelves. She swung with every ounce of strength she had
left. A satisfying crack resonated up the metal tubing and into her
arm. The attacking werepanther howled and pulled back the broken
arm, cradling it with its other hand.

This had been the second assault on the barricaded room. The
first had been more of a test of the defenses. This last one had been
better planned, with multiple werecats attacking the narrow
entrance to the storeroom at once.

Jaz had been lucky. Given her only weapon were the two metal
tubes that had been card table legs, she should have been pleased
with the outcome she'd had. If she'd had even just her grandmother's Katana, she'd have killed several werepanthers by now, and this
assault on their position would be over.

As it was, she'd broken a few bones, but caused no lasting
damage to anyone. She might hold them off one more time. This
last time, they'd partially dismantled the shelving she'd piled in the
doorway. It wouldn't take too much more work to pull the rest away,
and then they'd be able to rush in on her.

Jaz glanced back at Hangbe. Her breathing was ragged at this point. Each inhalation seemed a struggle. Anger filled Jaz rather than sorrow. She'd rather avenge her friend and fight to the end herself than give in to self-pity. Hangbe had been sure a rescue was imminent, but Jaz had yet to see any evidence anyone was close.

Artur stepped into view in the corridor outside. Two attractive female vampires flanked him. "Jaswinder, my child. I commend you on an admirable defense, however there's no way you're getting out of there alive. The only thing you're doing at this point is injuring my friends. They will recover and break through, eventually. They're not going to be gentle once they do get in."

Jaz dug her hand into her pocket, wrapping her hand around the makeshift stake she'd crafted from five tongue depressors she'd found in the medical kit. Taped together and hastily sharpened against the rough concrete walls, they made a passable shiv. Under the right circumstances, and with a little luck, she was pretty sure she could reach Artur's heart with it.

"I'll tell you what, Artur. You send your minions away, and I'll come out so just you and I can play. Surely, you're not afraid of a woman armed only with a table leg?"

A fourth vampire, this one a male, stepped into view and leaned in to whisper something to Artur. The ancient vampire's eyes glanced at the newcomer for a second before returning to glare at Jaz.

"Bad new, Artur?" A flash of anger across his face rewarded her guess.

"It is nothing." He waved his hand, dismissing the newcomer. Footsteps ran back up the corridor towards the central lair. "I tire of this, perhaps I will deal with you later. I have some pressing matters that I must attend to."

Jaz smiled. She had a good idea now what the whispered message must have been. "They're here, aren't they? My husband and friends wouldn't sit idly by and let you hold me for long."

When Artur didn't respond right away, Jaz continued. "My guess is they have you trapped down here. You're not getting away this time. This time you're going to die along with your minions."

A moment of irritation was replaced by a sly grin. "I've lived for thousands of years. My plans span centuries. I do not care if this one incursion upsets the balance momentarily. I will merely reset the chess pieces and begin again. That is the advantage I have over those of you with puny, human lives."

Artur flicked his head to the side and the two women with him ran off in the opposite direction, continuing past the storeroom. That rough concrete corridor went on for some distance, Jaz knew.

Shouts and the clash of steel on steel echoed down the corridor outside. Whatever was happening was coming closer.

The vampire's canines glistened as the grin broadened. "It seems, Jaswinder Errington, I must leave. Have no fear, though. I shall return. I have unfinished business with your family line, and I will come for you again."

With a curt nod in her direction, Artur's form blurred as he moved with a speed she could never have matched. He was out of sight before she could blink an eye.

For an instant, she considered tearing down the makeshift barricade to go after him. She decided there was no way she could dig her way out in time to catch up with him. Instead, she went over to Hangbe and did what she could to keep her comfortable until help arrived.

Chapter 38

DEAN JUMPED BACKWARD AS the limp body slid across the floor towards him. Gibbie, armed with the broken arm from a chair, had staked the vampire as he tried to race past and get at the paramedic to the rear.

"You good back there, Dean?" Gibbie called out as he engaged the next of Artur's undead minions.

"I'm still here. We have to break through. We must be getting close."

Gibbie didn't answer. The final vampire had pressed him back against the wall and wrestled to pull away the makeshift stake. He pummeled at Gibbie's face and head again and again with his free hand.

Dean looked around for help. The Casados had run farther down the concrete corridor. The two werejaguars battled a cluster of werepanthers gathered in front of several doors on either side.

Realizing if Gibbie was going to get help, it was going to have to come from him, Dean slid the trauma bag off his shoulder and bunched up the long strap in both hands. Letting out a guttural shout, he charged at the vampire's back.

The heavy bag struck the vampire from behind at the same time he'd pried the wooden stake from Gibbie's hand. The blow caused the chair arm to fall clattering the floor, leaving both vampires unarmed. Gibbie took one more blow to the head. His eyes rolled up in his head and he slumped to the floor.

Dean stepped back to swing the bag around for another strike. The vampire spun on him, leaving him no time to bring the heavy trauma kit around in time to stop the charge.

Before he knew what happened, Dean found himself on his back struggling to hold the vampire at bay. He pressed at the weight laying atop him with one hand on the creature's neck. The corded muscles resisted his fingers digging at the cold flesh.

The face and its dripping fangs dipped down towards Dean's neck despite every ounce of strength he poured into his arms to hold off the vampire.

"You smell tasty, human," the raspy voice whispered as the mouth passed his ear. "Do I detect a hint of something Unusual? Let's see what your vintage really is."

Dean wrenched his head to the side and slammed it back into the vampire's temple. He might as well have bashed it against a brick wall. All he did was knock himself into a daze.

He closed his eyes and tried to gather his wits, expecting to feel the piercing fangs at his neck any second.

Instead of pain, there was a splash of wetness against the side of his face and the full weight of the vampire fell upon him.

Opening his eyes, he blinked to clear away whatever had splashed on his face. His cloudy vision cleared as his tears wiped away the blood from his eyes.

Ingrid stood over him, her blazing silver heavenly sword in her hands.

Dean glanced to the side and gasped. The wide-eyed face of the vampire stared back at him from where the severed head lay beside him.

Groaning, he shoved the headless body away and sat up so no more of the foul vampire blood poured out onto him.

"A thank you would be nice," Ingrid said.

"Thank you," Dean replied as he tried to wipe blood from his face with the back of his hand. All he seemed to do was smear it around. He stopped and reached up to Ingrid. "Can you help me up?"

The Valkyrie extended her hand and pulled him to his feet with ease. Ashley knelt by Gibbie, checking his injuries. Gabe stood watching, his sword hanging in its scabbard at his side.

"Maybe you two could help the Casados?" Dean nodded towards the two werejaguars fighting a desperate battle down the corridor.

"They seem to be holding their own," Gabe said with the barest glance down at the battling werecats.

"If you don't, I'll consider your bargain void," Dean said. "The fight isn't over until Jaz and Hangbe are free and Artur dealt with."

With a gasp of exasperation, Gabe drew his gleaming blade, this one golden. "Shall we, cousin?" he asked Ingrid.

"Always up for a fight."

Together the two strode down the hallway towards the fighting.

Dean retrieved his trauma bag and knelt beside Gibbie with Ashley. "How is he?"

"His injuries are severe and he has a concussion, but he'll live. Most of what he's sustained should resolve after a few feedings."

"Do you think it's safe to leave him here?" Dean wanted to keep searching for Jaz.

Ashley smiled and nodded. "Go. I'll stay with him until he wakes up."

"Thank you." Dean ran down the hallway. The addition of the two Eldara had turned the tide against the werepanthers. They now fought a sort of fighting retreat, trying to disengage from the Casados and the two angels.

He caught up with them as the fight reached a bend in the hallway and turned the corner. He passed a room with junk piled in the doorway.

"Dean!"

He skidded to a stop and returned to the opening. Jaz's beautiful face appeared in between one gap in what he realized was a hastily constructed barricade.

"Are you alright?"

She smiled. "I am. It's good to see you. I knew you'd find me."

"Always. Where's Hangbe? Is she…?" He didn't want to finish the question.

"She's in here with me. She's hurt and bleeding internally. Do you have any fluids in that bag?"

Dean nodded. He pulled at the stacked shelves and boxes. "Clear me a way in so I can check on her."

It took several minutes to widen an opening for him to climb into the room. Dean rushed over to Hangbe and began assessing her. The ashen color of her dark skin told him she'd lost a lot of blood. She felt cold to the touch, but she still breathed and had a flicker of a thready pulse.

"Jaz, go back down the hallway. Find Ashley. I need her to help. I can give some fluids, but this is beyond me. She needs a full trauma suite."

Jaz disappeared as Dean set up the fluid drip and got the IV started. He continued his assessment. Her abdomen felt rigid and distended under his palpating fingers. She definitely had an internal bleed. The fluids might help to stabilize her blood pressure for a brief time, but she'd die without special intervention.

It didn't take long for Ashley to arrive.

Dean twisted his head around and asked, "Where's Jaz?"

"I left her with Gibbie. He's still out cold. What's going on with your friend here?"

"She's in shock, thready pulse, probable internal bleed in the abdomen. She needs surgery and I don't think there's any way to get her there in time."

Ashley knelt beside Dean and placed one hand on Hangbe's head. The other rested on her belly. The Eldara Sister closed her eyes and bowed her head. Dean watched as a golden glow formed beneath Ashley's palms. The glow remained for about ten seconds, then it faded away.

The Eldara slumped a little as she pulled her hands back. Dean knew she'd spent some of her corporeal life energy to heal some of Hangbe's injuries.

The Amazon's eyes fluttered open and seemed confused for a few seconds as she looked around. "Where's Jaz? She was just here."

Dean rested his hand on the woman's shoulder. "Rest easy. She's helping Gibbie. He's injured, too."

At mention of Gibbie, Hangbe tried again to rise.

Dean pressed her back to the floor. "You need to lay still until we can get an ambulance here for you. Ashley was able to heal you a bit, but you're going to need a trauma center to fix what's wrong with you."

Hangbe relaxed and lay back. "How bad is he?"

Ashley said, "He took a knock to the head. He's pretty banged up. I wouldn't worry, though. We'll take him to the hospital, too. A few bags of blood and he'll be good as new."

Hangbe relaxed at the news. Dean continued monitoring the woman's condition while he and Ashely waited for the others to return.

Carlos was the first to come back up the corridor, with Leah close behind. They both had shifted back to human form, though their eyes still glowed yellow.

"Did you find your woman?"

"I did. We found both of them. Jaz is down the hall looking after Gibbie. Leah, do you think you can run down there and check on him?"

The other paramedic nodded and jogged out of sight.

Dean checked the corridor behind Carlos. "What about Artur?"

"I think he made his escape into the night. We caught up to a pair of female vampires. After we dealt with them, we found an exit into the basement of a building about a block away from this one. The two Eldara gave chase, but I fear with a head start, they will not catch him. That one is too slippery by far."

"You're not kidding," Ashley said. She stood, shaking her head. "My sister and I have almost caught him several times in the last two centuries. Each time, he has weaseled out of trouble, either by escaping or using some obscure rule of protection to keep us from dispatching him on sight."

"Well, now he has the Casado Cartel to worry about. I care not about rules or how powerful he is. For the right price, everyone can be found and killed."

Ashley and Dean exchanged glances. The discussion of contract killing, even for someone as reprehensible as Artur, made them both uncomfortable.

Dean changed the subject. "What about the werepanthers behind the trafficking ring? Did you regain control over them?"

"They will no longer bother this area, or any other. They're an example for others who think they'd prefer working away from our oversight. I'm especially pleased with the way Leah has shown her leadership potential in the cartel tonight. Don't you agree?"

Dean hesitated to answer. He knew Leah's feelings about this, and he suspected they hadn't changed despite her participation in the fighting tonight. Aware of the elder Casado's eyes on him, Dean said, "She has a bright future in whatever she does."

Carlos frowned, but said nothing else. Dean decided to look busy and get another round of vitals on Hangbe. Her condition had improved since Ashley's supernatural intervention, but she was still borderline unstable. As soon as Leah returned, he'd leave her with Hangbe while he tracked down Brynne and got an ambulance for both Gibbie and the inspector. James and the others could deal with the cleanup down here.

Chapter 39

DEAN REACHED out to grab Jaz's hand where it rested on her knee as she steered the SUV with her left hand.

She gave his searching fingers a gentle squeeze and glanced his way. "You okay?"

"I'm fine now that you're home safe and sound. I'm not sure how I feel about you leaving again to track down the European side of this trafficking ring."

"Dean, it's been two weeks since the rescue. Hangbe's recovered fully, and she's finally prised herself away from Gibbie's side to get back to work."

"I know," Dean said. "I don't know why you have to go with her back to Ireland. You should be able to let your Dublin team handle things. We found Kaylee's family and Verity. Can't we leave the rest to someone else?"

Jaz shook her head. "There's too much riding on this. We have to follow up and track down the other side of this operation. We didn't have to do that here. Carlos Casado's ruthless retaliation against the remaining werepanthers left us no one to arrest. His cartel doesn't reach outside of the Americas, though. That leaves that clean up to Errington and Hangbe's Interpol connections."

Dean recalled all the news of random gang carnage in the area. He knew it was Carlos cleaning house and making sure everyone left alive had no doubts about who was in charge of the werecats in the western hemisphere. "Do you think we're going to have any trouble from the Cartel now that Carlos has taken things into his own hands?"

"Maybe." Jaz shook her head and sighed. "I'll give him credit for one thing. His hit teams were careful and avoided all collateral damage. We wouldn't have known they were here if it weren't for the bodies they left behind. That's why I didn't have to intervene."

She took her Hunter lineage seriously. As long as no one outside the gangs was hurt, she'd stand down.

Jaz pulled into a parking space at the rear of the Irish Shop. They had allowed Dougie to reopen after a long meeting with James about his part in the illegal activity. Dean thought the leprechaun had gotten off easy with the threat of future sanctions from James and the agreement that Rudy and his werewolves would watch to make sure things remained legal. Part of that agreement was to keep the door to Dublin locked except for specific uses arranged with James or Rudy in advance. To make sure he complied, James held on to Dougie's recovered pot-o-gold as collateral.

Dean hopped out. Gibbie's white van was already here, parked right next to the shop's rear door. Dean figured the vampire and Hangbe must be inside already.

When the back door of the van popped open and a shirtless Gibbie hopped out, Dean shouted and jumped backward.

Hangbe climbed out, pulling a black t-shirt over her sports bra. Gibbie pulled her close and planted a long, energetic kiss on her full lips.

When they parted, Gibbie turned and noticed Dean and Jaz for the first time. "Oh, hey guys. Hangbe and I were just, uh, saying goodbye."

Dean held up a hand. He really didn't need the mental image to go along with what he imagined had just been happening in the back of the van.

Hangbe winked at Jaz. "I'm going to miss this one." She

wrapped her arm around Gibbie's neck and pulled him in for another kiss, even more passionate than the last.

Jaz cleared her throat. "Maybe we should postpone the trip for a little while?"

Hangbe held out a hand with her forefinger extended as she continued to press her lips against the vampire's. Dean and Jaz waited.

Thirty seconds later, she came up for air and smiled. "I wanted him to remember what he's waiting for until I return."

Dean couldn't hide his surprise. He'd thought this whole affair with the frumpy vampire had been a fling. "You're coming back?"

"Of, course. Gibson and I have a wedding to plan."

Gibbie blushed, reaching out to clutch at her hand. "I cannot wait. It'll be the event of the year, I promise."

"I don't want a fuss, my love. I just want you."

Dean glanced and Jaz and rolled his eyes as Hangbe leaned in to kiss Gibbie again. The Hunter returned the expression.

Finally, they all went inside and headed to the storeroom with the door to Ireland. Dougie sat at a desk nearby, looking over his books. He stood as the four of them entered.

"It's wonderful to see you all back to visit. James gave me a heads up you'd be here to travel through the portal. Do you know when you'll be returning?"

Jaz shook her head. "I'll have Dean arrange a time with you once I know how long it's likely to take on the far side. Hangbe and I have a lot to do in coordination with Irish and UK authorities."

Dougie nodded and produced the key that unlocked the door. He twisted it in the keyhole and pulled the door open.

Dean decided he'd better make a good show of this after all the attention Gibbie had given Hangbe. He reached out for Jaz and pulled her into an embrace. "Hurry back."

"I will. I'll reach out with a message every day so you know what's going on."

Dean smiled. "I'll hold you to that."

They separated and waited while Gibbie and Hangbe exchanged goodbyes three more times. Finally, Hangbe came over to join Jaz with her bag on her shoulder and suitcase rolling behind her. Jaz grabbed her gear, too, and with a wave, the pair disappeared through the door, pulling it closed behind them.

Dougie locked the portal and returned the old key to his pocket. "What are you two going to do while the ladies are gone?"

Gibbie smiled. "I have to find a new apartment. Hangbe made it clear that my place was way too small for us to stay there long term. Maybe I'll get a new bed, too. We kind of wrecked the one I had."

Dean winced. He really didn't want to know.

"What about you, Dean?" Dougie asked.

"The work of a paramedic never ends. I've got a new shift tomorrow and Leah is still on probationary status. She's good, but there's a lot to learn to be as great as I expect her to be."

"She's a good kid, Dean," Gibbie said. "I'm sure she'll do fine."

"I hope so. There are some conflicts with her family that need to get worked out. As long as her father lets her live her life, she should be fine." Dean shrugged. There wasn't much he could do about that. "You up for a quick bite at Hank's place?"

Gibbie smiled. "I could have a little something. Not too much, though. Hangbe has me on a strict diet. She says she wants me in shape for our wedding night."

Dean shook his head as Gibbie described in too much detail all the things he loved about his new girlfriend. He didn't complain, though. It was all part of his life as a Station U paramedic. He wouldn't have it any other way.

Epilogue

GABE TRUDGED up the stairs and opened the door to his apartment above the music store. He snorted in disgust at the pitiful accommodations. An archangel should live in a palace. He was Eldara royalty and yet here he was.

Dropping his keys on the kitchenette counter, he bent down and picked up the mail someone had shoved beneath the door for him. Seeing nothing but bills and junk mail, he threw the stack of envelopes on the counter beside the keys.

"You never got back to me about your mission," a woman said from across the room.

Gabe resisted the urge to startle, instead slowly turning to stare at the person who'd let themselves in to his inner sanctum. "You came to me. It's not my job to track you down."

The woman, who looked to be in her mid-thirties, stood. She wore scarred tactical body armor from her shoulders down. Her close-cropped blonde hair had been shaved close on one side, and a scarlet streak swept across the other. She glared at Gabriel with her one good eye, the other covered with a black leather patch.

"Did you get him to agree to help you reopen the ways to the upper and lower planes?"

"I got him to say he would try. Neither of us know how he might do that, by the way."

The woman shook her head. "That's for me to work out. I have to make all this right. The problem started the moment he closed off earth from heaven and hell. Until I fix it, nothing will ever be normal again."

Gabe pulled a beer from the fridge for himself and held out another one for the woman. She shook her head. Shrugging, he opened his and took a long pull from the bottle. "Given what little you've told me, I'm not sure I want things to change. I can see across the boundaries of time, at least a little. There's much from the future you describe I like."

The woman stormed across at him, raising her hand to grab at the hilt of the Katana across her back. "Your kind is the reason I'm here. The archangels started it all. Maybe if I kill you now, I won't have to fix anything."

A flash of gold lit up the room as Gabe summoned his heavenly blade. He swept it at the woman's exposed neck. She finished drawing her own sword and blocked his strike with surprising ease. He filed that bit of information away for future reference.

"I'm not so easily dispatched, Gabriel. You're not the first of your kind I've tangled with. I'm still here, which should tell you not to cross me."

Gabe stepped back, lowering his blade a little as he took another sip from his beer. "You're fast, faster than a human should be. What have you done to enhance yourself?"

"What was necessary after the Eldara betrayed humanity." She also stepped back, but kept her sword between them, ready for another attack.

"You can lower your weapon, girl. My attack was just a test. You passed it."

"I won't lower my guard until Dean completes the task he agreed to. Until then, dearest Grandfather, you're stuck with me."

Be ready for more in the *Extreme Medical Services* series. Book 9, *The Paramedic's Sorceress*, comes out in late 2021.

Want more?

Check out the Eldara Sisters series and follow the historical adventures of Ashley and Ingrid.

—

Eldara Sister Series
The Nightingale's Angel
Blue and Gray Angel

Find more great fun fantasy reads. Join the reading list at
https://jamiedavisbooks.com/list/

Also by Jamie Davis

Get a free book and updates for new books.

visit JamieDavisBooks.com/send-free-book/

Extreme Medical Services Series

Book 1 - *Extreme Medical Services*

Book 2 - *The Paramedic's Angel*

Book 3 - *The Paramedic's Choice*

Book 4 - *The Paramedic's Hunter*

Book 5 - *The Paramedic's Witch*

Book 6 - *The Paramedic's Nemesis*

Book 7 - *The Paramedic's Doom*

Book 8 - *The Paramedic's Amazon*

Eldara Sister Series

The Nightingale's Angel

Blue and Gray Angel

The Huntress Clan Saga

(A 6-book Urban Fantasy series starting with)

Huntress Initiate

The Broken Throne Series

(A 5-Book Dystopian Urban Fantasy

starting with)

The Charm Runner

The Accidental Traveler LitRPG Series

(with C.J. Davis)

(A 6-book Epic Fantasy Series starting with)

The Accidental Thief

Follow on Facebook for updates, news, and upcoming book excerpts

Facebook.com/jamiedavisbooks

Help the With A Review

I Need Your Help ...

Without reviews indie books like this one are almost impossible to market.

Leaving a review will only take a minute — it doesn't have to be long or involved, just a sentence or two that tells people what you liked about the book, to help other readers know why they might like it, too. It also helps me write more of what you love.

The truth is, VERY few readers leave reviews. Please help me out by being the exception.

Thank you in advance!

Jamie Davis

About the Author

Jamie Davis is a nurse, retired paramedic, author, and nationally recognized medical educator who began teaching new emergency responders as a training officer for his local EMS program. He loves everything fantasy and sci-fi and especially the places where stories intersect with his love of medicine or gaming.

Jamie lives in a home in the woods in Maryland with his wife, three children, and dog. He is an avid gamer, preferring historical and fantasy miniature gaming, as well as tabletop games. He writes LitRPG, GameLit, urban, and contemporary paranormal fantasy stories, among other things. His Future Race Game rules were written to satisfy a desire to play a version of the pod races from Star Wars episode 1.

www.jamiedavisbooks.com

Made in the USA
Monee, IL
02 May 2022